07/01

SO-AJV-142

WITHDRAWN

STARTING OUT
IN THE EVENING

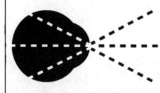

This Large Print Book carries the
Seal of Approval of N.A.V.H.

STARTING OUT IN THE EVENING

BRIAN MORTON

WITHDRAWN

Thorndike Press • Thorndike, Maine

Copyright © 1998 by Brian Morton

All rights reserved.

Published in 1998 by arangement with Crown Publishers, a division of Random House, Inc.

Thorndike Large Print ® Senior Lifestyles Series.

The tree indicium is a trademark of Thorndike Press.

The text of this Large Print edition is unabridged.
Other aspects of the book may vary from the original edition.

Set in 16 pt. Plantin by Juanita Macdonald.

Printed in the United States on permanent paper.

Library of Congress Cataloging in Publication Data

Morton, Brian, 1955–
    Starting out in the evening : a novel / Brian Morton.
      p.   cm.
    ISBN 0-7862-1451-1 (lg. print : hc : alk. paper)
    1. Dissertations, Academic — Authorship — Fiction.
  2. Authors — Fiction.   3. Large type books. I. Title.
    [PS3563.O88186S73   1998b]
    813′.54—dc21   98-14066

STARTING OUT
IN THE EVENING

1

Heather was wearing the wrong dress. It had seemed like a good idea in the morning — it was a tight little black thing; she'd looked fantastic in the mirror — but now she was thinking that she should have worn something demure. This was a foolish dress to meet your intellectual hero in.

Waiting in the coffee shop for the great man to arrive, Heather was squirming with nervousness, and she began to wonder why she was here — why she had gone to such lengths to meet this man, when she knew he couldn't possibly be as interesting in person as he was in his books. She had a wild urge to flee — to scribble a note of apology, leave it with the waiter, and drive all the way back to Providence. But she stayed where she was. She was nervous; she was a little scared; but she could live with that. Fear of any undertaking, to her way of thinking, was usually a reason to go ahead with it.

The door opened and a man came in from the cold. He was wearing an enormous coat — a coat that was like a house — and a big, furry, many-flapped hat. He peeled off the hat and stopped for a moment in front of the cash register, stamping off the snow. He was wearing galoshes.

They had never met, but he picked her out instantly, and he came toward her, smiling. Old, fat, bald, leaning awkwardly on a cane. The man of her dreams.

2

"I can't believe it's you," she said, as he pressed her hand and sat heavily across from her.

What she wanted to say was: You've been dear to me since I was a girl. You were one of my life-teachers. You understood me; you helped me understand myself. If reading a book is a naked encounter between two people, I have known you nakedly for years.

She wanted to say wild things to him, but here he was, struggling out of his coat, and he seemed terribly old and terribly frail, and above all terribly unfamiliar, and she suddenly felt shy. When she read his work, it was as if he poured his soul directly into hers, and they mixed. Now there were bodies in the way.

She felt as if she were in the middle of an earthquake. The furniture in her mind was sliding around. Reading his work, she had always thought of him as a contemporary. In fact — as she'd known, of course, with her rational mind — he was closer to her grandparents' age. And though she'd entertained many imaginary pictures of him over the years, it had never occurred to her that he might be fat. To her mind, genius was gaunt.

He was older and larger than she'd imagined, and somehow both softer and harder. His hand was soft when she shook it; his face was saggy, like a poached egg. In his eyes, though, there was something chilly and ironic. He was an odd combination of the soft and the shrewd. He looked like a gangster's uncle.

"I can't believe it's me either," Schiller said — breathing heavily, looking for a place to rest his cane.

3

Heather ordered a salad, a BLT, and coffee; Schiller asked for a baked potato — no butter, no sour cream — and tea. "I'm on the Pritikin diet," he said to her after the waiter left. "I had a heart attack last year, and the year before that. I'm not allowed to put butter on anything anymore."

"That must have been very scary," she said, trying to sound like the most sympathetic woman ever born.

"They do tend to concentrate the mind."

This was a literary reference, but she couldn't remember from where. Her mind was reeling. She was sitting across from him! He was here! He was here, but he was dying. She felt thankful that she had come to him in time.

The waiter returned with her salad, his potato, her coffee and his tea, and in the momentary confusion of platters she tried to bring herself down to earth.

"Are you working on a new novel?" she said.

"I'm working on a novel, yes. But I've been working on it so long I'm not sure you could call it new." He sipped his tea, with, she thought, a notable delicacy.

Remember the way he drinks his tea. Remember the softness of his hands. Remember the way he looks down at the table when he speaks. Remember.

He asked her a few questions about herself: where she was born, where she'd gone to school, whether she liked New York. It struck her as odd that she should have to tell him these things. Didn't he know her? During the years she'd been reading his work, he had so often helped her understand herself that she'd sometimes felt as if *he* cared about *her*.

"So," he said finally, "you've embarked on a project of questionable merit. You're working on a study. Of me." He shook his big head sadly.

This was why she was here. This was why she had worked up the courage to find him, and this was why she had come to New York. She was writing her master's thesis about Schiller's novels.

The thesis, in her mind, was only the first step: her real goal was to write a book about his work. She was twenty-four years old; she hoped to have her thesis written before her twenty-fifth birthday and a book contract in her hands before her twenty-sixth.

She had grandiose daydreams. Schiller had written four novels, and all of them were out of print. In the 1940s, when most of William Faulkner's work was out of print, the critic Malcolm Cowley reintroduced him to the public with a volume called *The Portable Faulkner*. It was this collection that made American readers see they had a genius in their midst; if not for Cowley, Faulkner might have died in obscurity. Heather was already thinking about a *Portable Schiller*.

"I think it's a very worthy project," she said, lamely.

He took off his glasses and polished them slovenly with a handkerchief. "I'm flattered by your interest. And if you're intent on doing this study, I won't try to talk you out of it. But I'm sorry to have to say that I won't be able to help you with it either."

She tried to take this in. He hadn't been encouraging on the phone, but neither had he told her flatly that he wouldn't help.

"Why?"

"Ten years ago, it would have made me very happy. But I'm an old man now."

"What does being old have to do with it?"

"I'm trying to finish a novel," he said. "It will probably be the last novel I write. My only remaining goal in life is to finish it. I'm not in good health, and I need to avoid anything that distracts me from that goal. Your project would be a distraction, Miss Wolfe. A very flattering distraction, but a distraction nonetheless. "

He sighed. It struck her as a poetic sigh, but she was prepared to find poetry in anything he did.

She looked at him closely. The folds of skin on his face sagged disastrously; like many old men, he looked strangely like an old woman.

In a way, what he'd said was what she would have wanted him to say. She thought his devotion to his art was beautiful. He was a hero: a wounded hero, dragging his frail body toward his goal.

"I understand. And I respect your decision. But I can't help thinking that you've made up your mind too quickly. Maybe the best thing for your health would be to have a fascinating young woman in your life."

He'd been about to put his glasses back on, but now he put them down and examined her, with an expression of curiosity and amusement. It was as if he was looking at her for the first time.

She didn't look away. It occurred to her that the eyes don't really age. These were the eyes that his friends and lovers had looked into when he was young.

With no attempt to hide her scrutiny, she studied his face. What she saw there, what she thought she saw, was strength, pain, loneliness, bitterness, and the struggle against bitterness. And, of course, time. In the slackness of his skin, in his fallen, half-womanly face, she saw the way time breaks the body down.

For a moment the stare felt like a sexualized encounter. By the time Schiller looked away, she felt as if they had passed beyond sex. She didn't know what she meant by that, but that was how it felt.

"Give me a chance, damn it. You'll be happy you got to know me."

She wanted to take things further; she wanted to say something she might regret. She knew what she wanted to say; she just didn't know if she should say it.

But whenever Heather felt uncertain about whether to do something, she did it. She had decided long ago that you never learn anything by holding back.

"Maybe," she said, "you'll even fall in love with me."

"You're an odd young woman," he murmured, with a look of prim disapproval. He was blushing. She had never seen an old man blush.

15

4

Schiller made his way gingerly on the icy sidewalk. She wanted to take his arm, to steady him, but she didn't know if he'd appreciate being treated like an old man. At four-thirty it was already dark; the air was so cold you had a taste of metal in your mouth. Schiller concentrated on each step. A bunch of kids tumbled out of a pizza place, and he pulled up short. Heather thought of the way he described New York in *Two Marriages* — the almost sexual pleasure he took in the energy of the street. But that was a long time ago.

He was taking her to his apartment. She had told him that she didn't own a copy of *The Lost City*, and he'd said he might have one at home.

He wasn't sure whether he had a copy of one of his own books. This impressed her: it seemed like a mark of a true artist.

He took her to a building on Broadway and 94th, and they took the elevator to the fifteenth floor.

Schiller helped Heather off with her coat and laboriously removed his hat and his

16

coat and his galoshes.

The first thing she noticed about his apartment was the smell. Heavy, airless, slightly sour: the sad smell of an old man living alone.

The second thing was the books. There were bookshelves against every wall; there were piles of books on every table. Old faded hardcovers and gleaming new paperbacks; triple-decker nineteenth-century novels — one shelf held the complete works of Balzac, another the complete works of Henry James — and slim collections of poetry. One wall seemed to be devoted entirely to politics and history. Another was taken up with literary criticism, from Matthew Arnold to V. S. Pritchett. More books than she had ever seen in one place, outside of a bookstore or library.

It was thrilling to be in his apartment. She felt as if she were in a seat of power: not worldly power, but the power of the imagination. Writers are the unacknowledged legislators of the world, and Schiller was the most unacknowledged of them all. She felt as if he were an exiled king, but no less a king for being in exile.

"If I do have a copy, it should be in my bedroom," he said. "I'll be right back. Make yourself at home."

She touched his arm. "Do you think I could have a look at the room where you write?" She spoke in an awestruck whisper: hushed, husky, reverent, rapt, and about 49 percent fake. She *did* want to see his study, and she *did* think of it as a sort of holy place — but she was also pouring it on thick.

He seemed unimpressed with her worshipfulness. "First door on the right," he said. "Don't touch anything."

She examined the room without stepping past the threshold. It was tiny — it must have been meant to be a maid's room — and stunningly bare. Against the wall was a wooden table with a huge manual typewriter and a stack of paper. Two cardboard boxes full of paper were on the floor. In front of the table was a straight-backed wooden chair. There was nothing on the wall: no photographs, no paintings. It was like a monk's cell, or a prison cell.

This wasn't what she'd expected. She'd expected a room filled with books, with beloved objects, with the disorderly evidence of labor.

He was still in his bedroom, wherever that was. She drifted into the kitchen; on the table was a shoe box filled with photographs. She sat down and started flipping through them quickly, as if she were looking for something in particular, which she wasn't.

Which she was. Except she hadn't known until she found it: a photo of him as a young man, almost as young as she was now.

He was handsome; he had a look of arrogance, of sexual challenge, that she found thrilling. He looked like a young athlete.

Wanting to hold some part of him, to possess him, she found herself pressing the picture against her heart, and then she found herself slipping it into her purse.

There were footsteps in the hall, rapid and light — not Schiller's footsteps. Heather quickly stood up, which made her look more awkward and suspicious than she would have looked if she'd stayed in her chair.

A woman in tights and sneakers came into the room. "Hello," she said.

Heather, because her purse had become strangely, distractingly heavy, couldn't think of a response.

"Are you a burglar?" the woman said.

"Not professionally," she said.

"Well, it's good to have a hobby."

They stood there, facing each other, and they might have remained like that for a long time if Schiller hadn't come back.

"Ariel," he said.

Heather felt as if she'd stepped through the looking glass. This was Ariel.

Heather knew her well. She knew about her difficult birth; she knew about her early wish to be a dancer. This was the girl whose childhood was chronicled in the long last chapter of Schiller's second book. This was Schiller's daughter.

And here she was, a grown woman — a positively middle-aged woman. She was probably almost forty.

"To what do I owe the pleasure?" Schiller said.

"I can only stay a minute. I have a new client on 92nd and I just finished up with her. So I thought I'd drop in and say hi. And have a snack." She began to take things out of her backpack: peanut butter, honey, brown bread, Marshmallow Fluff, a banana. "I had a yen for a Fluffernutter."

Heather was studying her. She was attractive — athletic-looking, with a sort of free-spirited air — but she was a slob. Her leotard was stained and covered with a fine layer of cat hair; her hair needed brushing.

Schiller introduced them. "Your timing is providential," he said to his daughter. "Heather is the young woman I told you about. Do you still have that copy of *The Lost City*?"

"I haven't read it yet," Ariel said.

"I'd like to lend it to Heather. I can give

20

it back to you after she's done. Is that all right?"

"Sure. Sorry."

"Don't be sorry," Schiller said, in a quiet, comforting voice.

Heather didn't like this voice: it was too protective, too syrupy.

"I'll get it right back to you," she said to Ariel. "I've already read it. I just want to be able to refer to it when I'm writing."

"It's like a sacred text," Schiller said. "There's only one copy in the world."

Ariel got out a knife and a plate and started to assemble her sandwich. "I didn't mean to interrupt anything," she said. "Don't mind me."

"No, it's all right," Schiller said. "Heather was about to leave."

"Do you mind if I make a phone call?" Heather said.

She went into the living room. She had no call to make. She was unhappy.

She could hear Schiller and his daughter talking in the kitchen. "Oprah upset me yesterday," Ariel said. "She said that any woman who doesn't have a child by the age of thirty-nine doesn't really want one, whether she admits it or not."

"Surely, even Oprah ventures a mistaken opinion on occasion," Schiller said.

Heather resented it that this woman was his daughter. How does a writer of the most subtle, serious fiction end up with a daughter who watches *Oprah*? I'd be a better daughter for him than she is.

And she was mad at Schiller for dismissing her. "Heather was about to leave." She was sure she could get him to reconsider if she spent more time with him.

She didn't need his cooperation to write her thesis. But she wanted his blessing.

On the coffee table were some things that Ariel, slobly, had dumped there. Her scarf, her jacket, a Snickers wrapper, and a catalog for the Learning Annex, with the ridiculous headline: HARNESS THE POWER OF MIND CONTROL!

She sat glumly with the phone at her ear, pretending to make a call.

Harness the power of mind control. She decided to send Schiller a thought-message to come and sit down with her in the living room. If he responded, it would mean that he was psychically available to her, and that he might help her after all. If he didn't respond, she would leave him alone.

She sent her thoughts into the other room, where she could hear him talking; she imagined them rushing like a mighty river, the Monongahela or something, into his mind.

She waited — one minute, two. He didn't appear.

Oh well. She decided to call her answering machine to see if she had any messages.

Schiller appeared at the threshold of the room. She smiled at him, willing him to come in and sit down.

"Well," he said, and he came in. The mind control was working! Now she had to get him to sit down.

"It was nice meeting you," he said. "I'll get your coat."

Apparently it hadn't worked. Unhappily, she followed him into the hall. She had met him, but that was all. She wanted to get to know him; she wanted him to approve of her project. There was only a moment left. She didn't know what to do. He carefully removed her coat from the hanger and extended it toward her, but instead of turning around to allow him to help her on with it, she clutched his hand and brought it to her lips. Absurdly, in the unlit hallway, she was kissing his hand.

"Promise me you'll give me a chance," she said.

Schiller pulled his hand away; he dropped her coat. He took a long step backward. She thought he was horrified. But then, in a gesture that, in Heather's view, was just as odd as hers, he placed the palm of his other hand on her face, covering her eyes. She didn't know if he was trying to commune with her or trying to hold her off.

5

Ariel had a graceful, gliding way of walking, and Heather realized that the girlish strivings that Schiller had described in his second book had come to fruition: she had become a dancer after all.

They were on the street, walking toward Heather's car — Heather still had the rental car she'd driven down from Providence. When Heather had gone back to the kitchen to say good-bye, Ariel had said that she was leaving too, and Heather had offered her a ride.

"I love your father's books," Heather said when she got behind the wheel.

"He says you're writing something about them?" Ariel said.

"I am. For graduate school. I hope to write a book about your father someday. I know an editor at the University of Chicago Press who's very interested."

"Cool," Ariel said.

Heather was proud of herself for acting like a normal person. She didn't feel like a normal person at the moment. Most of her mind was elsewhere: she was trying to absorb the meaning of that strange encounter in the hallway — if it had any meaning at all.

"What's it like to be the daughter of a great writer?" she said.

"You think he's a great writer?" Ariel looked delighted, but also, oddly, a little surprised.

"Don't you?"

"*I* do, but he's my father." A pause. "I'm not much of a reader, actually. I've actually only read two of his books."

Heather's estimation of her, low from the moment she'd set eyes on her, got lower.

The streets were bright with ice; ahead of them, a van slid slowly, with a stately grace, into a taxi.

"Are you a dancer?" Heather said.

"I used to be. I'm an aerobics teacher now. That's what happens to dancers when they die." She ran her hands through her hair. "At the moment I don't feel like anything. I'm not a dancer, I'm not a therapist, I'm not a mother. I feel like a collection of negatives."

If you really listen, you find that most people tell you their life stories as soon as they meet you. Ariel, clearly, was another boring forty-year-old obsessed with her "biological clock."

Heather couldn't relate to this. If the point

26

of your life is to produce another life, then what's the point of your life? All you're doing is passing the buck.

They were near Columbus Circle, where the traffic merges confusingly. Heather was braking for the oncoming traffic when two men carrying what appeared to be a six-foot hoagie trotted in front of the car. She turned the wheel to the left, and the back of the car swerved to the right. They were out of control.

"You have to go with the skid," Ariel said.

"That's a myth," Heather said, and she jerked the wheel to make the car go straight. She knew you were *supposed* to turn into the skid, but that seemed too wimpy to consider.

The car lurched in the wrong direction, and Heather had a sickening feeling in her stomach. "You have to go with the skid," Ariel said again, and this time Heather thought it might not be a bad idea to give the conventional wisdom a try. She turned into the skid, and the car, though still out of control, was suddenly moving more calmly. Two thousand pounds of calm, graceful metal, it glided, silent, majestic, slow, toward a U-Haul truck parked near the corner. Heather gently pressed the brake, but they kept moving.

They were about to have an accident.

There was nothing she could do to stop it. The black night air was clear, and every sound she heard — a car horn, the hum of the traffic — was distinct, and ghostly, and like music. Heather could almost hear the sound that was about to come, the peculiarly satisfying sound of metal on metal. And then, an inch or two away from the truck, the car stopped moving, as if it had decided it was just browsing, and didn't really want to have an accident today.

They sat there for a moment without speaking. Although they hadn't hit anything, the impact had seemed so certain that Heather's imagination had supplied the sound and feel of it, and in the moment of stupidity that follows any physical crisis she was wondering whether she could have gotten whiplash from the *thought* that they had been about to crash.

During the rest of the drive, Heather drove slowly and carefully. When they reached 23rd Street, Ariel thanked her for the ride and got out of the car. But before she closed the door, she stuck her head back in.

"We had an adventure," she said.

6

Ariel let herself into her apartment and put her backpack down. Her cat, Sancho, hurried up to her and pushed his head against her shins.

"Miracle cat," she said absently.

She was still musing about what had just happened. It was amazing.

The little miniskirted biographer had almost killed them. But that wasn't the amazing thing. The amazing thing was that she wouldn't go with the skid. It was as if she knew what to do but refused to do it.

How could something that was so natural to one person be so difficult for someone else? A couple of years ago Ariel had lost control of a car on an icy road in Vermont, and she'd turned toward the skid instinctively. It was so natural that she probably would've done it even if she hadn't known it was the right thing to do. If life had taught her anything — if she had a philosophy of life — it probably boiled down to that: Go with the skid.

The Lost City. She had no idea where the book was. During her year in California a small army of her friends had trooped through this apartment, and for all she knew someone had walked off with it. She looked through her not too many books and couldn't find it.

Maybe it was in the closet. She had an enormous closet, and sometimes things ended up there because they made her feel guilty when they were out on view. She went into the closet, got down on her knees, and started going through the boxes.

She was still annoyed about the way her father had acted around the miniskirted scholar. He'd acted like he wanted to date her. "Surely, even Oprah ventures a mistaken opinion on occasion." That wasn't even the way he *talked*. *Nobody* talked like that. He'd looked embarrassed that she'd even mentioned Oprah, and he'd changed the subject as fast as he could. He never would have dismissed her like that if the little biographer hadn't been in the next room.

It was strange, the way a new person can bring out a new, unpleasant side of someone you love.

Sitting on her knees, going through her closet, she was trying to figure out why that hot-wired little intellectual had thrown her for a loop. It was probably her own possessiveness. When Ariel had returned to New

Whenever she visited her father she liked to check out his night table to see what he was reading. When he was in the hospital, the book he'd left on his night table at home was the autobiography of William Butler Yeats. Leafing through it, she came across a passage he'd underlined: "In Paris Synge once said to me, 'We should unite stoicism, asceticism and ecstasy. Two of them have often come together, but the three never.' "

She was surprised that he'd underlined this. She knew that her father was a stoic and an ascetic, but she wouldn't have thought of him as someone who yearned for ecstasy.

For Ariel, ecstasy was the only one of those qualities that mattered.

She was touched to learn that he was still spiritually youthful enough to be underlining passages like this. Young enough to be seeking guidelines for living.

After the operation there was no ecstasy; there wasn't even stoicism. He was depressed for months: he didn't write; he didn't return phone calls; he read nothing more taxing than the newspaper. He spent most of his time watching TV — which amazed her, because he'd hardly ever watched TV before. But she thought she understood what he was going through. She'd once heard that

York last fall, the rock she thought she could cling to was her father: his love of her, and his need of her.

In the past year he'd had a heart attack — his second — and two operations: a quadruple bypass and then an operation to repair a damaged aorta, whatever that was. When he'd told her about the problem with his aorta, he said it was what Einstein had died of. "I suppose I should be flattered to be in such distinguished company, but it's an honor I'd just as soon forgo." She was touched by his good humor, his courage. Listening to him on the phone, three thousand miles away, she had resolved to be strong for him, to keep her own trivial problems in perspective.

The resolution lasted five minutes — as soon as she got off the phone she was back into her crack-up. Peter, the guy she'd been living with, the guy she'd been talking about having a child with, had started sleeping with some underage cutie, a girl with noteworthy hair. Peter had come home one night and started criticizing Ariel's hair.

Which was nasty, because he knew that her hair was a source of perpetual woe.

She got up from the closet and went into the bathroom to check her hair. Her hair was aimlessly frizzy, and there was nothing she could do to bring it to heel. In her nearly four decades on this planet, she'd never been able to figure out where to put the part in her hair. Her new hairdresser claimed that she didn't need to worry about a part — he said she'd look great if she just gently "tossed" her hair, like a salad. It was a comforting theory, but Ariel wasn't sure she believed it.

"Lettuce head," she said to herself in the mirror. Then she went back to the closet and resumed her search.

So Peter gave her the old heave-ho, and her father was sick, and she was getting sick of her job, and finally she stopped working. For a month she mostly stayed in bed, ordering in Chinese food and watching Nick at Nite — she kept herself together every day by counting the hours till *Mary Tyler Moore* — and the only reason she got out of bed was to check her hair, and she began to suspect that she was having a nervous breakdown; and when her father had his second operation in three months, the one on his aorta, she came east to see him; and walking on Irving Place on a particularly nasty day in March she realized that she didn't want to live in California anymore, land of the eternal sun, and that she could move back to New York, take care of her father in his convalescence, forget Peter, afresh.

In the space of three months went from a vigorous seventy to a seventy-one. He became a man outlived his body. His body was bloa purple-veined and his legs didn't loo like legs anymore but like rotted log inexplicable protrusions, and after he little weight everything turned to flab a somehow looked fatter than he'd lo when he was fatter. He hadn't abused body over the years so much as ignorec but it came to the same thing. When thought of some of the older dancers s knew, people who'd become choreographe but who still danced for pleasure — peopl who respected their bodies — her fathei seemed to belong to a different species. When she'd danced in Erick Hawkins's company he was deep into his sixties and still a lithe, sexy man.

During her first two weeks back in New York, when her father was in the hospital, she stayed in his apartment while the guy who was subletting her place looked for something else. It was an oddly comforting way to come home. Though she was terrified that her father was going to die, it was calming to live in his apartment.

when you have heart surgery — your chest sawed open, your ribs cracked, the action of your heart replaced for hours by the action of a machine — the suffering you undergo for the next few months, that peculiarly spiritual sorrow, is the sorrow of a body in mourning for itself, a body that believes it has died.

Somehow even times of grief can be sweet to remember. She visited him every day in the hospital, bringing him little fat-free treats, sitting by his bed and kibitzing with him and the old friends of his who dropped by; and when he was back home, in his depression, she was there constantly, shopping for him, cooking for him, keeping him company. It was a terrible time, but it was also a loving, cozy time. She bought him a VCR and rented movies for him; in the more than two decades since her mother died, he'd gone to the movies about once a year, so there was a lot of great stuff he'd never seen. They watched a lot of Woody Allen movies, a few by John Sayles, and a bunch of old Bette Davis weepers that he'd ignored in his youth. She was amazed by how out of it he was, movie-wise. He reminded her of one of those Japanese soldiers who used to wander out of the hills after spending thirty years in hiding, thinking that the Second World War was still on. Her father had been hiding out for thirty years in his writing room, thinking that the war of high culture versus low was still raging away. He hadn't gotten the news that the war was over: that high culture, which he had cherished, fought for, given his life for, had been crushed.

Despite the circumstances, it was delicious just to be with him. He'd never had much time for her when she was growing up. Through most of her childhood and youth her father had been represented by a closed door and the thin metallic slapping noise of his typewriter keys.

She couldn't find the damn book.

She was embarrassed that she'd never read it. And that lipsticked intellectual had made her feel worse. "I've already read it. I just want to be able to refer to it when I'm writing." Fuck you.

Heather. Even her name was idiotic. Every third jerk on the street was named Heather.

Ariel had disliked her on sight: she'd had a sneaky, guilty look in her eyes during that first moment in the kitchen. She must have been stealing cookies.

But it wasn't just that. After that first awkward second, you could tell that she was extremely pleased with herself. She was one of those people — you could tell — for whom everything had gone right in life. She radiated smugness; she radiated success. "I know an editor who's very interested." When she'd said that, in a smug, fake-blasé tone of voice, Ariel had wanted to smack her.

She did have a certain style — that was undeniable. Her compact little body — a swimmer's body; her Mr. Spock haircut; the three tiny earrings in her right ear; the mysterious little scar under her lip: even her imperfections had style. Ariel had noticed everything about her, the way one woman notices another.

She was further along in life than Ariel was. How could that be? By the time Heather was born, Ariel had already had about ten years of dance lessons, had seemed well along on the road of life — she'd seemed precocious, even. And now this girl was full of energy and promise, and Ariel was a has-been, a washed-up former dancer, yesterday's news. How did that little girl get ahead of me, when I had a fifteen-year head start?

But on the other hand, Heather couldn't go with the skid. And if not for Ariel, all that bright promise would have ended up in a bony bloody pulp on the windshield.

While she was still on her knees, rustling around in the closet, she heard her answering machine going through its conniptions —

37

she had an ancient answering machine that hurled itself around on her desk when it took a call. She hadn't heard the phone ring. She went out to pick up the phone, but when she heard who was leaving the message she decided not to.

It was Victor. Victor Mature.

Victor was a guy she'd had dinner with twice. She was beginning to think he was her fate. There was something uninspiring about him, but he seemed like a decent guy, and he seemed to like her, and he'd mentioned, on their second date, that he was at the time of life when he wanted to start a family. So she was beginning to think that marrying him would be the mature thing to do. That was why she thought of him as Victor Mature.

He was the first guy she'd met in a while who wasn't disgusting. That was a point in his favor. And though some part of her mind, when she contemplated marrying him — when she even contemplated sleeping with him — though some clear voice in her mind shouted "No!," she thought the voice could be overruled.

She stood next to the answering machine, listening to his smooth, rich, chocolatey, man-from-nowhere voice, and she wondered whether she could spend the rest of her life with that slightly too perfect voice.

On the phone the other day he'd said that *Husbands and Wives* was his favorite movie. Ariel loved Woody Allen — *Annie Hall* was *her* favorite movie — but she hated *Husbands and Wives*. She hated the part where one of the husbands has an affair with an aerobics teacher, who's portrayed as a brainless bimbo. When Ariel saw it, everybody in the audience seemed to think the aerobics teacher scenes were hilarious. It didn't seem to matter to them that the character was a caricature, a cliché. And it apparently hadn't occurred to Woody Allen that your thoughts and your emotions and your life can be serious and worthy of respect even if you don't know how to sit around talking about your problems in terms of the theories of Jean-Paul Sartre.

It wasn't really the fact that Victor liked the movie that bothered her: she didn't expect him to go through life campaigning for the rights of aerobics teachers. But when she'd tried to explain how she felt, he'd told her she was overreacting.

Nevertheless, he was the best prospect she'd come upon in months, and she was trying to give him a chance.

Sometimes she thought about getting back in touch with Casey Davis — the most interesting, truest-hearted man she'd ever found. But things hadn't worked out with Casey the first time, so there was no reason to think they could work out if they tried again. Anyway, he was probably married by now. Everyone was married by now.

She was full of anxiety, full of self-pity, and she decided to try to calm herself through meditation. She was always trying to work meditation into her life, as an every-day discipline, but it was hard to find the time.

The idea is to sit quietly with your eyes closed and pay attention only to your breath, letting your thoughts pass lightly across the stage of your mind. Ariel had always found this hard to do. Whenever she tried to medi-tate, all she could think about was that she didn't meditate enough. She had no disci-pline; she couldn't set a goal and stay with it. When she came east she'd planned to start afresh, maybe go to social-work school or find another way to become a therapist, but here she was, having done nothing to get closer to that goal, teaching aerobics again.

She tried to focus on her breath, but the stage of her mind wouldn't stay empty. Her father came on, limping, with his weak liga-ments and his weak heart, and the mini-skirted scholar came on, full of an obscure hunger, and Sancho came on — actually, he had jumped on her lap — and Victor Mature came on, smiling with an eager hopefulness, and everyone was milling around — it was like a housewarming party — and all Ariel could do, finally, was listen to them all, let them have their way, admit them.

After she had been meditating for ten minutes, a new thought bubbled into her mind. She realized why she was so upset about this young woman. It wasn't just possessiveness after all. When, a couple of weeks ago, her father had mentioned casually that he'd heard from someone who was writing a study of his work — he'd mentioned it so casually that she knew it was important to him — she'd immediately become afraid. Though it would be great if someone, even this Heather person, wrote a book about him someday — her father's life had been so difficult for so long; he deserved something wonderful — Ariel didn't believe it would happen. Maybe it was just a peculiarly Jewish sense of disaster that had been planted deep inside her by thousands of years of tribal memory, and that remained untouchable in the core of her, despite all her years of interest in Buddhism, Hinduism, Taoism, yoga, tai chi, Codependents Anonymous, Rolfing, Authentic Movement, and the Alexander Technique, but the very fact that something good was seemingly going to happen for her father, after all this time, filled Ariel with a superstitious dread. It wasn't the lipsticked scholar's fault, but Ariel felt as if this young woman were the angel of death.

7

As Schiller walked through the hospital corridors toward the room of his dying friend, he felt his spirit expand with joy. Schiller was an atheist: his parents had raised him to be an atheist and his faithlessness had never wavered. But he had worshipful inclinations, and certain events and places were like temples to him. The kind of reverence that someone else might describe as religious came over him most strongly at weddings, at funerals, and in hospitals. Here you felt the fleetingness of life, and therefore its holiness; here you saw that life and death are married. Whenever he entered a hospital — whether to visit someone who was dying or someone who had given birth — he felt the touch of the sacred. He had even felt it, at moments, during his own long confinement in the spring.

Or maybe he was joyful today simply because his friend Levin was still, for the moment, alive.

Levin was sitting up in bed, reading. The table next to him was piled high with books.

Schiller hung back in the doorway. Levin

was reading the one-volume edition of Leon Edel's biography of Henry James. As Schiller watched, Levin scribbled something in a notepad. He wrote with difficulty because of the I.V. tube in his arm.

Schiller had always admired his friend, but never more than now. Levin didn't have much time left, but this hadn't dimmed the joy he took in learning. As long as he had the strength to follow his vocation, he would follow it, patiently and serenely.

Schiller didn't move. This was the way he wanted to remember his friend: reading, with perfect concentration, perfect calm. He would have liked the moment to last a long time.

Levin finally looked up. "Leonard." He took off his reading glasses. "Have you been spying on me?"

"I was wondering how you do it," Schiller said. He touched Levin's hand and sat in a chair near the bed. "When I was sick last year I couldn't even read the sports page."

"That's not the way I remember it. I seem to remember you hunched over a little green notebook, working on the fifty-seventh draft of your novel."

It wasn't true, but it was nice of Levin to remember it that way.

"Thanks for the book, by the way."

Schiller had given him the James biography the week before.

"How are you doing?" Schiller said.

"I go in and out. They're having a little trouble regulating the drugs. I spent most of the day yesterday staring at my feet." He poked his toes out from under the blanket. "They're not very interesting."

"Is there anything I can get you?"

"Some apple juice would be good."

There was a bottle on the night table; Schiller poured some juice into a plastic glass and handed it to him. Levin gripped the cup with difficulty: his hands were bloated and stiff from chemotherapy.

"What's new in the world?" he said. "Did Murray finish his piece?"

Murray was a friend whose healthy sense of his own importance had entertained them both for almost forty years.

"Yes. Murray finished his piece. He called the other day to read some of it to me. He reads to me for about five minutes, and then he says, 'There's a lot more, and it's just as moving!' "

Schiller visited Levin once a week. He still couldn't quite absorb the fact that his young friend was dying. Levin was in his sixties, but Schiller still thought of him, and would always think of him, as his young friend.

Levin had never produced much — he'd never written a book, and he'd never been concerned about writing one. He had devoted himself to his teaching; he had written his elegant reviews and essays, three or four a year; and the very spareness of his output had finally begun to seem a mark of his intellectual delicacy, the fineness of his discriminations. Every writer writes with mixed motives, with some combination of purity and self-aggrandizement; Levin was no exception, but he was much more pure than most. He would have been reading and writing in the same way — for pleasure and self-clarification — if you had put him on a desert island. He had spent little time pushing himself forward in the world, "managing his career"; that would have been a disagreeable distraction from reading and writing and teaching, from the work he loved.

He was beautiful even in his refusals. In the sixties he'd signed a contract for a book on Leigh Hunt, the nineteenth-century essayist and friend of Keats; he wrote two hundred pages and finally decided that only in the twenty-page first chapter had he said anything new. He published the chapter in *Partisan Review*, returned his advance, and bowed out of the contract. The essay had become a minor classic; at least one scholar of the Romantic period had made his reputation by expanding on the hints Levin had dropped there.

"Are you hungry?" he said. "There's fruit."

Schiller detached a pear from a large fruit basket, found a knife, and went to work on the pear, sharing bite-sized pieces with Levin. When they were done he found a paper towel and cleaned off Levin's hands.

Schiller thought of mentioning his lunch with the young woman, whose name he couldn't recall at the moment. He decided not to: it would sound as if he were boasting.

They spent half an hour talking. They talked about sports; about Levin's three children and Schiller's daughter; about the latest controversy in what was left of their part of the literary world. Lionel Abel had insulted the memory of Harold Rosenberg in a letter to *Commentary*, Rosenberg's literary executor had written an angry response, and everyone in the little crowd of people who remembered Rosenberg was all aflutter. It was an exciting feeling; it made everyone feel as if it were 1957 again.

Schiller thought that such scuffles were ridiculous at this late date, but they still held his interest, as quarrels among younger writers did not. His world was ending, and it was hard not to feel as if the world of intelligent discourse itself was coming to an end. The younger generation seemed so bent on celebrity, as opposed to lasting achievement. But of course, every generation believes itself to be the last truly cultivated generation. It's a form of vanity that's hard to resist.

Levin closed his eyes, and Schiller thought he had gone to sleep. But he hadn't gone to sleep.

"I'm trying not to be morbid," he said, "but it's difficult. I've been reading the James book. Did I thank you for that, by the way?"

"Yes, you thanked me."

"After William died, Henry got a letter from H. G. Wells — I think it was Wells — in which he said . . . I can't remember exactly what he said. But he said something about how unjust it was that all that 'ripened understanding' should be lost." He reached for the book and looked through it for a minute, trying to find the passage, but with an expression of frustration he finally put it back down. "That's how I feel now. About myself. I don't feel like an old man. I feel as if I'm still ripening. I feel as if I'm just starting to understand things. But what's the use of this ripeness? It doesn't give birth to anything. It doesn't nourish anything. It just disappears."

"You *have* given birth, George. Think of all your students. Think of your friends. Think of all the people who've profited from the things you've written. Think of all the people who've learned from your example."

Levin shook his head. "Oh please," he said. "Don't get corny on me now."

A tiny nurse came into the room. "Look at your hair," she said. "It's a disaster area." This was true. His latest bout of chemotherapy had ravaged his hair. There were only a few sparse patches left, and not for long: he was sure to be bald within a day or two.

"Karen is concerned about my grooming," Levin said.

"Someone has to be." She opened the top drawer of his night table, extracted a comb, and ran it through the few sad tufts of hair that remained on his head.

He closed his eyes and smiled weakly. "Ardent brushing does not mitigate my troubles. But thank you anyway, dear."

Ardent brushing does not mitigate my troubles. Schiller thought he recognized the phrase. It was from the Henry James biography. It was something James said to his sister-in-law during his last illness — one of the few coherent remarks he made during the last months of his life.

Levin was one of the people Schiller had

49

taken the entire journey with. Who would there be to talk to after he was gone?

Many years before, in the late fifties, the two of them had played chess almost every week. Levin was maddeningly slow, and when the game wasn't going well for him, he became slower. He was preoccupied with the thought that at every point of the game there was at least one perfect move, one "brilliancy," which he could find if he pondered the position deeply enough. Even when he found himself in an impossible fix, when there was nothing to do except resign, he would sit for twenty minutes studying the board. "What are you waiting for?" Schiller would finally say. "You *lost.*"

Levin would slowly, abstractedly lift his eyes from the board. "I'm searching for a brilliancy," he would say.

Now, as the young nurse shifted him in his bed with careful hands, making sure not to disturb the I.V. tube in his arm or the catheter in his penis, Levin looked at Schiller and raised his hands in a gesture of gentle patient helplessness and said, "I'm searching for a brilliancy."

Schiller excused himself and went to a lounge down the hall. What he had said to Levin was true: he would be wrong to feel as if his life had come to nothing. The people

50

who knew him had been permanently enriched by his example. But he could understand Levin's feeling that this was not enough. His work wouldn't live on. He would never find his brilliancy. This was where it would end for him, in this room. He would be remembered by the people who loved him, but he would never pass his existence on to the future. He was trapped in his time, trapped in his body, and when his body and the bodies of those who loved him were gone, all trace of him would be lost.

Schiller thought of the young woman he had seen the day before. Wolfe. Something Wolfe. Heather Wolfe.

It was strange to think that his work meant something to anyone that young. She was so young that it was almost as if she were an emissary from the future. It was hard to imagine how his work could mean anything to her when she didn't know anything about his milieu, about the world he had come of age in.

But then again, then again. There was something intoxicating about that thought — that this emissary from the future felt strongly about his work. As if she had traveled back in time to pluck him out, to liberate him from his context, to carry him forward into the next century.

It was an exhilarating feeling.

The lounge overlooked the East River; the midmorning sun was burning; the river seemed to be on fire. He felt an intense, selfish joy. She might carry him into the future. She might keep him alive. Even if she did write a book about him someday, he knew there wasn't much chance that it would make a difference, but any small chance was better than nothing. It was like a message in a bottle. One more chance that he'd be remembered; one more chance that he would find a fate like that of Henry Roth or Nathanael West, like that of any of those writers who were "discovered" in their dotage or after they died. When he'd talked with her on the phone last week he'd been skeptical — why waste time talking about your work with some overheated young academic who wanted "background" for her thesis, when the thing that mattered was not what he had to say about it, but the work itself? He'd carried that skepticism into their meeting, but she had seemed so bright and so energetic and so . . . daring, that she'd overturned his doubts. That strange scene in the hallway — as he thought about it now, his hand still seemed to be buzzing on the spot where, bizarrely, she had kissed it. She was an unusual young woman, and he found it exciting to think that she wanted to write about his work. And thinking about Levin, how Levin in a few months would be powder while he himself would have a chance of living on, he was shaken by a horrible guilty flooding feeling of triumph. His friendship with Levin had always had an element of rivalry, and he felt drunk with the thought that he might have won the race with his old friend after all. His friend was dying fifty feet away, but he felt like dancing.

After a few minutes he made his way back to Levin's room. The nurse was gone. Schiller settled back into the chair; he felt his bad conscience pouring out of him in waves, and he wondered if Levin, with the sharpened senses of a dying man, might be able to smell it.

"Are you still in the mood to do me a favor?" Levin said.

Schiller raised his eyebrows obligingly.

"My feet are killing me."

Schiller drew his chair closer to the bed and began to massage his friend's feet. His feet were very white and dry.

"Thank you," Levin said. "Thank you."

8

Schiller met his daughter that evening outside the Joyce Theater, on 19th Street and Eighth Avenue. He was taking her to a dance concert for a belated birthday present. As he approached he saw her waiting on the street: dressed in a baggy purple jumpsuit, she looked as if she was ready to strap on a parachute and leap from a plane.

"Happy birthday, my dear," he said, and he kissed her dryly on the cheek. Whenever he saw her, he tried to give his affection a dry, formal, almost ironic cast. What he felt was precisely the opposite: the sight of his daughter always brought on a dizzying rush of tenderness and protectiveness and love. He tried to appear less moved than he was, because he believed that fathers should be a little distant, should give their children room to breathe.

"You snuck up on me," she said. "On little cat feet."

They found their seats. They were attending a performance of the Erick Hawkins Dance Company. Ariel had been a member of the company during her twenties and early thirties, until the protests of her knees became too insistent to ignore; now she liked to see them at least once a year.

Schiller took off his coat and settled in for an hour or two of dreaming. He knew he wouldn't be able to concentrate tonight.

When the lights went down, his thoughts went back to the hospital. He kept thinking of Levin, alone now, staring up at the ceiling. He thought of his own long stay in the hospital last spring. He'd had plenty of visitors — Ariel, old friends, former students — but it didn't make any difference. Every night he was left alone with his damaged heart, left alone to think about death.

All he hoped was that he wouldn't die slowly, as Levin was dying. He didn't want to endure another prolonged spell of decrepitude. Let it come quickly when it comes.

When he finally turned his attention to the dancers, he found that they annoyed him. Their very proficiency annoyed him: their fantastically muscular legs, their unbelievable lightness. It was such a deceptive representation of life, such a small part of it all. Somewhere on the stage, a dying man or woman should be lying on a bed, working hard for each breath.

When the lights came up for the intermission Ariel asked him if he had enjoyed it.

"Of course. It was wonderful."

"I'm not so sure," she said. "I think you were writing or something."

The lobby was crowded; Schiller and his daughter went outside for some air. She took his hand and pulled him across the street, into a little Cuban-Chinese restaurant where she ordered a *café con leche* to go. "I need a pick-me-up," she said. Schiller ordered a black coffee. Coffee was forbidden on his Pritikin diet, but he hadn't been able to give it up completely.

They went back into the cold night and stood outside the theater. The coffee was too hot to drink; Ariel blew on hers with a hopeful expression. He remembered how he'd taught her to blow on her soup, when she was four or five.

The lights in the lobby started flashing. "So much for coffee," Schiller said. He leaned over at the curb and started to pour his coffee into the sewer.

"Why don't we just leave it here?" Ariel said. "We can drink it after." She put her cup on top of a green metal box, a signal box, attached to a traffic-light post. "We can drink it cold."

"Just leave it here on the street? We can't do that."

"Why? What could happen?"

"I don't know. Anything." He poured the rest of his coffee away. "I'll buy you a fresh cup later. I can spring for the seventy-five cents."

He came close to his daughter and brushed a strand of hair from her face. "You trust the world," he said.

They smiled at each other — each of them quizzical, puzzled by the other's sense of life.

They found their seats, the concert resumed, but now Schiller couldn't pay attention to the dance at all. He was stunned with tenderness for his daughter. The idea that they could leave the coffee outside, on a New York street, and find it safe an hour later! He hadn't had an answer to her question, "What could happen?" In New York, what could happen was wilder than anything he could imagine. A few months ago, after getting a busy signal at a pay phone on 72nd Street, he'd put his finger in the coin-return slot to retrieve his quarter and dipped it into something soft and warm and sticky. Extracting the finger, he saw that whatever was on it was soft and warm and sticky and *brown;* he walked into a bar and went straight to the men's room and spent a ridiculous five minutes washing and rewashing his hands. Why should anyone have gone to the trouble to stuff something revolting into a coin-return slot? In New York, such a question made no sense. The answer was simply "Because it is there." What was surprising was that things like this didn't happen more often. He wondered how civility survived in the city at all: when someone preceding him out the rear door of a bus held it open for him, or when the people on a subway platform waited until he left the train before they got on, Schiller always had a moment of baffled gratitude.

As he watched the dancers — the beautiful long-legged women, the superfluous men — all he could think about was his daughter. He often worried that she wasn't strong enough for the world. Was this just what any father thinks about his daughter, or was it the truth about Ariel? He feared it was the truth about Ariel. With her near breakdowns — she'd had two of them now, one during her first semester of college, and then another last year — and with her curiously tattered history of relationships, she was always on the edge of a fall. And he didn't know how to help her.

She was so unequipped for life — she was more like a child than a woman. Her habits weren't New York habits: she kept her keys in the back pocket of her knapsack, and she usually kept the pocket unzipped; she talked to strangers on the street. They weren't the habits of a woman who knew how to protect herself.

When she came east last spring it was heartbreaking to see her. She had supposedly come to take care of him during his convalescence, but he could see that she was barely holding herself together, and that she needed those long nights of movies and togetherness as much as he did.

After the concert they went to a Chinese restaurant on Hudson Street. When they were seated, under the unforgiving fluorescent light, he could see that she was suffering the harsh effects of winter. Her skin had temporarily lost its softness; the cold had made it taut; there were new lines around her eyes, lines of tense and tired white skin.

Probably some of his dizzy protectiveness came from having seen her at his house the day before. It had been unsettling to see her alongside that young woman, Heather. Heather, who was fully a generation younger, seemed so much more self-possessed, more purposeful than his daughter.

He wanted her to ask him about Heather; he wanted to mention that he'd decided to help her with her project. But she didn't ask, and something warned him away from bringing up the young woman's name.

"So what's your story, lass?" he said. His habit of calling younger people "lass" or "lad" was one of those things about himself that he found charming, but which, he sometimes suspected, charmed other people less. "What have you been up to?"

"I'm storyless, Dad."

"How could that be? A lively young woman like yourself?"

"I *am* storyless. That's exactly the word for me. I was thinking about it the other day. I went to MoMA to see a show by some hot young artist. That German guy. It turned out to be really stupid — it was all gimmicks. One piece had a TV in it, another had a trash basket that you could throw stuff in.

"When you leave the exhibit you walk right into the permanent collection. Just behind me there was this kid in his twenties, with this scraggly beard. He comes storming out of the trash basket show and goes up to a Van Gogh and says to himself, 'Finally! Fucking *art!*' "

She nodded, as if the point of this story were obvious.

"And?" Schiller said.

"*That's* one of the stories the world likes to hear. The young man burning with promise. The young beginner, burning to make fucking art. And that used to be *my* story. I was the young dancer, and all I thought about was fucking art. But what am I now? What do I do now? I'm an exercise teacher. I jump around all day yelling, 'One more time, ladies!' If you're thirty-nine, and you're not successful, and you still don't know what you want to do with your life, that's not a story the world wants to hear. It's not a story *I* want to hear.

"When you're in your twenties, when you're in your early thirties, you can tell yourself a nice story about your life: 'I'm young, I have promise, I have everything going for me.' But when you can't tell yourself that story anymore, what *are* you? You're storyless."

"That can't be true. There has to be a story for your time of life."

"Tell me what it is then."

He tried to think of what it could be. "A beautiful, intelligent young woman, who's already had two successful careers, as a dancer and an exercise teacher, is searching for a new life."

"And a decent boyfriend," she put in quickly. It reminded him of the days when he used to tuck her in and tell her a bedtime story, and she'd eagerly add the crucial details.

"And a decent boyfriend. One of the remarkable things about this young woman is that she's always known what she's wanted to do in life. She wanted to be a dancer from the age of five, and she became one. Then she wanted to combine her dance abilities with some kind of helping work, and she did that too." Ariel's aerobics class was for overweight women and older women; she gave them a place where they could work out without feeling judged. "Now she wants to do something new, and she's in the unfamiliar position of not knowing exactly what she wants. It's scary, but she knows that growth is always scary. She's struggling, but she knows that without struggle there's no life."

Ariel brightened momentarily. He was happy to see her happy, but he wished she weren't so susceptible to the appeal of pop psychology.

"Thank you," she said quietly. "When you tell me I'm doing okay, I can almost believe it."

"Of course you are," he said, almost believing it himself.

She did seem cheered. The waiter arrived with their food, and Ariel eagerly reached for the dumplings. "I love this restaurant," she said. "It's a dumpling haven."

"How's the boyfriend situation?" Schiller

said. "Any prospects?"

"Yes. I've met my future husband, in fact," she said.

"Congratulations. Anyone I know?"

"I've told you about him. That guy Victor. That lawyer."

He remembered vaguely. "You didn't seem that taken with him."

"Maybe you reach an age where you have to compromise. Isn't that the essence of maturity?"

He didn't know what to say. He didn't like to see her selling herself short, but he knew how much she wanted to have kids. He had no advice about such matters. He'd been alone for so many years that he'd lost all sense of what to do about the quandaries of longing.

More than once he'd thought of asking if she'd considered having a child on her own. If she were a different kind of woman, he would have asked. But he didn't think she was strong enough to undertake that.

"I do know what I'd like to do next in life, actually. I want to be a healer."

"You are a healer. You give a great deal to your clients."

"Don't humor me. I'm a glorified gym teacher. I want to be a real therapist, but I can't afford it. I never even paid off my student loans from college."

He knew this already, and she knew he knew it, but she couldn't help telling him again. It made him feel miserable, though he was sure that wasn't her intention. A father worth his salt would be able to pay his daughter's way through social-work school. A father who hadn't spent his prime earning years on the poverty line, living like Raskolnikov, indulging himself in the effort to make fucking art.

"But anyway, even if I don't marry Victor Mature, I'm going to have everything figured out pretty soon. Did I tell you I made an appointment to see a psychic?"

He raised his eyebrows.

"Millie Meeker. She's supposed to be famous in the psychic community. She's the psychic that all the other psychics consult. They swear by her."

"They swear by her, do they? That sounds marvelous."

"Oh yeah — marvelous. You think your daughter is a ditz."

"Not at all. Marxism is dead, Freudianism is dead — all the great explanatory systems have broken down. We all need to find new myths. I wouldn't mind consulting a psychic myself."

"You're a nice man," Ariel said.

"I'm not being nice. I'm being serious. Almost."

On the street, having carried the conversation further in her mind, she said, "I guess you've been known to do an unconventional thing or two yourself. Are you going to keep your date in Paris?"

"I plan to. Do you think I'm crazy?"

"You're not crazy. You're a romantic."

Many years ago, he and Stella — Ariel's mother, his wife — had picked a far-off date and agreed to spend it together in Paris. Now the day was near. Stella was no longer alive to keep the appointment, but he intended to keep it himself, for both of them. He supposed he was a romantic at that.

He kissed his daughter good-bye, and she ran off to catch a bus that was just opening its doors near the bus shelter. He took pleasure in watching her run. When she was a kid she was a bit of a clown, and he used to tell her that she was the greatest physical comedian since Chaplin; and through all the disappointments of her life — she'd endured more than her share of disappointments — she'd retained the physical exuberance of her youth. Beneath the struggling, churning surface, she seemed to have an inalienable core of well-being; when you watched her move, you found it hard to believe she could ever be unhappy.

9

When Heather was ten years old, her fifth-grade teacher — a would-be poet who had long ago endured some sort of literary drubbing in New York and retreated to Cleveland Heights to nurse his psychic wounds — took the class to a lecture that Jorge Luis Borges was giving at Oberlin College. He said that Borges was the greatest writer alive.

Most of what Borges talked about that day was over her head, but he told one story that she never forgot. He said that he had once encountered a young man who said he had no interest in reading about Hamlet, "because Hamlet wasn't real." Borges took a sip of water and paused dramatically, looking around the crowded hall. "I said, 'You are mistaken, my young friend. Prince Hamlet is more real than you are.' "

There was a reception after the event; Borges was sitting in a tiny chair, surrounded by admirers. Squeezing nimbly between the grown-ups, Heather made her way to his side.

"Are *you* as real as Hamlet?" she demanded.

Blind, frail, ancient, the writer smiled at her mournfully. "No, my dear. Hamlet is more real than I am. Even the Borges in my stories is more real than I."

He asked her her name, and, bowing slightly in his chair, he lifted her hand to his lips and kissed it.

A few years later, when she heard he had died, she thought, If it wasn't true then, it's true now. The Borges in his stories is still alive.

As a young girl, Heather lived in books. She read at the dinner table; she read as she walked to the grocery store; she tried to figure out a way to read in the shower. She didn't really belong to the modern world: when she read magazine articles that offered portraits of her generation she didn't recognize herself at all. She would discover that she was supposed to be "affectless," when what she felt in herself was a wild intensity. She would discover that she was supposed to lack the attention span for "linear narratives," when in fact she loved nothing more than to lose herself in mammoth books. At thirteen she read *Middlemarch* and imagined herself as Dorothea Brooke, trying to find a way to live virtuously; at fourteen she read *The Rainbow* and became Ursula Brangwen, passionately searching for a wider life.

She was a wild, rebellious, intense, unhappy girl with a conviction that she was fated for great things. She didn't know what she wanted, but she felt sure that the stage on which she would play out her aspirations was far from Cleveland Heights.

Heather's parents were good people — warm-hearted and generous — but their lives were lives of comfortable disappointment. Her mother had dreamed of being a lawyer, but she'd sacrificed herself to be her husband's helpmate while he went through medical school. He, in turn, had had plans to do important research, but he'd fribbled away his gifts and become a dermatologist. Heather loved them without ever quite believing she was their natural daughter.

On her fourteenth birthday, she stood in front of the mirror with a cigarette in her hand. She didn't like the way it tasted, but she liked the way she looked when she held it. "Freedom has always been my theme in life," she said, imagining a day when she could speak these words to a man. A man who would understand her.

During her high school years she spent every Saturday in the Cleveland Heights Public Library, looking for books that would release her, that would spring her from her life. This was where she fell in love with

Leonard Schiller.

On a sleety, gray Saturday in late November, Heather was prowling around in the library stacks, picking out novels at random, reading a few pages of each, hoping to find something that would speak to her. She came across a book called *Tenderness*. She liked the cover — a mild, faded blue. When she turned to the first page, she immediately found herself drawn in by the description of a young couple having coffee in a café in Paris — their conversation humorous, loving, but also somehow tense.

The light in the stacks was bad, but she didn't want to bring the book out to the reading room; she didn't want to break the spell. She sat on the floor in the weak light and read until closing time.

On the day when Heather discovered the book, she was suffering. She'd been suffering for weeks. She'd been admitted to Brown that fall through a special "early entrance" program that allowed you to skip your last year of high school. She was eager to go, but now there was a complication. Her boyfriend was having problems. He was a brilliant but high-strung boy whom she'd been seeing for a year and a half; he had always been the star in their relationship, Heather the side-kick; but now, at the prospect of losing her, he was coming apart. He tried to paste himself together through an elaborate series of rituals, but this was only making things worse. One day he forgot to pat his dog on the head before leaving for school, and he spent the next week convinced that this meant he'd do horribly on his SATs; and when the day of the tests arrived he was too sick with worry to even take them.

Heather had never been confronted by anything as alarming as her boyfriend's deterioration; she didn't understand that she was only the occasion for it, not the cause. She'd just about decided to change her plans and stay in high school for another year, to help him maintain his equilibrium; but she was miserably unhappy about it.

This was what she was going through when she discovered Schiller's novel.

Sometimes, said Thoreau, you can date a new era in your life from the reading of a book. Heather dated an era in her life from the reading of *Tenderness*.

The novel was about an American couple spending a year in France. The woman, Ellen, is completing a dissertation on the philosophy of existentialism. In combination with the intellectual and moral atmosphere of Paris, the ideas she is studying become combustible; she begins to discover that, if she means to take these ideas seriously, she must live in a different way.

But living in a different way means making difficult choices. She decides to remain in France, putting both her academic career and her marriage at risk. She loves her husband; she loves her career; what she's giving up is much clearer to her than what she's seeking; and she knows that her choice will bring grief, to her husband and to herself. But she obscurely senses that she needs to stay.

Near the end of the novel she learns that she's pregnant. This makes the burden of her choice more difficult, but it doesn't make her change her mind.

It was very much a novel of the 1950s, but at the age of sixteen Heather didn't understand this, and if she had understood it she wouldn't have cared. She read the book in a day, and by the end of the day she had decided to go away to college the next year. *Tenderness* gave her courage; it taught her that she was responsible only for her own life, and that she couldn't protect her boyfriend from his fate. In the heroine of the book, she could see herself — she could see herself not as a selfish girl, walking away from someone who needed her, but as a tragic figure, making a wrenching choice. It was as if Schiller had explained her life to her more sympathetically than she'd been able to explain it to herself.

No one she knew had ever heard of him — not her parents, not her teachers. It surprised her, but it didn't really displease her. It made her feel as if he were her secret.

The novel stayed alive in her mind. The summer after her sophomore year in college she took a trip to Europe, and making her way around Paris she discovered that the book had formed her picture of the place, more than anything else she'd read, more than the movies she'd seen. When she sat in cafés there she didn't think of Jean-Paul Sartre or Jean-Paul Belmondo: she thought of the couple from *Tenderness*. In the Luxembourg Garden, she remembered the conversation they had there near the end of the book — when Ellen told her husband that he was "angelic," and he realized that she wasn't going back home with him. Walking across the Pont Neuf, she realized that this was the bridge from which Ellen threw her watch into the Seine.

For years the book was one of her closest companions. Once a year or so she reread it from cover to cover; more often she'd dip into it for ten- or twenty- or fifty-page visits. She loved to return to the world of the book, a world in which people were willing to let go of everything in order to follow their passions.

It was a long time before she came upon another of Schiller's books. In the fall of her senior year at Brown she spent a weekend in Manhattan. Rooting around in a used-book store on Broadway, she found Schiller's second novel, *Two Marriages.*

She bought it and took it back to the apartment where she was staying — a friend's parents' place — and instead of spending the afternoon visiting museums, as she'd planned, she stayed inside and spent the day with Schiller.

She was in another time of confusion. She had no idea what she wanted to do with her life after college. Her mother was urging her to go to law school — she'd never stopped mourning the fact that she herself had not become a lawyer — but Heather wasn't sure. When she came across Schiller's second novel, she hoped it would speak to her as much as *Tenderness* had. She wasn't disappointed.

One of the characters in *Two Marriages* is a young man whose father was a gifted sculptor who died young. The young man has come to believe that his duty in life is to champion his father's reputation. The turning point — not of the book, but of his strand of the book — comes during a conversation with his mother, when she helps him see that the only battles he needs to fight are his own.

When the young man takes this in, his liberation is by no means simple or simply happy: the guiding purpose of his life is suddenly gone. But it's clear that, in the moral scale of the novel, his new uncertainty represents growth.

The book as a whole inspired her — the central characters were penniless young artists in New York, living the kind of life she'd always dreamed about — but the part that dealt with the young man seemed to be addressed to her directly. It was like a letter from a friend. For the second time, Schiller had helped her find the courage to live her own life.

She finally decided to stay at Brown and get her M.A. in comparative literature. Brown gave her a full scholarship, which made the decision easier. During her senior year in the program, her thesis advisor, an aging hipster named James Bonner, who'd told her that she was the most brilliant student he'd worked with in twenty years of teaching, but who was probably just in love with her, began editing a series of book-length essays for the University of Chicago Press. The series had the general title *Rediscoveries*; each book was to be devoted to the work of some neglected American writer.

This gave Heather the idea for her master's thesis: she asked if she could write a study of Leonard Schiller. Bonner had heard of Schiller vaguely, but he hadn't read his work. Heather lent him *Tenderness* and *Two Marriages* — she'd lifted *Tenderness* from the library the previous winter after ascertaining that she was the only person to have checked it out in the last twenty years. He read them over the weekend and delivered his verdict: "He's seventh-rate."

In Bonner's scale of literary merit, Shakespeare and Tolstoy were first-rate; Dostoevsky and George Eliot and Proust were second-rate. Melville was third-rate; Henry James fourth-rate; Virginia Woolf fifth-rate. To be called seventh-rate was high praise. He gave her permission to write her thesis about Schiller, and he even suggested that she might consider writing a book about him someday.

Now she had to approach Schiller's work not as an admirer, but as a scholar. She tracked down his last two books and read them — with disappointment. They were good . . . she told herself they were good; but they didn't quite do for her what the first two had.

The frustrating thing was that she couldn't tell whether the last two books were *objectively* worse. The problem may have been simply that they weren't addressed to her condition.

His third book, *Stories from the Lives of My Friends*, was a social novel about New York at the end of the sixties, and she had no interest in it at all.

"It feels like it was written by a different person," she said to Bonner.

"The sixties drove a lot of people crazy," Bonner said.

He didn't seem inclined to say more: he liked to make gnomic pronouncements. But she asked him what he meant.

"What was he then, in his forties? All his life he was probably looking forward to being middle-aged, because those were the days when middle-aged white men were supposed to inherit the earth. But as soon as his generation attained that condition, the rug was pulled out from under them. All of a sudden the world belonged to the young."

Schiller's fourth novel, *The Lost City*, seemed to be a return to his family roots. It was about his parents, or people who could have been his parents: a Jewish couple living on New York's Lower East Side in the early 1920s. Garment workers, labor struggles, the Yiddish theater — it was tender, and loving, and careful, and it meant very little to her.

These last two books brought her news about the world. That was fine, she supposed, but his first two had done something more valuable: they had brought her news about herself.

This wasn't a fair way to judge an author's work. Probably.

Her disappointment didn't change the way she felt about his first two novels, and it didn't dim her desire to write her thesis about his work.

After she finished her course work, she decided to move to New York, write the thesis, and, if possible, meet Schiller. She called his publishing company, but no one there had ever heard of him. Maybe that shouldn't have been shocking — his last book had come out in the early eighties — but she was shocked. She didn't know how to proceed, until Bonner suggested she call New York City information.

She was surprised when this worked. She knew that Schiller wasn't famous, but he was famous in her mind, and therefore she didn't think his phone number would be listed.

"It's nice to be naive," Bonner said.

She had enough money to live on for a few months. She couldn't afford Manhattan, but she found a nice little studio in Hoboken on the block where Frank Sinatra was born. At least that was what her landlady told her. Later she learned that everybody in Hoboken thinks they're living on the block where Frank Sinatra was born.

Other than *Tenderness*, all of Schiller's books were set in New York. During her first few weeks there, she felt as if she were living inside his mind. Sometimes she walked on streets he'd mentioned just because he'd mentioned them. The city was just as he'd described it: the mazy streets of the West Village; the long brown reaches of the Upper West Side. In one scene in his third novel, an elderly Jewish immigrant from Czechoslovakia makes his first visit to New York; walking on Broadway, he is stunned to see so many men and women who have the same features as the people he lost in his youth. On the Upper West Side, Heather examined the old people closely. Two old men playing chess in a delicatessen on 72nd Street — without Schiller's book, she wouldn't have noticed them; now she watched them, haunted, for a long time.

This was the second city he had given to her; the second city to which he'd been her guide.

Two days after they met, Schiller called her. He told her he'd found a copy of his last book. "And I've given the matter more thought. It would be my pleasure to help you with your project, if you're still interested."

She wasn't surprised to learn he'd changed his mind. She'd had a feeling he would. Taking the bus into New York to see him again, she felt that life was scandalously easy. If you know what you want, you can get it.

10

When Heather arrived at his apartment, Schiller seemed both courtly and nervous. He stood at arm's length from her as he took her coat. He seemed to be trying to keep a lot of space between them, as if he were afraid she'd make another lunge at him to kiss his hand.

Just as on her first visit, she was impressed by the library and depressed by the smell.

The smell of the place — the smell, the smell, the smell! It wasn't that it smelled *bad:* it didn't smell rank or foul or unclean. It just smelled like a place where an old man lived.

So much of human life is animal life: we respond to each other as animals. She felt as if she loved this man, but the animal in her was repelled by him.

Without being obvious about it, Heather took several deep breaths of the sour, heavy air: so she could take it in, so she could experience it to the utmost, so she could forget it.

"I usually," he said, "when I see a fellow writer, I ask how the work is going. But if I

were to ask you, it would sound self-inter-
ested."

As he said this he sounded owlish, profes-
sorial, arch. But she was thrilled to hear him
call her a fellow writer.

They went to the kitchen and he asked if
she'd like something to drink. She asked if
he had any club soda.

"Jewish club soda," he said. He poured
two glasses of seltzer. But to put it this way
is to describe too coarsely a subtle and elaborate procedure.

He brought two glasses down from the
cupboard, and he put ice cubes in each,
handling the ice with metal tongs. Then he
took a bottle of seltzer from the refrigerator.

She'd never seen anyone open a bottle of
seltzer as patiently as Schiller opened his. He
turned the cap slightly; a hiss of air was
released from the bottle, and, inside, a team
of bubbles raced madly to the surface. He
waited until the race was done, and then he
turned the cap, very slightly, again. Another
hiss of air, but weaker; another bubble race,
but not so furious. Again he waited, and after
he had waited, again he carefully released
more air. The whole process took about a
minute.

This is what an artist is, she thought. This
is the temperament you need to spend a

whole day tinkering with a sentence, making sure that both the meaning and the music are right; to spend three or seven or ten years working on a book.

She was aware that it might be a little extreme to be impressed by the way a man opens a bottle of seltzer, but she couldn't help but be impressed. When she opened a seltzer bottle, she usually ended up wet.

Sitting at his kitchen table, she took off her sweater. She was wearing a sleeveless shirt; she wanted to show off her bare arms. She had muscular arms for a woman, from years of working out.

This is what a seductress is, she thought.

It wasn't that she wanted to seduce him — not literally. But flirting was a pleasure, and flirting with intelligent people — male or female — was one of the supreme pleasures of life. Ever since she was in high school — ever since fifth grade, really, with her failed poet of an English teacher — intellectual communion and intense flirtation had grown from the same root. She'd always had a love of learning, a love of knowledge, but it was always an *embodied* love: she desired this man's learning or that woman's. The desire to learn from people was always bound up with the desire to seem special to them. Heather didn't merely want her teachers to teach her: she wanted them to single her out.

She had broken a few of her teachers' hearts with all this.

"Shall we begin?" she said. She opened up her notebook. "I thought I'd start by asking some questions about how you write."

This was to break the ice. From reading the interviews in *The Paris Review*, she knew that writers like to talk about their work habits, perhaps more than about their work. Do you do your first drafts in longhand? (No, he said. Typewriter.) Do you prefer to work in the morning or at night? (Morning and afternoon.) Do you break for lunch?

Here Schiller looked at her skeptically. "Do I break for lunch," he said. It was clear he didn't intend to answer.

"Thomas Mann," he said, "used to write fiction in a suit and tie. Now that you know that, do you know anything more about his work? I don't think so. At any rate, it's no substitute for two or three close readings of *The Magic Mountain*."

She didn't know him well enough to know whether he was irritated with her or just teasing, but she understood that she shouldn't ask him any more trivial questions.

"When you start a book, what do you start

with? Do you have the story clearly in mind?"

This question, apparently, was permitted. "Never. I wish I did. I start with a character. Usually just a fleeting glimpse of a character. With *Tenderness*, I had a picture of a woman being asked to leave a museum because she'd run her hand over one of the statues. I had no idea who she was or why she was touching the statue. I wrote the book to find out."

"How do you find out?"

"You just sit down at the typewriter and follow the character around. It's like being a detective. You write page after page after page just finding out who they are. You wait for them to do something interesting." He sighed. "That's one reason why it takes me so long. Sometimes they don't do anything interesting for a long time. And sometimes they never do. There are five or six books that I've begun but never finished. I would spend a year or two, even longer, following these characters around, but they finally never did anything that was interesting enough."

He looked unhappy. Try something else. "When you wrote *Tenderness*, were you reading a lot of D. H. Lawrence?"

"D. H. Lawrence?"

"Why are you smiling?"

"A New York Jew," he said, "imitates D. H. Lawrence at his peril."

"I didn't say you imitated him. But there's something in the flavor of your early work that reminds me of him."

"And what would that be?" He was trying to look amused, but he was interested. She could tell.

She had first read *Women in Love* shortly after she'd read *Tenderness*. Reading the way you read when you're sixteen, when you immerse yourself so deeply in a book that you hardly even notice the author's name, she had put the two books together in her mind, and it never occurred to her that they were vastly different in stature. Even now, though she'd never admit this to any of her old literature professors, she still didn't think of them as vastly different in stature. Maybe it was only because she'd read them at the same time of life, but the two books still kept each other company in her mind.

"You remind me of Lawrence in the way you give your characters room. Room to reject things — even the things I suspect you value. Like the way Ellen walks away from her marriage. I had the feeling that you sympathized most of all with Ira. But you let Ellen walk away from him without portraying her as cruel."

"She did what she needed to do."

"That's what I mean. You give your characters freedom. I think you'd give them the freedom to walk right out of your books if they wanted to."

"And that reminds you of D. H. Lawrence?"

"I think D. H. Lawrence does the same thing. He doesn't hover over them with judgments. At least not the characters he loves. What other people might see as cruelty, he sees as . . . people doing what they need to do."

Schiller considered this silently. Not quite silently: he was a large, overweight man, and he made a lot of noise when he breathed. Simply sitting and thinking seemed to require great labor.

"I'm flattered and all that, but . . . no. In the fifties I was reading Chekhov, James, Turgenev — the great hesitaters. At that time in my life I wouldn't go near Lawrence."

"Why?" She felt hurt, the way you feel when you introduce two of your friends to each other and they don't get along.

"There was a period, in the fifties, when almost every writer in New York was trying to relinquish his mind. Everybody wanted to be intoxicated with 'the wisdom of the blood.' Isaac Rosenfeld sitting in an orgone

86

box, trying to gather up his psychosexual energy. Norman Mailer writing 'The White Negro,' telling us that when a hoodlum robs a grocery store and beats the owner to death, he's engaging in an act of existential bravery. I thought it was unseemly for Jewish intellectuals, of all people, to comport themselves that way. I know there's more to Lawrence than the wisdom of the blood, but I was a very straitlaced young man, and in those days I simply had no time for him."

She wasn't happy about this answer. She had never heard of Isaac Rosenfeld, and Mailer had never meant much to her — his writing seemed both too literary and too crude, a weird combination of filigree and sweat.

But it wasn't just that she wasn't interested in those people. It unsettled her to hear Schiller putting himself in this *context*. When she thought about Schiller as a writer, she liked to imagine him in the "one big room" that E. M. Forster speaks of in *Aspects of the Novel* — the room in which all novelists, past and present, are writing side by side. In her mind Schiller's place was somewhere in eternity, next to Lawrence and Melville, not in the 1950s, next to Isaac Rosenfeld.

"I'm a little tired," he said. He stood up — lifted himself up with an effort, keeping one hand on the table to steady himself. "Why don't we make this your last question? We can get together again next week if you like."

"Ellen, in your first book, seems very similar to Beth in your second. But no character resembling her appears in either of your next two books. Why not?"

It was an obvious question: it was a question, she would have thought, that he'd been asked many times before. But Schiller seemed surprised. "You really have read the books," he said.

"What did you think I'd read? The Cliff Notes?"

And then she realized how stupid she'd been. She knew that his wife had died in the seventies. The character had never reappeared because she was drawn from life, and her real-life model had died. And he was still in mourning.

"I'm sorry," she said.

He didn't say anything, and this made her sure that she'd been right to apologize.

Schiller looked unsettled. He went to the sink and ran the water and filled a glass. She understood that he was doing this so he could keep his back turned to her for a minute.

She had the power to unsettle him. It was

almost dizzying. This man, who had been reading and writing and thinking before her parents were born, still had the ability to be shaken.

He sat back down at the table. She had arrived in the late afternoon, when there was still natural light in the room. Now it was early evening. They sat without speaking in the dimly lit room.

She was touched by his delicacy. Maybe *this* is what an artist is, she thought. It reminded her of something she'd once read, about how an artist doesn't really need a great deal of experience. One heartbreak can produce many novels. But you have to have a heart that can break.

11

She came to see him two afternoons a week. Her visits seemed to mean a lot to him. He seemed excited when he opened the door, and when she called on the phone she always heard a little lift in his voice, a note of happiness and surprise.

She always came with questions. Sometimes he answered them, and sometimes he answered them with questions of his own, which *she* would answer, slowly, thoughtfully, as if it were she who was being interviewed. What began as a series of interviews became a series of conversations.

She stopped bringing her notebook. She was flattered that he allowed her to keep visiting. When she mentioned this on the phone to a friend, her friend said, "You may not believe this, but he probably doesn't have that many twenty-four-year-old women coming to worship him."

The more she saw of him, the more she was puzzled by his life.

She had a mental picture of the artist's life, and it was nothing like Schiller's. He didn't drink; he didn't smoke; he didn't seem to do anything to excess. The only thing excessive about him was his cautiousness.

He was a man of routines. When she visited him, she couldn't show up before four-fifteen, because he wrote — "tried to write," as he put it — between ten in the morning and four in the afternoon, every day of the week.

He seemed to have a dull life. She saw that his calendar was mostly blank. He got together with his daughter about once a week; he had a friend in the hospital he visited every Friday. But his life consisted, for the most part, of writing and reading. He wrote during the day, read at night, went to bed early, and did the same thing the next day.

She would have thought his life would be more romantic. He seemed to know other writers, but he didn't hang around with them. The high point of his social life, as far as she could determine, was when, after four, he took his daily "constitutional" — a little walk down Broadway, or into Riverside Park if the weather was nice — and then stopped off at the Argo coffee shop for a green salad, a baked potato, and a fruit cup, maybe with some Sanka as a treat. After that he went home, read, watched the news, and went to bed. And that was his life. The monotony of it, the unvarying sameness, would have driven her out of her skull.

What did this man have to do with the man who had written the books? The books — the two she loved, at least — were about freedom, about the value of a certain kind of recklessness. She sometimes felt as if she were visiting, not the man who had written the books, but his grandfather. Don't artists have to *live*, not just write?

He *had* lived, apparently, twenty or thirty years ago. When he talked about his life as a writer, he all too often dropped the names of Famous Fossils He Had Known. It distressed her — first, because he was trying too hard (he'd tell her about how he had published his first stories in "Saul's old magazine, *The Noble Savage*," as if he were racking up coolness points by not saying "Saul Bellow"), and second, because it showed how out of touch he was. He didn't realize that these names didn't impress her. In the academic circles in which she'd moved until now, most of these people were considered passé. They were old dead white men, even the ones who were still alive.

But of course, if they were, he was too. One afternoon he excused himself to make a call about a doctor's appointment and left her in the kitchen alone. She opened the refrigerator to put back a carton of juice. The inside of his refrigerator was a sad place. Skim milk, fat-free yogurt, Pritikin spaghetti sauce, carrots, seltzer, caffeine-free Diet Coke, medicine, not much else. It was the refrigerator of a man who was worried about his health.

It was also the refrigerator of a man from another generation. The kind of man who, though he might live alone for thirty years, would never really learn how to cook.

"Are you looking for something to eat?" Schiller said, standing at the kitchen door.

She closed the refrigerator, with what she was sure was a guilty look on her face.

"Ah," he said. "You were engaging in refrigerator analysis."

One evening she took a walk with him and they ended up in the Argo. While Schiller was sipping his Sanka, a man walked over to their table — a very tall man with an expensive suit and an expensive tan. "I got your message," he said to Schiller. "Morally earnest as always. That's why I offer you these things. I love to hear how considerately you say no." He was bouncing on his toes, as if he was nervous. He didn't seem worthy of the suit.

"It was nice of you to think of me,

though," Schiller said.

The man patted Schiller on the shoulder. "Well, if you ever do decide to sell your soul, you know where to find me."

"What was that about?" Heather said after he left.

"A high school friend of my daughter's. He edits some sort of advertising supplement for American Express. He asked me to write something for it."

"He wanted you to write advertising copy?" Heather was amused.

"Not exactly. Just a few paragraphs about Central Park. I wouldn't have had to mention American Express, but the piece would have been part of the supplement, so it would have been advertising all the same."

"A few paragraphs about Central Park? That's all?"

"Yes. It would have paid nicely, too."

"That doesn't sound so bad to me. Why didn't you do it?"

"I have this old-fashioned idea that art and commerce are at war."

She sipped her coffee and tried to take this in. The younger man, despite his Armani suit and his midwinter tan, had seemed nervous — jangly and eager to please. Schiller, old and pale and fat and frail, had seemed rocklike. If you stick to your guns in life —

this was the moral she drew — you become strong.

She was moved by his dedication to the life he had chosen. She wondered if she could turn down easy money for the sake of an ideal.

She decided that yes, she could.

The people she admired in his books were people who walked away from the lives that other people expected them to live — Ellen in his first novel, the bohemian painters in his second. He had dwelled — in those early books, at least — on the glory of choosing your own life, even when it takes ruthlessness to do it.

But now it occurred to her that he had only written about the beginning of the journey. He had never shown the consequences of the choice — never shown what happened to these people ten and twenty and thirty years down the line. And she felt that she was seeing the consequences, every day, in what she was seeing of him.

You seize your freedom in a spirit of rebelliousness, exuberance, defiant joy. But to live that choice — over the weeks and months and years to come — requires different qualities. It requires that you turn hard, turn rigid. Because it isn't a choice that the world encourages, you have to wear a suit of armor to defend it.

When they were leaving the restaurant, he held the door for her, and he continued to hold it open for a scruffy teenage boy in an army surplus jacket who was leaving at the same time. In her five or six visits, which had included two or three trips to coffee shops, Heather had never seen Schiller precede anyone, male or female, through a door. He lived by his own code, with intricate proprieties and prohibitions. It might have been outmoded, but it was his. His social bearing seemed of a piece, somehow, with his unwillingness to write advertising copy. Even in your smallest gestures, you express your sense of honor, if you have one.

They walked in silence across the street, and as she mused on all this her feeling of respect for him grew, and her feeling of *sympathy* for him — he seemed like a modern Don Quixote.

Back in his living room, he looked at his watch, but she didn't feel ready to leave.

"I've never told you why I liked your work so much," she said. "Your novels set me free."

She told him about it: how his books had helped her find the courage to live her own life, not anyone else's. "I felt as if your books were written just for me. I've always thought the subject of your books was freedom. And freedom has always been my theme in life."

It was only after she said this that she realized it was the same thing she had said to herself in the mirror on her fourteenth birthday. She felt her face grow warm, but Schiller was smiling, and he wasn't smiling unkindly.

And though this wasn't quite what she'd had in mind at the time — he wasn't the man she'd pictured when she first spoke those words — it was close enough. He *could* have been the man for her, if only he'd been about four hundred years younger. Whenever she spoke to him, she could feel the pleasure he took in looking at her, and she could feel how carefully, how closely, he listened. And if she looked only at his eyes — ignoring the great Humpty Dumpty dome of his skull and the layers of his cheeks and chins — she could see the young man he used to be, the man with whom anything might have been possible.

They were standing awkwardly in the middle of the living room. She was looking into his eyes. There was something soft and welcoming and puzzled there.

She almost wanted him to touch her. She didn't desire him, she didn't want to touch him, but she almost wanted him to touch her. She wanted to close her eyes and imagine that he was the man he used to be. His eyes were the eyes he'd had when he was young; and if, in his youth, he had known how to touch a woman, his hands must have retained that knowledge. How strange.

She almost said, "Do you want to touch me?"

You could transform any relationship with a word or two.

"It's time for you to go," he said.

On the bus, heading back toward Hoboken, she said to herself: "Are you *crazy?* What were you *thinking?*"

Her unconscious mind did nothing to clarify matters: that night she dreamed she was having an affair with a four-year-old girl.

"This is wrong," she told the girl, whose name, for whatever reason, was Bean.

"We love each other," Bean said. "How can that be wrong?"

12

In one of the dialogues of Plato, Socrates remarks that the task of the philosopher is to "practice dying." The philosopher must wean himself from his attachments to the phenomenological world — the realm of mere appearances — and turn his thoughts toward the realm of the unchanging, the transcendent, the eternal.

By this standard, Schiller would have made a good philosopher. He had practiced dying for a long time.

During the years in which he had learned his craft, he had gone without most of the normal material comforts. He and Stella and Ariel had lived without a television until Ariel was in her teens. He still didn't have an air conditioner. His manual typewriter had served him well since the 1960s. He hadn't bought a new suit in fifteen years.

When his books went out of print he had learned, painfully, to starve his own need for recognition, until he thought he had finally killed it.

And after Stella died, he had weaned himself, he thought, of the need for romantic love. Ariel, a few old friends, and a few old students who had become old friends provided all the warmth he desired.

All that remained was his work. And now he just wanted to finish one book. If he could finish the thing he was working on, he thought, he would be ready to die.

He thought he'd be able to finish it shortly after his trip to France. If he'd wanted to, he could have simply imagined what it would be like to keep the appointment he'd made with Stella, and saved himself the expense of actually keeping it. But honoring their agreement was important to him. There are obligations that extend beyond the grave.

He was acutely conscious of the uncertain state of his health: he knew he might not have much time. He wanted to live without distractions; he wanted to focus all the life-force he had left on this last book. But now it was hard to concentrate. There was something new in his life. There was the painful distraction of desire.

He had found himself ridiculously interested in impressing this young woman. She would blow in like a little whirlwind, eager to hear him say wise things; and he wanted to have wise things to say — he wanted to be worthy of her admiration.

More than that. He wanted her to be in love with him. Idiotic, but true.

"Ah, to be sixty again," he said, as he stooped, with difficulty, to pick up a little piece of fluff from the floor.

No: even sixty would be too old. If he were forty, or even fifty, he could be a dashing older man; he could introduce her to a wider life. But as it was, what could he give her? Not very much. He could give her his back issues of *Modern Maturity* . . .

It was absurd. There was something *un-dignified* about this feeling. He was almost fifty years older than she was. Shouldn't those years have given him wisdom, wisdom that would make it impossible for him to be interested in a mere girl? Well, they hadn't.

She wasn't even beautiful. If someone else, someone less spirited, less bold, had inhabited her body, she wouldn't have been attractive at all. But as it was she had a sort of radiant ugliness that he found captivating.

Sometimes he had the odd feeling that *she* was somehow attracted to *him*. But that was impossible. Put it out of your mind. If you can't put it out of your mind, then look at your face in the mirror. That will cure you of your delusions.

She was picking him up that evening, and

he was taking her to a party.

At about two in the afternoon he gave up all pretense of trying to work, and he took another shower, brushed his teeth again, gargled with Listerine, clipped a few hairs from his nostrils and earlobes, tidied up the house, and opened the windows to freshen the air.

The stirrings of desire, after a long frost. One morning this week, for the first time in months, he'd awakened with an erection.

He had to be careful not to make a fool of himself.

As he was tidying up he got a call from Ariel.

"Pain," she said.

"What pain, my dear?"

"Spiritual pain. Emotional pain. The pain of being thirty-nine."

He was smiling. "It's not nice to complain about being thirty-nine to a man who's past seventy."

"You're a young seventy-one. I'm an old thirty-nine."

Neither statement was true.

Behind her he heard traffic, sirens, horns.

"Where are you?"

"I'm at my office."

Which was her way of saying she was at a pay phone. With the exception of drug dealers and the city's few remaining bookies, she was the foremost patron of Manhattan's pay phones: she'd call you from the street and chat for half an hour, feeding nickels into the phone every five minutes when the mechanical voice cut in.

"Pain," she sang.

"I'm sorry you're in pain," he said, but he was laughing.

"It's not funny! You don't know what it's like. I'm thirty-nine, and my womb is drying up."

He felt a sudden spasm of discomfort. It wasn't the kind of thing a daughter should say to a father.

"I'm coming to the end of the line here," she said. "There's a Holocaust on my womb."

He had such a complicated reaction to this that he couldn't speak. He disapproved of the metaphor: he wanted to tell her that one shouldn't compare one's personal unhappiness to the most horrible crime in history. Following closely behind that thought was a sense of sadness that his daughter wasn't an intellectual, and that if he tried to tell her why he objected to her metaphor she would probably find him pedantic and cold. But competing with all this was the recognition that whatever he might think about the figure of speech she'd used, she *was* in pain. He was struck by his own obliviousness: she gave him so much delight, so much comfort, even when she was in misery herself, that he usually failed to see her misery until she called his attention to it with a shout. And he thought about how odd it was that Ariel could so often give joy when she wasn't feeling any. Yeats wrote somewhere that "Man can embody the truth but he cannot know it." Schiller had never understood what he'd meant by that, but the idea made sense when applied to Ariel. She gave joy more often than she felt it.

He felt as if he should ask her over — that would be the fatherly thing to do. But he was looking forward to seeing the young woman tonight.

Occasionally she could almost read his mind. "Can I come over?" she said.

"I have an appointment tonight." He didn't want to say that he was seeing Heather; he didn't want to say that the appointment was a party. "I should be home by eleven. I'd love to see you then."

"It's okay," she said forlornly. "I'm busy later. I have a date with Victor Mature. I have a client in your neighborhood tomorrow morning. Maybe we could have a little bite for lunch?"

He hesitated, and she caught the hesitation. "I know. You have to write. A real writer doesn't break for lunch. Sorry, sorry, sorry."

In his own muted way, he was a tyrant, and he had always been a tyrant. Everyone around him had always been at the mercy of his inflexible schedule.

"Maybe we could get together tomorrow night," she said.

"I'd like that."

"I'll call you in the afternoon."

He felt ashamed of the way he had reduced her to begging for his time.

When he got off the phone he felt dizzy and he lay down.

Heather arrived a little before seven, and he buzzed her up. He was gift-wrapping a bottle of wine for the party; the elevators in the building were sluggish, and by the time she rang at his front door he was finished.

She stood on his threshold, glowing from the cold. Her cheeks and the tip of her nose were touched with red; her eyes were so blue the blueness seemed unreal — tinted contact lenses, probably. With her cheeks so red you wanted to bite them, with her tigerishly glittering eyes, with her slightly sarcastic smile, she was almost unbearably full of life. "Hello old man," she said, and even this, this meaningless greeting, he found wonderfully intimate and frank.

"I'm glad the refrigerator took so long," Schiller said. "I was still gift-wrapping the wine."

There was a moment of silence.

"Did I say refrigerator?" he said. "I meant elevator."

"Refrigerator, elevator. It's the same idea."

"Would you like a drink?" he said. He headed toward the kitchen; he wanted to hide his face. He was a senile old man, and someday he was going to leave the house without his pants. "I have some white wine," he said, "here in the dishwasher."

The phone rang once — a tiny spurt, a half ring — and then stopped. He knew it was his daughter. When she was in distress she called people — not just him — and hung up before they could answer.

Heather leaned against the refrigerator, smiling, as he opened the wine. She was alight with confidence, ambition, and an exhilarated consciousness of her own youth. She seemed ready to lay siege to the world.

His daughter, even if the world began to show her its mildest face, would always be tangled in coils of unhappiness. He felt as if he bore the blame: he had failed as a father.

The party was on 65th and Central Park

West. In the cab Schiller felt proud to be able to give her this — a glimpse of literary New York. He wasn't completely out of circulation yet.

He also felt a little nervous about her. He wondered whether she'd impress people, or impress them merely as being very young. She impressed *him*, but in the cab he began to wonder whether this was just because she had touched his vanity. Would he look like an ass at the party — an elderly oaf trailing impotently after a teenybopper?

"Teenybopper": a word he thought of as newly coined, and which probably hadn't been used by anyone else in twenty-five years.

Leslie greeted him at the door; she looked as fresh as she had when she was his student, twenty years ago. She could have been the Ivory Girl. He introduced her to Heather, and Leslie, with her matchless social grace, greeted her as if she were a valued friend.

Leslie put her arm through Schiller's as she led them to a bedroom to leave their coats. "How *are* you?" she said. She had been his student in an American literature class in 1975, at Hunter College. After she graduated she went into publishing; she'd been an editor for twenty years now.

The company she worked for didn't value

serious writing. For a few years she'd struggled to carve out a space for higher standards: she'd even started her own imprint, which, however, quickly succumbed to the pressures of the market. Eventually she accepted defeat, and tried to keep her spirits up by publishing amusing nonsense rather than pernicious nonsense. Much of her company's revenue came from self-help books and celebrity confessions; she liked to publish parody self-help books, parody confessions.

The way she treated Schiller varied according to how she was feeling about herself. She was always friendly, pleasant, interested; but he could tell that there were times when he had power in her mind, and times when he didn't. Every year or two, when her literary conscience was aching, when she was in mourning for the life she'd envisioned when she'd gone into publishing in the first place, Schiller would rise up in her mind as a figure of lonely integrity, and she would call him up and ask him out to dinner at Aquavit or the Union Square Cafe — restaurants he never would have ventured into otherwise: they were beyond his means — and she'd compulsively tell him about how unhappy she was to be publishing the stuff she published. But when things were going well at work, when she was being praised around town as a gifted editor of hip and wicked satires, then she regarded Schiller — he could sense it — as an amiable fossil, a figure of fun. He was sure she sometimes joked about him behind his back. But the thought didn't bother him much, because he was also sure that beneath all this wavering, at the core of her feelings for him, there was a steady affection and respect.

The only thing that stayed constant was that she didn't publish him. He didn't take this personally: he knew that his work simply didn't sell much, and that she had an obligation to publish things that would sell. Of course in his worst moods he lay awake cursing her and every other editor he knew, remembering how William Kennedy had been "discovered" after four novels, and Barbara Pym, and Henry Roth, and Daniel Fuchs — he would go over that long list of once-obscure writers who, because of one impassioned editor, had been rediscovered and turned into "hot," best-selling authors, with profiles in *Vanity Fair* and front-page reviews in the *Times Book Review* of books they had written years or decades earlier. He would lie awake at three in the morning, burning with a sense of having been wronged. But tonight he kissed Leslie on the cheek and said, "Marvelous. You look wonderful."

"Are you working on a novel?" she asked brightly.

"Always."

"What's it about?" She said this with a teasing smile: he had always told his students that writers shouldn't talk about what they were writing; that one was all too likely to talk one's books away. He didn't bother answering; she didn't expect an answer. And really, she didn't care.

He looked around the room. There were several people he knew: editors, writers, critics. Only one person in the room was older than Schiller — Alfred Kazin, who was standing in a corner with a few young people, holding forth with his usual curious mixture of aggressiveness and shyness.

"A man resembles his time more than he resembles his father," says the Arab proverb: if this was true, then Schiller and Kazin resembled each other. They had been formed in the same fires. Children of immigrant parents, children of the Depression, mad for writing — in all these ways, they were members of the same tribe.

Which is not to say that they were friends. Kazin had never paid Schiller any mind. For one thing, Kazin was almost ten years older than Schiller; for another, with his lifelong immersion in the work of the Great Dead — Thoreau and Whitman and Melville and Faulkner and Hemingway and Dreiser — he'd barely looked up at the living. He had admitted a few living novelists into his canon — Bellow, Mailer, Roth — but not Schiller. The only public notice Kazin had ever taken of his work was a passing remark in a broad overview of the literary scene he'd written in 1967, in which he'd lumped Schiller together with several other writers who were "conscientious craftsmen" but who were too preoccupied with their own personal questions to shed any light on the larger problems of the time.

Schiller greeted him with a wave, and didn't try to talk to him.

Leslie was talking with Heather. "Technically, I'm still in school," he heard Heather say. "I'm writing my master's thesis."

Leslie looked genuinely interested. There was something wonderful about her, about the way she was so welcoming to someone she didn't know. Even if her warmth was to some degree a social mask, it was the loveliest mask imaginable. "About what?"

Heather pointed toward Schiller. "Him."

"Fantastic," Leslie said, squeezing Schiller's arm. "It's about time, too. Soon they'll have courses about your work."

"There'll be entire departments devoted to the study of my work," Schiller said.

"Has he actually *told* you anything about himself?" Leslie said to Heather. "Have you managed to solve any of Leonard's mysteries? Have you persuaded him to explain why he never leaves the house before dark?"

"He *can't* go out," Heather said. "He only writes for ten minutes a day, but it's an important ten minutes, and he never knows when they'll come."

This was not so far from true — all too much of his day was spent pacing — but he didn't know how she knew it.

Leslie introduced Heather to Sam Dreier, an editor at Farrar Straus. Dreier was an extremely self-confident young man who wrote long, dyspeptic essays on the state of contemporary culture for *The New York Review of Books,* and who had turned down Schiller's last novel. Schiller began to wonder whether bringing Heather here had been such a good idea. He was throbbing with a sense of his grievances; he couldn't let them go. There had to be a mind exercise, a meditation, that would help you to stop seeing all things and all people through the lens of your own self-interest. All he could think was: that woman did me a good turn; that man let me down. It was all so irrelevant, really: each of us stoking our own little furnaces of ambition; but he couldn't let it go.

"Oh my God," he heard Heather saying. She was kissing someone on the cheek. It was someone Schiller didn't know: a heavy-set woman in her middle or late thirties, in warriorlike makeup and leather pants.

"This is Harriet Bandler," Heather said to Schiller. "She's an editor at *Bomb*. We met at a poetry reading last week." The woman nodded at him; it was a chilling experience. There wasn't a hint of interest in her eyes, not even a pretense.

Bomb. An East Village literary magazine that he'd heard about but never seen. He retreated to the buffet and busied himself with a complicated seafood salad. Impaling a squirmy chunk of lobster meat and trying to wipe it onto a piece of bread, he felt stunned. *Bomb!* He had thought he was the only literary person Heather knew — he'd thought he *was* literature, in Heather's eyes. But in the evenings, while he was in his kitchen heating up his pan of skim milk before bed, she was in bars in the East Village, making postmodern remarks with people from *Bomb*.

With no one to talk to, he examined Leslie's bookshelves. Bitterly.

Every young editor in New York, Schiller

had often thought, has the same library. All the books on their shelves are glossy hardcovers. There's nothing wrong with their books: they've got Updike and Carver and Roth, Atwood and Drabble and Munro, Rushdie and Amis and Barnes: the cream of the last three generations. But that's all they've got. The most ancient writer on their shelves is F. Scott Fitzgerald; or if they have anything older than that, it's because they've mooched free copies of the new Library of America series, so they have James and Melville in those enormous tomes — two or three novels per volume — that are so unwieldy they can only be displayed, not read. What appalled Schiller about these libraries was that they featured nothing off the beaten track: no tattered paperbacks; no evidence of distinctive personal interests; no tokens of long intellectual detours passionately explored. If under cover of night you switched the libraries of any two young editors in New York, neither of them would notice.

This, at least, was how it seemed to Schiller. But part of what was making him so mad, he knew, was that Leslie's alphabetized collection went from J. D. Salinger to Mona Simpson. She used to have his books on her shelf, but he'd been removed to make room for the young.

Across the room, Heather was still talking to the woman from *Bomb*, whose name he had already forgotten. Heather was looking at her with the same intensity she habitually trained on Schiller. She was running her hands through her own hair. Somehow she looked as if she'd just gone swimming.

He was jealous. The realization made him put down his plate.

He told himself that it wasn't logical to be jealous: she was talking, after all, to a woman. But then he realized how naive *that* was. So what if it was a woman? The sexuality of the young was incomprehensible. Browsing aimlessly through a list of academic job openings the other day, he'd noticed that Cornell University was seeking a specialist in "queer theory." A branch of thought that wasn't part of the canon when he was going to school. People under thirty, in Schiller's view, were probably all versed in queer theory. They were sexually fluid: they didn't care if their mates were male or female, because they thought the very idea of gender was an arbitrary social fiction.

Though one might have thought that the fact that Heather was talking to a woman would give his jealousy a slightly new inflection, a new texture, he discovered now that jealousy comes in only one flavor.

And the flavor doesn't fade with time. It felt exactly as it had always felt. He remembered an afternoon of agony at Camp Kinder Ring — a socialist youth camp he went to in the mid-1930s — after he saw Rachel Solomon holding hands with Bernie Sachs. He had stalked away in anguish when everyone was singing folk songs, and he'd spent a long afternoon on the mountain, throwing rocks at birds.

He talked to a few people, for ten minutes, twenty; Heather was still in animated conversation with her friend. She was puzzlingly well connected for someone who'd come to New York only last month. He wanted to slip out without letting her know — which, of course, would be nothing more than a bid for her attention. At a party in Montrouge in 1956, Stella had spent the evening flirting with a young philosopher; Schiller abruptly told her he was going home, and she blithely said she could get a ride later from . . . what was his name? Pierre-Antoine. What stupid faggy names those Frenchmen had! Schiller went out and sat in their little car, that tiny white Renault, without putting the key in the ignition; he sat huddled up in his coat as the snow battered the windshield, covering it up completely so he couldn't see.

And now Heather was laughing with this

woman, rolling her head around as if she had a crick in her neck — in some ritual of body language that Schiller didn't comprehend, but that was probably second nature to the young.

Schiller finally got into a conversation he could enjoy, with a couple named Paula and Martin Cohen. Paula Cohen was one of the few editors Schiller respected: she was a woman who fought for her convictions. A few of her writers had brought in a great deal of money for her company; this gave her the freedom to publish and nurture the other writers in her stable, most of whom didn't sell much. She fought for her writers; she kept their work in print. Schiller would have liked to work with her, but his novels had never been her cup of tea: she preferred more avant-garde stuff. He regretted this, but he wasn't bitter about it, because he respected her integrity: if she didn't publish him it was for literary rather than commercial reasons. Schiller liked her a great deal. He spent ten or fifteen minutes catching up with her and her husband, and his soul was rested.

He drifted back toward Heather, who was still talking with that scary young woman from *Bomb*. A violent light of pleasure was in Heather's eyes. She looked up as he approached; he was on the alert for evidence that she didn't want him there, but he didn't detect any.

"I need to go," he said. "It's late for an old man." Which was a stupid thing to say: there's nothing more annoying than an old person who makes lame jests about his age. "When I was young, back in the Middle Ages." "When I was young — I *was* young once, you know." Remarks like this irritate you when you're young, but somehow you can't help making them when you're old.

"But there's no need for *you* to leave," he said.

"No, I need to come back with you," she said. "I left my bag in your kitchen."

As they got their coats he was seething, and he could barely look at her. She was leaving with him because she'd forgotten her bag. Yes: it was the same feeling, down to the sensation of being *physically* bruised, that he'd had when Rachel Solomon toyed with his emotions more than fifty years ago. Rachel Solomon, whom he had stayed in touch with. Whose grandchildren he had met. Whose burial he had attended, seven years ago, on a hilltop graveyard in Paramus.

And he himself was still alive, at the mercy of the same emotions she had stirred in him sixty years earlier. The child he had been was still alive in him, and Rachel was dead. Simple, banal, unfathomable.

He stepped off the sidewalk and walked into the street to hail a cab. He was happy to have a reason not to stand next to her.

"Is something wrong?" she said in the cab.

"Not that I know of," he said. He couldn't admit that he was jealous; he was sealed in the cave of his pride.

When they got back to his place he quickly found her bag and held it out at arm's length. "Well then."

"But you haven't fed me," she said.

In spite of himself, he was charmed. "I thought you ate at the party."

"I didn't like the look of that seafood salad. All I had to eat there was a lettuce leaf."

"We can't send you home starving," he said, softening.

There wasn't much in his refrigerator, except for the fixings from Ariel's Fluffernutter.

"Maybe a little sandwich," she said. She took some things out of the refrigerator and the cupboards; she was comfortable enough in his place by now to help herself. It gave him pleasure to watch her moving easily about in his kitchen.

She was comfortable enough, in fact, to slip off her shoes. He was taken aback by this. He felt like an Edwardian gentleman —

the man of fashion out of fashion, unfit for the modern world.

His back hurt and he wanted to sit on the couch, so they brought the things into the living room and put them on the coffee table: peanut butter, honey, brown bread, and a bowl of trail mix that Ariel had left here recently.

"You looked sad tonight," she said. "The knight of the mournful countenance."

"Honestly, I can't stop thinking about my daughter." This wasn't honest at all, but he didn't want to tell her that she'd made him jealous. He couldn't believe that he was trading on his daughter's problems like this, but once he'd begun he couldn't stop himself, and soon he was saying things he hadn't intended to say. "I think I messed her up from the beginning. Her mother died when Ariel was still in her teens. And I can't say I did a very good job after that. I wasn't very attentive. I was more concerned . . . let's say I was concerned with the perfection of the work, not of the life. So I messed up my daughter's life. And it's not exactly as if I achieved perfection of the work in the process."

Heather rested her hand on his; she squeezed his hand supportively. "Supportively" — the word was an abomination, a product of the contemporary culture of therapy. There were too many words in the world that were impossible to abide and impossible to avoid. He was losing his language. It was time to go.

But the fact remained that she was squeezing his hand supportively. "You're very hard on yourself," she said. She had been making a peanut butter and honey sandwich; some of the honey had dripped onto her fingers, and now, when she withdrew her hand from his, she saw that she'd left small dots of it on his knuckles. "Sorry," she said. She smiled at him speculatively, dipped her fingers into the jar, said, "Sorry for getting honey on you," and then she touched his face.

With the soft stickiness of her fingertips, she painted his forehead, his jawline, his lips.

This is the only way it could have happened. If there had been no honey, there could have been no physical communion, for the honey made the moment half-comic.

They were seated awkwardly on the couch. It had been years and years and years since a woman had touched him. Schiller was petrified with surprise. Sex, he was thinking, is never what you think it is.

What *is* sex? This was a question that had baffled him all his life. When he was young his sexual energy had been boundless: if his desire could have been converted to electricity he could have kept all the lights in New York City blazing full-time. He was so crudely hungry with sexual need in those days that he must have been a lousy lover — but that was in the forties and fifties, when everybody was a lousy lover. And then there were the eighteen years with Stella: the early days of groping awkwardly in bed, and then the slow and blessed learning. He remembered the night he confessed to her that a woman's sex was still as mysterious to him as the source of the Nile, and she took his hands and guided him through her pleasures. They were both shy, but the memory of how they overcame their shyness together was moving for him still.

And for years, he burned for her. He remembered an afternoon in the early sixties when he returned home from some appointment and her Uncle Manny was in the living room, gleefully describing one of his new inventions. ("It can't miss!" That was Uncle Manny's mantra — every one of his inventions couldn't miss. Poor Uncle Manny, also gone.) Stella was sitting on the couch, her long legs tucked beneath her, an expression of humor and interest and irony on her face — she was in the fullest flower of her gorgeousness, and she struck him as the most desirable woman he'd ever seen. He couldn't wait to be alone with her, and though she was listening to Manny attentively — one of the amazing things about her was that she never seemed to give anyone less than her full attention — he understood somehow that she shared his feeling. He considered picking Manny up, holding him out the window, and letting go: he was a tiny man — he weighed about as much as a tissue — and he favored baggy clothing, so there was a fair chance that he'd float gently and unharmed to earth. Finally he left by the front door; after seeing him out, Schiller turned and looked at Stella on the couch. No. He didn't simply look at her: he beheld her. She was wearing a sundress: she was a little too large, too big-boned, for the delicate sundress look, but with her gleaming shoulders and her long brown arms, and the long, sturdy, somehow noble line of her neck, and her eyes alight with wit — taking her in, Schiller felt that he was not a bounded entity, that he existed in her as much as he existed in his own body. And though he could remember now, years later, that they went eagerly and happily and immediately to bed, his memory of the love-making itself, curiously, was not nearly as strong as the memory of desiring her.

Over the years, in the usual, gradual way — it was somehow both predictable and shocking — his sexual vitality had declined. In part this may have been because he never fell in love again after Stella died, but in part it was the inexorable running-down of the body. It was hard to accept; it was hard to believe. In his youth his sexual vitality had seemed as essential a part of him as his ability to use language, so it was hard to comprehend its waning — especially since his love of *looking* at beautiful women was as strong as ever.

After Stella, there were three or four affairs, one of which lasted for more than a year. But the sex that he had during those years always seemed somehow post-sexual; the period in which sex was a major part of his life had passed.

When he was being honest with himself, he admitted that he didn't completely regret its passing. The sexual encounter had always struck him as extraordinarily complex. Movies, bad novels, even good novels usually represented sex as something that simply flowed — something that came as easily as Robert Frost said a poem should come to a poet: like an ice cube melting on a hot stove. For Schiller, though it had provided him with moments, hours, of pleasure and communion, it had rarely simply flowed. To sit across the table and talk with someone you love is itself a complex engagement, with an exhaustingly subtle flow of information; to go to bed with someone — to carry your conversation into the realm of the body, a realm of insecurity and fear as well as pleasure — was always fraught with the sad evidence of how difficult it is to understand another person and make yourself understood. And now, though he was amazed and grateful that this young woman was touching him, he had the sense of being asked to return to an arena that he had been glad to quit.

If all this was passing through his mind as he sat on the couch beside Heather, it was only in the most fragmentary way. She was touching his face with her soft, sticky fingertips, and he wanted to kiss her, but he was afraid he had old man's breath — cat food breath, he thought — and he was afraid, also, that she would recoil in horror if he tried to kiss her — that she'd tell him he'd misunderstood her, that that wasn't what she'd meant at all — so he didn't do anything, and although she was touching his face tenderly, his uncertainty about what she wanted made the experience a kind of torture. How could she be doing this? How could she be enduring the experience of touching his skin? I'm old enough to be her ancestor.

Her body, in its nearness, radiated a peculiar force. It was like sitting next to an engine.

Heather put her arms around him, to the extent that she could. He was too large to be embraced by one woman: it would take a team.

Outside his window, fifteen floors below, a car plowed into another car. There was a horrible sound of metal on metal and the long depression of a car horn. They separated for a moment, and Schiller felt as if injury or death had entered the room.

"Excuse me," Heather said, now that they had paused; she squeezed his hand and rose, to go to the bathroom.

But before she walked away, he made a mistake. He looked toward the window. In the dark window, the two of them were reflected: a lovely, alert-looking young woman and an elderly clown. He had a double chin, and a bulbous nose, and a huge smooth head.

She left the room; waiting for her, he had a little munch of the trail mix. It wasn't bad. He carried another handful nervously to his mouth. He was still looking at himself in the glass, trying to find an angle from which he might appear less gruesome. He looked like a rabbit under the influence of mind-altering drugs.

"A rabbit under the influence," he said quietly.

"Excuse me?" Heather said, standing in the hall.

"I was just . . . I don't know. Pardon me." And he went to the bathroom himself, touching her shoulder awkwardly, not quite familiarly, as he passed her.

He closed the bathroom door and wiped the honey off his face with a towel. He wasn't sure whether he should — he might seem to be rebuffing her, erasing her strange and tender gesture — but if he came out of the bathroom without having cleaned his face, he'd probably look like an ass.

Now he had a decision to make about *how* to urinate. In the last five years he had found himself needing to urinate more frequently, but he'd also found that he urinated with less force. Giving forth little dribbles, he'd all too often spotted his pants. Therefore, he now routinely sat down to urinate. Tonight he would have preferred to do the manly thing and pee standing up, but cautiousness prevailed. He undid his pants and, feeling like a little old lady, sat down.

When he stood, he looked at his gray, fat penis, a smoked-out stub of an antique cigar.

Old man, he thought, are you still with me? I may have to call on you to perform an unusual task.

It was too absurd. He was an elderly clown, and he should try to preserve one last fragment of his dignity in the only way available to him: by accepting his essential clownishness, and not pretending to be an actual man.

When he emerged, she was sitting on the couch. "I'm sorry," he said, "but I think it's time for you to go."

"Oh dear. Did I do something wrong?"

"No, you've been very kind to me. It's just that I'm too old."

"Please." She got off the couch and walked toward him. "I'm not being kind. If you want me to go, I'll go. But I don't know what you mean when you say you're too old. I'm not expecting anything from you. I just want to hold you for a while. I was enjoying myself. I hope you were enjoying yourself too. I thought we could enjoy ourselves a while longer."

He was touched by her sensitivity, her tact. It was as if she'd read a guide. A money-making scheme popped into his mind: a guide to the things young women should say to old men. It doesn't matter to me that you can't get much of an erection, my love; all I really want is to hold you. Of course I don't mind speaking louder, my darling — I like a man who likes to hear me shout.

She put her arms around him, and they stood together in the center of the room. He noticed that her breathing was deeper and more regular than his. But as they remained pressed against each other, his breaths became deeper; he felt as if she were giving him life, breathing life into him. They stayed like that for a long time.

"Can we lie down?" she said, and thereby murdered his illusion that she couldn't make a false step. He didn't want to lie down. He felt so spent, so old. This young woman was offering him a gift; she was astonishingly kind; he thought of friends of his, other men in their late sixties or seventies, who simply wouldn't believe him if he told them about all this. Could he ever tell them that a lovely young woman had offered herself to him and that he'd been less than elated? The fact was that he wished she weren't there. He wished he were alone in bed, reading *Daniel Deronda*.

They went into the bedroom without turning on the light and lay side by side on the bed. He was ashamed of his body, ashamed of being old, as if it were a mistake he had made.

"We don't have to do anything," she said. "I just want to be near you." This was the perfect thing to say; and yet he had a spasm of irritation at the thought that she was treating him like an old man, a semi-impotent old man, which, he supposed, was what he was: he had a tenuous and dispirited half-erection, like an aged mole blinking uncertainly as it raised its head, coming up to see what the commotion was about. But her words, though they humiliated him a little, also, after a moment, had their intended effect: they relaxed him, and as he lay beside her in the dark he was able to think, finally, not of his shabby elderliness, but of her.

He touched her face. When he was a young man, a few months after the end of the Second World War, he had attended a fund-raising event for Europe's "displaced persons" and had met Helen Keller there. As her way of saying hello, she had put both her hands on his face and explored his features. Touching Heather's face now, he felt as if he were Helen Keller. He had forgotten what it was to know someone in this way; he had forgotten how much you could learn about someone with your hands. He could feel her youth, not only in the sharpness of her features and the suppleness of her skin, but in something that was harder to define, some force that seemed to radiate from her. He removed his hands from her face and held them in the air, still quite near her, and he could still feel that force, rising from her skin. He passed his hand in the air above her closed eyelids, and he felt their delicacy, their subtle trembling.

He wanted to take her clothes off. He didn't want to take his own clothes off. It would have been too painful to expose his bloated stomach, forty years pregnant; his chest where they had cracked him open like a lobster; the scar on his leg where they'd removed some of his arteries to replace the fat-clogged arteries around his heart.

She seemed to understand that he didn't want her to touch him. She lay on the bed with her eyes open and unbuttoned her dress. He ran his hands through the air a few inches above her, and he could have sworn that he could feel her body as he touched the air. Without placing his hands on her skin, he acquainted himself with her small breasts — he had always loved small breasts: large breasts he'd never known what to do with; with her protruding ribs — she was too skinny, she needed some meat on her bones (he found himself thinking this in a grand-fatherly way, concerned for her health if she should catch a flu); with her sinewy forearms; with the muscular thickness of her thighs.

As he moved his hand in the air above her he was reflecting on the fact that this well-muscled modern woman represented an entirely different variety of womanhood from the one he was familiar with.

As he did all this, she was watching him. She was looking into his eyes, and her gaze never wavered. She had looked directly into his eyes like this before — on the day they met, and again during one of her first visits. It unnerved him, and it thrilled him, to look unwaveringly into her eyes.

He didn't put his hand near what he was old-fashioned or prim enough to think of as her sex.

She closed her eyes. He lay beside her, propped on one arm, nervous, unsure of what was supposed to happen next.

"I think that was the most erotic thing that anyone's ever done to me," she said. Instantly, as if he'd been injected with a drug, he swelled with male pride: I'm still the cocksman I used to be! Move over, you whippersnappers, I'll teach you all a thing or two about loving! His penis swelled with hubris, but he just lay there beside her, unmoving, and in another few minutes, listening to her slow, even breathing, he realized that she was asleep.

He was still fully dressed: he still had his shoes on. The experience was a little easier to enjoy now that it was over. He could rely on the filtering processes of the mind to retain only the good parts of the evening.

He was astonished by her generosity. Surely it must have been horrible for her to be mauled like this by an old man.

Even though he hadn't actually touched her.

To be mauled by an old man's shadow.

He tried to calm down. His heart was jerking around in his chest; his jaw was numb. He sent up a prayer to the God he didn't believe in: Please don't let me have a heart attack tonight.

After a few minutes he became aware of the need to urinate. He decided to ignore it. She seemed to be sleeping very lightly; if he got out of bed he might wake her. He didn't want to wake her. The experience had ended nicely: he hadn't humiliated himself in any way, as far as he knew. He didn't want to push his luck.

The need to urinate became insistent. It was odd, because he hadn't had much to drink all night. He wondered whether this was a sign of prostate trouble. Probably it was just nervousness. Incontinence was one of the few geriatric disorders he hadn't experienced yet.

Or was that true? Certainly, in recent years, he had found it more difficult to control his bladder. He'd learned that after a meal at a restaurant he neglected to visit the bathroom at his peril, for if he did, the trip home would be extremely uncomfortable. And it was also true that there were moments when he couldn't quite keep his sphincter clamped shut. A sudden sneeze often caused him to leak.

So perhaps what he was feeling right now wasn't just nervousness: perhaps he *had* become incontinent, and was discovering it at a particularly inconvenient moment.

But this seemed doubtful. He turned over onto his stomach to put the pressure of his body on his penis, in the hope that this might stifle the need to pee. It worked, but it made her stir in her sleep.

He began to think about how humiliating it would be if he leaked in bed.

He got out of bed as quietly as possible and went down the hall to the bathroom. He kept the light off and didn't look in the mirror.

He came back to the bed and got in next to her, as gently as he could.

Almost every night, for the last few decades, he'd spent an hour or so reading in bed and then gone to sleep while listening to classical music on the radio. He didn't know if he could fall asleep without his routine.

He looked out the window — from his bedroom window he could see a sliver of New Jersey — and listened to the sounds of the street.

After a few minutes, he needed to urinate again.

He was in despair. This is what becomes of the most exalted moment of the last season of your life. This was the first time he had been with a woman in more than fifteen years. In the future, he was sure, he would cherish the memory of this evening. He would remember this evening as proof of the bounty of life, proof that life keeps offering unexpected gifts. He would forget, as soon as he could, that much of the actual experience had been torture.

Shifting and squirming, he couldn't take it anymore. He left the bed again, went to the bathroom, and found, not to his surprise, that he didn't have to urinate at all.

He removed his shirt and his pants, leaving his socks and his underwear on, and took down his robe from the hook on the bathroom door. A thick blue terry-cloth robe that

Ariel had given him during his last stay in the hospital. Instead of trying to go to sleep — he knew that was impossible — he went to the kitchen and poured a little skim milk into a pan on the stove. He got some fat-free cookies from the cupboard.

Her bag was lying near the doorway, next to her shoes; he thought about looking through it, but the urge quickly passed. When he was younger he used to do that kind of detective work without thinking twice: as soon as he'd slept with a woman he'd be poking through her pocketbook on the sly, nosing through her diaries, holding sealed letters to the light. It used to be the kind of thing he expected of himself, as an artist. But he left Heather's bag undisturbed. Was this because he respected her; or because he'd outgrown his pretentious belief that artists are exempt from social conventions; or because he'd lost his curiosity? He didn't know. We congratulate ourselves on having abandoned our vices, when it is they who have abandoned us. Some witty literary man had said that; he couldn't remember who. Probably Wilde. Probably Shaw. Probably Wilde.

13

Ariel was meeting Victor for a late drink at the Shark Bar on Amsterdam and 74th. She found him sitting in a booth, squinting at a copy of *Barron's* in the dim light.

According to the three-date rule, Ariel had to sleep with Victor tonight. Promulgated by one of Ariel's girlfriends, the rule stipulated that you can't sleep with a guy until the third date, but you have to sleep with him on the third date if you're going to sleep with him at all.

She asked him what was new, and he started talking about one of his cases: he was defending a high-level drug dealer named Ishmael.

"I find the drug dealers to be the nicest guys," he said. "They're always polite, and they don't tell you they're innocent. I hate it when *you* know the guy is guilty and *he* knows you know he's guilty, but he keeps claiming he didn't do it.

"The guys from the Mafia aren't so nice. They expect you to treat them like royalty — all those Godfather movies must've gone to their heads."

Ariel pushed her lime slice around with her straw. She didn't understand why this man didn't inspire her. He was a good guy, he had a sense of humor, he even had artistic leanings — last month she'd journeyed up to Westchester to see him playing the Dick York role in an amateur stage production of *Inherit the Wind.* So what could be wrong?

"Why'd you become a lawyer?" she said, with an uneasy feeling that she had asked him this already.

"I was always deeply in love with the majesty of the law."

"Really?" Suddenly he seemed more interesting, even more handsome.

"Yeah, right. I was an English major. What can an English major do in the real world? Nothing. So I applied to law school."

She could understand that well enough, but it disappointed her. She wished he *were* in love with the majesty of the law. She didn't think she could be with someone who was just killing time with his life. She needed someone who was living out a passion: an artist or a scientist or a therapist or a teacher. The problem wasn't that he was a lawyer: the problem was that he wasn't in love with what he did.

He went back to talking about his client, and although he was a very nice guy and she hoped he'd find his Juliet, it wasn't going to be her. She wasn't going to sleep with him tonight, and probably she wasn't going to see him again. When they finished their drinks he asked her if she wanted to come over to his place, and she said no. "I have a client tomorrow morning at eight," she said. "I should go home." He smiled with resignation, and she knew that he knew that they weren't going to see each other again.

Out on the street, when they kissed good night, she discovered that he didn't know any such thing: he kissed her with his mouth open and fleetingly gave her his tongue. Apparently he wasn't acquainted with the three-date rule, and therefore didn't realize that his failure to get her into bed tonight spelled the doom of his boyfriendly hopes.

She said good night and broke away from him quickly, skipping nervously across the street while the DON'T WALK sign flashed. In her ten-second journey from the west side of Amsterdam to the east side, she traveled to 1972 and back again. The tongue flick during a street-corner kiss as an invitation or statement of intent: it was like something out of high school.

She walked aimlessly north. Weird kiss.

It was a little after eleven. She didn't really have a client at eight, and now that she'd gotten rid of Victor she realized she wasn't quite ready to go home.

When was she going to find a decent guy? She felt as if doors were closing in her life.

Ariel had been married once, for two and a half years, in her late twenties. Her husband, Ted, who was in his forties when they met, wanted kids as much as she did. For the first year they had a great time trying; when nothing happened they started going to specialists. During the second year they supplemented their efforts with the most advanced techniques and equipment, and she spent a great deal of time in glaring white rooms with her feet up in stirrups, but still with no luck. By this time she'd begun to believe that there was nothing wrong with their reproductive systems — it was just that her eggs and his sperm didn't want anything to do with each other. They'd gotten married much too fast, and now their relationship had deteriorated to the point where the desire to have children was one of the few things they shared. "I can't wait till we get pregnant," Ted kept saying — and this formulation, as if both of them would be getting pregnant, began to strike her as geeky and insulting, even though she knew that this way of putting it was close to obligatory for the sensitive modern husband.

Old Ted. She thought of him about once a year now, if that.

After she and Ted split up, she fell in love with someone — Casey Davis — who already had a kid and didn't want to have another; and she went out with a couple of guys who wanted kids but whom she didn't want to have kids with; and she spent some time with two or three jerks who weren't nice to her and whom she didn't even like; and somehow ten years had flown by.

She was still walking uptown. She had a membership at a video rental store on Columbus and 82nd — she used to get videos there when she was taking care of her father between his operations. Just to go somewhere, she walked to the store — she thought she'd spend half an hour browsing through the new releases — and when she got there it occurred to her that it would be nice to go over to her father's and watch a video with him. He never went to sleep before midnight. She knew he'd be happy to see her. That was one of the few things she could count on in life. She picked out *Mrs. Miniver*, Greer Garson, Walter Pidgeon, 1942, which always made her cry.

She walked up to his place and let herself in. The lights were on in the living room and the kitchen: he was up. She put her backpack down in the hallway and went to find him. There were dishes on the coffee table, and jars of honey and peanut butter. It wasn't like him: he was a neatness freak, and peanut butter wasn't the kind of thing he ate anymore. There was a funny smell.

He was sitting in the kitchen in his bathrobe, having milk and cookies. He looked up at her. He looked . . . scared.

"Howdy," Ariel said.

On the floor near the table were a pair of shoes: black wing-tip boots, sexy little hipster boots with heels.

"I should have called," she said. Her father held his cookie in the air and stared at her, but he didn't speak. "I'll call you tomorrow," she said, and walked quickly — she didn't quite run, but almost — through the hallway and out the front door.

She hit the elevator button, but she was too spooked to wait. She lurched into the stairwell and walked down fifteen flights without thinking a single thought, and she was out on the street before she knew it.

He was *sleeping* with her? *She* was sleeping with *him?*

It wasn't even midnight yet, but Broadway seemed suddenly threatening. She flagged a cab, told the driver where to go, and closed her eyes. The taxi streaked wildly down

Broadway; she started to feel ill. She leaned toward the partition and said, "If we get into an accident and I die, I won't be able to tip you."

All she wanted was to go home and watch her video and try not to think. Then she realized that she didn't have the video. And then she realized that she didn't have her backpack, and, therefore, that she didn't have her purse or her keys. She must have left everything at her father's.

She tapped on the partition and said, "I'm really sorry, but I forgot my purse. I don't have any money. Do you think you could drive me back to 94th so I could get my purse?"

The cabbie had a turban, a beard, and long deep grimness lines about the mouth. He pulled over to the curb. "If you don't have money I can't drive you anywhere. This automobile is not a charitable organization."

"What do you think, I'm going to jump out and not come back? You think I just wanted to take a joyride? Look, I'm not going to disappear. I'll write down my address if you want." *Why am I giving him my address?*

"I don't want your address, or your phone number either. You are a pretty girl but not that pretty. You're a little bit over the hill."

She should have been relieved, but she was insulted. "I want you to pay the fare. That's all I ask."

"I'm sorry but I told you I forgot my purse."

He pressed a button and all the locks in the cab went down. "I can't let you out of my cab without collateral. What do you have? You have jewelry? You have rings?"

"I don't have any jewelry. I have a watch."

"Give me the watch and I'll wait for you."

She gave him the watch and he drove her back to 94th. She got out of the car and, standing outside her father's building, she realized that she didn't want to go back up.

"Look," she said to the cabbie, "I can't get the money now. Can I get your number and pay you tomorrow?"

He shook his head, with a righteous and disdainful smile.

She felt a surge of what can only be called racist rage — she felt outraged that this . . . *foreigner*, with that weird *shmatte* on his head, was lording it over *her*, an American citizen! But this wasn't at all like Ariel, and she came to her senses quickly. "Can't you just be nice?" she said.

"I am a philosopher!" he said. "In my country I am known as a philosopher! Do you think I was born to drive a cab? I speak seven languages! How many languages do *you* speak?"

"Just one," she admitted forlornly. "I studied French in high school, but I can't remember much of it." She wasn't sure why they were talking about this. *"Je suis Madame Thibault,"* she said — the only thing she remembered from high school French.

He told her that his name was . . . something: it flew out of her head as soon as he said it; and he said that if she called the Taxi and Limousine Commission she could leave him a message and he'd exchange her watch for the fare. She lamely agreed; she just wanted him to be gone. He stepped on the gas and sped away, and her watch rode out of her life.

Her father had bought her the watch at a street fair a few months ago, shortly after she came back to New York.

"Fuck," she said. "Fuck a duck." She had no idea where to go. She didn't have a dime. For a moment she thought she understood what it must be like to be homeless, but she quickly saw that that was a silly thought.

"Fuck it and duck it," she said. This was something she said to herself at moments of extreme frustration; she'd been saying it since she was ten. It occurred to her that no one in the world knew she said this: she didn't think she'd ever said it in anyone else's presence.

She felt reproached by the nakedness of her wrist. She felt as if she'd thrown away not just the gift but the tenderness of the moment when he'd given it to her. They were strolling through the Columbus Avenue Street Fair, near the Museum of Natural History, and she was complaining about how disorganized she was: always arriving late at her clients' apartments, hair unbrushed, breathless, gulping coffee from a cardboard cup. It was a beautiful blue afternoon in the middle of May; the city seemed a calm, friendly place; and she was miserable. She wanted to keep berating herself, but her father stopped her. "Ariel, my dear, it's not a moral problem, it's a technical problem. All you need is a watch." They stopped at an antiques stall run by a spaced-out Norseman from Vermont, and he bought her the watch. It wasn't a watch she would have bought for herself: for herself she would have bought a purple Swatch — something bright and disposable. He picked out the kind of thing he liked: tiny, ancient, sliver-thin, delicate, dear.

He was right: just having the watch helped her get her act together. She stopped being late so much; it helped her take herself and her profession more seriously.

She appreciated the way her father, in his gentleness, had told her that her work problem was only "technical." It was a way of telling her not to judge herself so harshly. And maybe the watch wouldn't have cleared things up as it did if she hadn't had the memory of his tenderness to think of when she looked at it.

And now she'd given it away.

She was walking down Broadway, trying to figure out what to do. She couldn't go back to her father's place, and she couldn't get into her own.

There wasn't really anyone she could call at this hour. When she'd moved back to New York last year she hadn't gotten back in touch with her old friends — she'd wanted to start over — and she hadn't made many new ones since then. All the lousy loneliness of her life was crashing down on her. In high school all the boys were in love with her. I used to be the belle of the ball, she thought.

Halfway down the block she saw an elegant-looking black man walking his dog, and for a second she thought it was her old boyfriend Casey. Casey! Wouldn't it be amazing to run into him now? Wouldn't it be amazing if he was still single? But this man wasn't Casey, and Casey probably wasn't single, and anyway, she and Casey had already had their chance.

She was still reeling from her father and the biographer. How could he . . . ? How could *she* . . . ? Ariel loved her father, but she couldn't imagine how any young woman in her right mind could get into bed with him.

Trudging down Broadway, she started thinking about her mother. She felt as if her father had betrayed her memory. It made no sense, but this was how she felt.

If it had been some dowdy sixty-year-old, some librarian, that would have been different. Ariel would have welcomed that — she would have taken the librarian out for lunch. But this was something else.

By now she was at 79th Street. She knew a couple who lived a block away, on West End. She could see their windows; their lights were on. She didn't know them well enough to disturb them at this hour, but she was drawn there anyway; she drifted down the block and stood across the street from their building, trying to see if they were moving around in their apartment.

The man was a client of hers — one of her few male clients. His doctor had told him to get some exercise, so he'd hired her to help him develop a strengthening and aerobics routine. His name was Ben. He was in his middle forties; Sally, his wife, was in her middle thirties. Ben worked for a labor union and Sally was a social worker. They had two sons. Ariel felt a kinship with them: they were idealists, left-wingers, sixties people at heart. She sort of wanted to be their friend.

Maybe the kids were in bed and the two of them were snuggled in front of the television set enjoying a cozy night together. Maybe they were making love. She would have liked to ring their doorbell and sleep on their couch, but she didn't know them well enough. She looked up at the window, envying the life she was locked out of.

14

Heather spent the night in a state between sleeping and waking, alone in Schiller's bed.

She was relieved when morning came, but she didn't get up right away. She had to sort out her feelings, and she had to decide on a face to present to him when she left the room.

The night before had been . . . *interesting.* Heather had slept with seventeen guys in her life — on an insomniac winter night last year, she'd counted — but no one had ever paid such close and loving attention to her before. Schiller had made her feel as if she were worthy of awe.

Even though he hadn't touched her. Precisely because he hadn't touched her. If he'd touched her it would have been something else entirely.

It hadn't precisely been a sexual experience for her. How could it have been? She'd been acutely conscious of his body: the old man's smell; his huge and withered old man's ears, like jumbo-sized dried apricots; the deadness of his old man's skin.

You're only ripe for a moment. Life made more sense in the Middle Ages, when no one lasted past forty.

But still, it had been interesting. More than interesting, really.

She buttoned up her dress — she'd unbuttoned it last night, but she'd never taken it off. She was nervous about what he might expect from her.

She looked for her shoes, couldn't find them, and walked barefoot into the kitchen. Her shoes were where she'd left them — now she remembered — near the kitchen door. Schiller was peering into his toaster oven, examining the progress of a slice of toast.

He looked bad. He was already shaved, showered, and dressed in a jacket and a tie, but somehow he looked undone. He looked as if he hadn't slept at all.

A moment after he looked up at her, he seemed transformed. He suddenly didn't look tired anymore. It was a pleasure to have this effect on someone.

He had coffee ready for her; he offered to make her something to eat but she told him she never ate breakfast. Moving around his small kitchen, he had an ungainly grace — if such a thing can be.

He sat across the table from her and watched her drink her coffee, and he seemed

151

to be cherishing her with his gaze: it was as if the night had lasted into the morning.

On the table next to his coffee cup was a novel by R. K. Narayan. "I love Narayan," she said. This was stretching it — she'd read only one of his novels, *The English Teacher*; but she really had loved it.

"You've read him?"

"Oh my God, yes. He's incredible. He reminds me of Chekhov. He's not as tough-minded as Chekhov, I guess, but he has more of a sense of humor."

Schiller was smiling at her oddly.

"What?" she said.

"It's nice to know a young person who wants to talk about R. K. Narayan at seven o'clock in the morning."

"I've always thought that people will still be reading him in a hundred years," she said. She'd never thought such a thing in her life; she didn't even know why she'd said it. And then she understood why she'd said it. It was so she could say the next thing.

"Do you ever wonder whether people will still be reading *you* in a hundred years?"

It struck her that this might be a rude question. But she wanted to know. And more than that, she liked the idea of herself as a person who asked rude questions at seven o'clock in the morning.

He scowled at her as he applied jam to a slice of toast. "What I wonder," he said, "is whether people will still be reading in a hundred years."

"But don't you think about it? Really."

"Why on earth *should* I?"

"I don't think you're being honest with me," she said.

"Maybe I'm not, but if I do think about these things, it would still be unseemly to talk about them. That's got nothing to do with what the whole enterprise is about."

"What *is* the whole enterprise about? Now that you mention it."

"It isn't something I can put into words. Not at seven o'clock in the morning."

"Of course you can."

He looked around helplessly, as if he were searching for something to distract her with. He didn't find anything. "Young lady," he said. "I'm an old man. I'm an old man trying to eat toast."

"To put it bluntly," she said, "your novels are out of print, and you've said that you don't even know if anyone is going to be interested in publishing the one you're working on now. So why do you keep going?"

"Heather, what can I say? Whatever I said would be too much or too little."

"But what if I write a book about you

someday? What should I say it was that kept you going?"

"Just say it was the madness of art." He raised his eyebrows with a meaningful look, as if this explained everything.

It didn't explain much. The madness of art. She thought of some of the aspiring artists she'd met since she came to New York — boys with buzz-saw haircuts and great expectations, who were always boasting about the epic poems they were writing or the movies they planned to make. One filmmaker she knew was putting together a film, if it could be called a film, made up entirely of still photographs of his own face. Every morning, first thing in the morning, he took a photograph of himself in the bathroom mirror. The film, which would not be complete until the end of his life but which he intended to show in installments before then, was titled *The Progress of Death*. He smoked too many cigarettes (Gauloises), drank too much (Jack Daniel's), and never took off his sunglasses, not even in the darkest bars. He would have been eager to nominate himself as an example of the madness of art, if he'd known the phrase. But Schiller? His work was careful, tender, sometimes breaking into passion, sometimes breaking into song — it was beautiful at its best, but it had little to do with madness, as far as she could see.

"The madness of art?" she said.

Schiller just shrugged, as if he were powerless to explain the idea.

She kicked him lightly on the shin, in a friendly way. "If I have to ask I'll never know — is that it?"

She didn't, in fact, take the phrase too seriously: she thought he was just putting on airs. He was intoxicated with himself because he'd had a fresh young thing in his bed.

She put her cup in the sink. "Time to go."

Ever since she was in her teens, Heather had considered herself a virtuoso of the abrupt exit. She liked to leave people wanting more.

Schiller looked disappointed — which was good. She wanted her leaving to be an exclamation mark. She wanted her life to be an exclamation mark.

She kissed him on the forehead — kissed him directly on a mottled age spot — and got her coat.

15

Now that the experience was over, it felt wonderful. She was intoxicated with her own generosity. She felt like a Florence Nightingale of sexual life.

She was sure that he had loved every minute of their night together. She had no idea that his feelings had been as mixed as hers.

She walked rapidly downtown. With each step she felt more amazing. She felt perfect, fluent, charmed. It was a nasty day: raw, bitter, grim, gray, grimacing. She didn't mind it at all. The air was entitled to its rawness; the sky was entitled to be grim. Everything was welcome; everything was entitled to unfold itself. Waiting to cross with the light, she heard bagpipes bleating from a second-story window. The sounds lurched toward her, sought out her ear; the music needed her — to confirm itself, to complete itself, to be.

She was a giver of life. She gave a dollar to a panhandler, who half-bowed and smiled at her — with a look of ironic recognition, as if the two of them might have been lovers in another life. "Mama," he said as she passed him, "you're a poem in the flesh."

The air parted to let her by. Manhattan was blessed. She took the subway to Hudson River Park and boarded a ferry to Hoboken; and as the ferry labored across the bucking river she reveled in the stripped stark harshness of the day. Watching the towers of Manhattan tremble in the brooding light, she wanted the skies to crack wide open; she wanted to be assaulted by rain and sleet and hail.

But the sky didn't open. By the time she arrived in Hoboken the day had turned warmer and milder, and she was left with a feeling of anticlimax as she stepped onto the pier.

She stopped at an Italian deli for some groceries, and waited on line behind a bedraggled-looking mother and her son. The boy was making a nuisance of himself, demanding that his mother buy him a pack of Twinkies. In a zombie monotone, he kept repeating, "Roy is a monkey boy; Twinkies and milk for Roy. Roy is a monkey boy; Twinkies and milk for Roy."

He was a uniquely unappealing child. As he chanted, he picked his nose with one hand and pawed at his mother's pocketbook with the other.

"You've been asking me for Twinkies all

day, and you're not going to get them," his mother said. "And if you ask again I'm going to smack you."

The child, undeterred, pressed his claim. "Roy is a peepee boy; Twinkies and milk for Roy." A peepee boy was apparently even more deserving than a monkey boy. Slap him, Heather thought. He needs it. Finally the woman drew her hand back as if to do just that, but then, as if overcome by the understanding that Roy had long ago emerged the victor from their battle of wills and that it would be a pointless gesture to slap him now, she let her hand drop back to her side.

Wimp, Heather thought. You two deserve each other.

At home she got under the covers and slept heavily for three hours. When she woke she noticed a curious change. She found it hard to remember the hour she had spent with Schiller on his bed. It was as if it had left no trace.

She was able to bring back a mental picture of it, but she couldn't recall it on her senses. The body remembers things in its own way, and her body didn't remember the experience at all.

This, when she thought about it, didn't seem surprising. After all, he hadn't touched her. When it was happening, when she was in his bed, she was impressed by the way he refrained from touching her: she thought it was the essence of delicacy. And that was true: he couldn't have been more delicate. But he could have been bolder.

She started to prepare a bath. She ran her hand experimentally through the stream of water. It was pleasantly warm. She got into the tub, sat down cross-legged under the stream, and turned the hot water knob until the heat was so fierce that it hurt her. Quickly she leaned forward and adjusted it, to make it hotter. The water scalded her arms and her thighs and left them bright red and burning. She leaned forward again to make it hotter.

16

During the mornings Heather worked on her thesis. The pages piled up effortlessly. She had decided on a focus for her study: the drama of personal liberation in Schiller's work. This would allow her to concentrate on what was most alive in his writing; it would give her license to compare him to other writers she loved, other writers whose best work was about breaking away from the dull compulsions of routine; and, though she wasn't going to write about herself explicitly — this was an academic study, after all — it would give her a way to put her own passions front and center in what she wrote.

She was at the midpoint of the thesis — she'd written about a hundred pages — when things started to slow down. She'd been moving along at the rate of five pages a day; but now she realized that she'd spent the last two days staring at a single paragraph. She decided to knock off for an hour, and she took a walk around Hoboken in the gorgeous cool day.

Everything about the day was gorgeous except Hoboken itself. She'd moved here because she'd heard it was a mecca for poor, fledgling artists, but she found it a creepy place. It had the grime of a city but not the excitement; it had the brain-dead aura of the suburbs, but not the green. It reminded her of Dickens's description of Coketown in *Hard Times*: "neither city nor country, but either spoiled." On the weekends college kids from all over Jersey came to party in the bars; at midnight you could see them vomiting into trash cans. In the afternoons big jock high school boys stood across the street from each other chucking footballs. They liked to skim the ball low, just above the heads of passersby.

The only person she cared for in Hoboken was a dog. When she took her stroll that day she passed him. He was an old, half-blind, dust-colored mutt with a badly scratched nose, as if some alley cat he'd tangled with had gotten the better of him. He was always at his post, just outside a pizza place on Washington Street, lying fatly with his legs splayed out as if he'd decided he'd walked far enough in life. He had a calm, reflective, tolerant demeanor as he watched the passing human show; he seemed like the neighborhood sage. The pizza place was named Benny Tudino's; Heather didn't know the dog's name, but she named him Benny in her mind. She touched his matted flank; he looked at her acceptingly. "Hello, Benny," she said.

She returned to her apartment eager to get back to work, but when she sat at her desk the problem was still there.

It was starting to disturb her. She had a feeling that it wasn't a literary problem. Maybe it was simply this: that she couldn't help thinking that something had gone wrong in Schiller's life.

She was still puzzled by the way he lived. She knew she never could have lived that way: just sitting at your desk, alone, day after day after day. Is that really the way to nourish your emotions — to nourish your art? Heather had always been a ferocious reader, but she never could have enjoyed a life that consisted only of reading. Part of the joy of reading was talking about what you'd read — in a classroom, in a bar, wherever. She loved solitude, but she also loved being with people, and a life spent entirely in solitude made no sense to her.

But it wasn't just his manner of life. What was troubling Heather was that she couldn't shake the sense that his *work* had gone dry somehow.

Of course, Schiller wasn't the only writer who'd done his best work early in life. She thought of some of the people she'd studied in her American literature classes. Hemingway had faded terribly: by the end of his life he was writing imitations of his early work. You could say something similar about Faulkner, or Sherwood Anderson, or Edith Wharton, or Richard Wright.

Maybe it's inevitable. Maybe you only feel things strongly when you're young.

That was a scary thought.

But as she thought about it over the next couple of days, she came to the conclusion that it didn't have to be true. Certain writers managed to stay fresh, even in old age. Yeats, for instance, grew younger as he grew older: his work grew stronger and more muscular as he aged. George Eliot got steadily better: more intelligent, more original, more daring. D. H. Lawrence and Virginia Woolf may not have gotten better, but they continued to experiment restlessly as long as they lived.

So you *can* keep going. You *can* stay young. There's no inevitable law of diminishment: everyone who fades fades for his own reasons. Certainly it was easier to peter out than to keep going; certainly the loss of sheer animal vitality must have a great deal to do with it. But there was more to it. There had to be more.

It was a question, she was aware, that

could be applied to any area of life. How many marriages, for example, remained creative, remained interesting to both partners? Probably few. What differentiated the few that remain creative from the many that sink into routine?

Precisely because she was just getting started in life, these questions seemed urgent to her. She had the sense that her first steps might determine everything to come.

It wasn't as if she did nothing in life but think about Schiller. She worked hard during the day, and in the evening she usually explored New York.

She'd been going to fiction or poetry readings almost every week. It seemed like a good way to meet people, to find her place in the city. That was how she'd met the woman from *Bomb*. A few days after her night at Schiller's, she went to a reading in the East Village sponsored by *The Village Voice*.

Ever since her junior year of high school, Heather had bought the *Voice* every week and studied it with a devotion that was part scholarly, part religious. She'd thought of it as a lifeline to sophistication, to freedom, to New York.

After the reading was over, she went up to the woman who'd introduced the readers.

"My name is Heather Wolfe," she said. "You rejected two of my book reviews."

The woman, Sandra Bennett, was in her mid-forties; she was slender, tall, with long black hair and enviable cheekbones. From the podium she'd radiated a sense of calm authority. She had, Heather thought, a certain stateliness — a word she never would have applied to anyone before.

"Heather Wolfe. I can't say I remember them. I guess they weren't very good."

Heather was unfazed by this. "I just wanted to tell you I loved the article you wrote last spring about Max's Kansas City. I loved the autobiographical parts the most. I think you should be writing your memoirs."

Each word of this was true, and yet it was pure flattery. Heather had only seconds to impress herself on Sandra's brain, and a few words of well-chosen flattery seemed like the best way to achieve that end.

Heather was a student of flattery — which is a subtle art. There's a fine line between effective flattery, which makes some important person feel that you've perceptively appreciated his work, and cringing flattery, which makes the person think you're a groupie — someone to be ignored, or used, but certainly not taken seriously.

"Thanks, I guess," Sandra said. "I hope

I'm a little young for my memoirs."

"But I also thought you weren't saying everything you knew about Lou Reed. That part could have been better. You kept hinting at something and then not saying it."

The criticism was just as calculated as the praise. She wanted to seem independent-minded and shrewd. But again, she was also speaking the truth: there *was* something off about the way Sandra had written about Lou Reed. It made Heather wonder if Sandra had had an affair with him.

Sandra looked at her with a skeptical, amused expression, and Heather had the impression that Sandra was bringing her into focus, putting her on file in her memory. She also had the impression that Sandra knew exactly what she was doing with this two-step of praise and critique.

"Maybe I do remember those reviews," Sandra said. "You're a graduate student somewhere, aren't you?"

"I was. At Brown. I finished my course work. Now I'm writing my thesis and living here."

"The young woman from the provinces, ready to make a name for herself in the city. I love it." Sandra seemed to be teasing her, but maybe not. It was hard to tell.

Now that she had Sandra's attention, she

started telling her about her thesis — as usual, she placed her emphasis on the idea that she had a good shot at turning it into a book. Heather couldn't tell whether Sandra had ever heard of Schiller: when she mentioned his name, Sandra nodded, but in a vague way.

A crowd of people from the reading were going out for a drink; Heather, still talking to Sandra, fell in step with her, and although she hadn't precisely been invited, she ended up sitting next to Sandra at a long table in a crowded bar.

The music was too loud; they had to bend their heads together to hear each other speak. But no one sitting nearby could eavesdrop. It was curious, the intimacy of a conversation conducted in shouts.

Heather knew all about Sandra. She was a former wunderkind: she'd been a staff writer at *The New Yorker* in the middle seventies, a protégée of William Shawn, and when Shawn was deposed, Sandra, along with a lot of other people, left in protest. When people think of the old *New Yorker* as staid and safe, they're forgetting about writers like Sandra. She wrote about rock music with literacy and wit; she was one of the first people to discover Patti Smith; she was one of the first people to write intelligently about punk music. Heather had once spent an afternoon in the library digging up Sandra's articles, and they still held up.

After Sandra left *The New Yorker* she bounced around for a few years at other magazines, finally ending up at the *Voice*. She didn't write much anymore — she published about an article a year. Supposedly she threw most of her energies into editing. She had a reputation as someone who nurtured young talent. And this was why Heather had approached her.

"So what do you see yourself doing in five years?" Sandra said. "Are you planning to become a literary critic?"

She hadn't really thought about it. Five years seemed a long way away.

"I'm not sure. Some days I want to be Elizabeth Bishop, some days I want to be Liz Phair. Some days I want to be Joan Didion, and some days I want to be —"

"Joan of Arc," Sandra said. "You've got the under-thirty disease. It'll pass."

Sandra seemed to be taking her seriously. But she seemed to take everyone seriously. A guy who had come along from the reading was leaving the bar; he sat down to talk with Sandra for a minute on his way out, and though Heather couldn't hear what they were saying, she saw that Sandra was speaking to him with complete absorption, as if he were the only person in the room. During the hour that Heather spent there, this happened several times: Sandra would engage in intense conversation with someone and Heather would sip her beer, biding her time, waiting for an opportunity to regain her attention.

After two drinks, Heather was telling Sandra what she liked about her work. "I love the way you go from books to movies to literature to history to politics to music. It's not like you're saying that the Sex Pistols were as great as Dostoevsky. But you do seem to be saying that it's perfectly fine to like the Sex Pistols *and* Dostoevsky. I love that. It's very freeing."

Freeing, Heather thought drunkenly. Whenever I want to flatter an older person I tell them they freed me. But it's true.

During the next half hour their talk went from Laurie Anderson to Mary Gaitskill to Willa Cather to Chantal Ackerman to Robert Bresson. Heather had the sense that she was being tested — but this was a test she could pass.

She flashed on Schiller, who was undoubtedly in bed by now. When she was with Schiller, she felt continually reproached — for not knowing enough about Delmore

Schwartz, for never having heard of Harvey Swados, for not understanding the long-ago cultural centrality of *Partisan Review*. Not that Schiller ever actually reproached her — it was just that she could feel his sadness that the constellations he had steered by were so faint to her.

"Time for bed," Sandra said. "Give me a call at the *Voice* this week. Maybe we can find something for you to write about."

"Really? That's really nice of you." Heather wasn't acting: she was genuinely thrilled.

"I like to give young people a hand."

"I've heard that about you. I've always wondered why."

"When I was young a few older people gave me a hand. It's the kind of thing you can't really repay, because the people who help you may never need your help. But what you *can* do is pass it on. So I try to pass it on."

They left the bar; at almost two in the morning Second Avenue was still throbbing, and Heather felt the power and splendor of the city as vividly as if she'd just arrived. Sandra had said that maybe she could write for the *Voice*. Heather thought the world could stop right now. Life was perfect; how could it get any better than this? But maybe the world shouldn't stop — because what made life perfect was this sense of possibility, this sense of the promise of the future. Maybe someday she could be like Sandra, welcoming some beginner, some young hopeful, to the pleasures of the life of the mind. She felt incredibly lucky. You can go from pleasure to pleasure to pleasure if you're lucky enough.

17

Ariel met her father at Williams Bar-B-Que on Broadway and 86th. They were visiting his friend Levin at Beth Israel North on the East Side. Schiller bought some food to take to the hospital: a roast chicken, kasha varnishkes, a three-bean salad, and a quart of gefilte fish. Ariel bought a bag of peanuts to eat on their walk through the park.

The day was oddly warm, wet, thick with mist.

"I'm sorry about the other weekend," he said. This was the first time she'd seen him since she'd stumbled into his love nest. She'd ended up sleeping that night at her exercise studio — a guard she knew had been on duty in the building — and she'd picked up her backpack the next day when she knew Schiller wouldn't be home — Jeff, the doorman, had a set of keys.

"Heather wasn't feeling well, so I put her up in the guest room."

Well, maybe it was true. Certainly it was easier to believe that than to believe the two of them were lovers. But on the other hand her father had looked guilty and strange when she'd barged in on him that night, and even now he was mumbling in a way that wasn't like him.

The soil in the park was mushy and he had to walk slowly; his cane sank into the ground each time he leaned on it, and he had to struggle to extract it with each step.

Why did she even care? He had his own life; whatever he was doing with that little freak was his own business.

The Great Lawn was deserted except for a few people playing Frisbee in the distance.

She didn't have a right to care, but she cared.

It was just *weird*, that's all. It was against nature.

By the time they reached Fifth Avenue he was tired, and they rested on a bench near the Metropolitan Museum.

"I have something for you," he said. He reached into an inside pocket of his suit jacket and withdrew a silver necklace, attached to which were two small pearls. "I was going through a trunk of your mother's things. I hadn't looked inside it in twenty years. I think I bought this for her the year you were born."

The pearls were beautiful: their purity, their subtlety, their modesty.

"Thank you," she said.

He unclasped the necklace and fitted it around her neck, and he examined her with a fatherly appreciativeness — his gaze moving from the pearls to her eyes to the pearls — and took a deep breath; and this long fluent breath reassured her more than anything he could have said to her. She needed to feel important to her father, and, in this moment, she did.

"Pearls symbolize hope," he said.

She wanted to make the moment last somehow. She took a peanut out of the little bag she'd bought at Williams.

"Did you ever see the man in the peanut?" she said. She shelled the peanut and then carefully broke it in half, along its seam. Inside was a little bump that looked like an old man with a beard. She showed it to her father.

"Mom showed me that," she said.

After he rested they resumed their walk. The hospital was all the way over by the East River, near Gracie Mansion. The streets here were stunningly calm and well-tended; it was hardly like being in New York.

The hospital itself was old-fashioned, neighborly, and quaint. In his room, Levin was sitting up in bed.

"Jesus H. Christ," he said. "Stella."

"It's not Stella," Schiller said. "It's Ariel.

It's my daughter." His voice was soft, but his face was grim.

"Goodness," Levin said. He closed his eyes and pressed his lips together with an expression of self-reproach. "Don't mind me. I'm just sloshing around through the decades here."

Another of her father's old friends, Sol Booth, was sitting in the corner. He shook Schiller's hand and gave Ariel a hug.

"George is tired because he's been taking an intellectual thrashing," Booth said.

"Sol waits until I'm in intensive care to lecture me about Israel."

Ariel had known these men all her life; she cared for them a great deal; but she had always been afraid of them as well. Their love of intellectual combat left her cold. They were always arguing about something; it seemed to make them feel more alive. She didn't like to argue.

"What's going on?" her father said, putting the bags of food on the table.

"Sol was calling me a political naif," Levin said.

"Look what I find on the man's night table." Booth held up a book. "Noam Chomsky!" he said.

"So?" Schiller said.

"Ach!" was all Booth could say.

175

Levin smiled, but she could see he was in great pain.

"I wasn't even reading it," he said. "My son sent it to me."

"You should have sent it back," Booth said.

"We brought some food," Schiller said.

Booth got up to help. He was noticeably sprier than her father and most of her father's other friends. He took a plastic container out of the bag and waved it at Ariel. "Gefilte fish. Can I interest you in some refreshing gefilte fish, my dear?" She smiled and said no, but he wouldn't take no for an answer. He took out a piece with a plastic fork, put it on a paper plate, and put the plate into her hand. "Eat, eat."

Gefilte fish was one of those Jewish specialties that had always baffled her. What *was* gefilte fish? Soft spongy slimy loaves of beige matter fixed in gelatin. Was it really even fish? No one knew.

As Booth and her father spread out the fish and the kasha varnishkes and the roast chicken, she wondered who would eat these things after their generation was gone. She saw herself in the distant future, in some delicatessen on Broadway, ordering gefilte fish to commune with her father's spirit.

Her father and Booth were talking about

176

Noam Chomsky, Israel, the peace process, and, somehow, linguistics; the conversation quickly found its way to realms where she couldn't follow. "Chomsky's linguistics never seemed much more to me than warmed-over Kant," Booth said.

She couldn't tell whether Levin was following them either. He looked back and forth at his friends as they spoke, smiling encouragingly, but he seemed very tired, and she suspected that his mind was far away. She suspected that this was the old story: the dying person acting strong in order to keep up the courage of his friends.

It was hard for her to understand how you could sit at the bedside of a dying friend and talk about politics. If she were in Levin's state, she thought, she'd be thinking about death, the possibility of life after death, and little else. All worldly things would be slipping away. She wouldn't want to have to pretend to pay attention while her friends talked about the Middle East. But these men coped with death by acting as if it didn't exist. When Levin died, her father and Booth and the rest of them would attend his funeral, and then they would go to a coffee shop and talk about Kafka, Beckett, Noam Chomsky, Edward Said, and all the other things they talked about every day of their lives.

To Ariel it seemed as if they were averting their eyes from the larger questions. But maybe their way was better than hers — maybe they were serving eternity precisely by staying faithful to daily life.

If she didn't understand her father's friends, she felt that they didn't even come close to understanding her. Though as intellectuals they probably liked to think that "nothing human was alien to them," she found them narrow in their interests: the only thing they thrilled to, really, was the written word. Ariel was outside their radar. When she was a dancer, they had occasionally tried to talk to her about her work, but the conversations never got very far: they were interested in dance in a theoretical or historical way — Diaghilev, Balanchine — and she loved dance only because she loved to *do* it. Now that she taught dance exercise, her conversations with them rarely passed beyond "How are you?" It wasn't that they were cold — they were quite the opposite. Booth and Levin, like most of her father's other friends, were always happy to see her; she didn't think it would be putting it too strongly to say that they loved her. It was just that they were all so relentlessly intellectual that she existed in a realm that had no meaning for them.

"Can I get you something to drink?" her father asked Levin.

"For about a week I've had a yen for Mission orange soda," he said.

Schiller looked at his friend for a long time. "Mission orange soda," he said to Ariel, "is a drink they probably haven't made since 1940. We used to drink it after we played stickball." He patted Levin on the hand. "I'll try to hunt up a reasonable substitute."

"I'll stretch my legs with you," Booth said; and she was alone in the room with Levin.

When she was a girl, Levin and his wife Abby used to come around about once a month. Ariel liked them, but she never saw them alone, and she never really had a conversation with either of them. Except once.

It was during her first semester of college, when she was home for fall break. She was desperately unhappy at Carnegie Mellon, and she wanted to drop out and travel for a while, and her father was freaking out about it. Maybe he thought that if she left school she'd never go back; maybe he thought that if she went traveling she'd wind up in trouble — it was impossible to tell what he thought. He was barely coherent about it; her desire to leave school was a blow to his inmost, most inarticulate soul. Their conversations during that period usually ended in shouts and tears — his shouts, her tears.

Levin dropped by to see her father one afternoon, but Schiller was out, so he sat around and talked with Ariel. He must have sensed that she was upset about something, and he encouraged her to talk. She told him her story, and he listened patiently — much more patiently than her father could have listened at the time.

In retrospect, the reasons she gave for wanting to drop out — she wanted to see more of "Life" outside the classroom, and so on — weren't the real reasons. Really, it was just that she'd been shaken by the sudden changes in her life. She'd been a star at the High School of Music and Art, and now, in her first semester of college, she was a nobody; she'd been happy living at home, and being in a strange place with strange people was more of a shock than she'd anticipated.

After listening to her story, Levin told her to do what she needed to do and not take her father's opinions too seriously. "He'll love you whatever you do. You just have to decide for yourself; he'll come around. And one thing you should keep in mind is that although he doesn't want you to do anything unconventional, he was doing the same things when he was your age."

She thought he was sweet to say this, but she didn't believe him. Her father was the high priest of sobriety.

She said something like this to Levin.

"Your father?" he said. "When I was a kid, I looked up to him, and the reason I looked up to him was that he was a maniac. If I told you about some of the stunts he used to pull, it would upset you. And even after he started to become serious and sober-minded and all that, do you think his parents approved of his choices? His father wanted him to be a rabbi. When he told him he wanted to be a writer, your grandfather, whom you're fortunate never to have met, stood up and said, 'My son is driving a stake through my heart.' I'm translating roughly, from the Yiddish. Your father made his own mistakes in his time, and you have to make your own mistakes in yours."

She only half-believed all this — she couldn't imagine her father as a wild man — but even so, it helped.

Sitting alone with Levin in his hospital room, she remembered that afternoon. She realized that when they had that conversation, he was only a little older than she was now. It was difficult to take this in. She felt very much in the disorderly middle of life.

But at the time she had thought of Levin as a grown-up, a settled man, an old man.

She hadn't known it at the time, but during that period Levin's marriage was going through its death throes; he and Abby split up for good about a year after that, around the time Ariel went back to college. So when he and Ariel had that conversation, he was suffering at least as deeply as she was. But in the midst of all that, in the midst of life's perplexities, they had shared a moment of calm. Everyone else she knew at the time was barking at her, telling her what to do. She could still remember the feeling of blessed relief at finding a grown-up who would simply listen.

Maybe the moment was alive somewhere. Levin was sitting upright in his bed with his eyes closed; he seemed to be listening to his pain. But Ariel felt sure that every moment is indestructible, and that somewhere in the universe, tucked away in some hidden fold of time, their moment together still endured. Somewhere she was still a young girl, hurled about by life, confessing her troubles, and he was a calm older man, listening to her as her father couldn't listen and telling her to have courage. Somewhere the two of them were still talking in the quiet of that fall afternoon.

Levin, in his bed, opened his eyes. He had huge beautiful brown eyes — Ariel had always loved his eyes. "Sorry I called you Stella," he said. "These drugs take the pain away, but they take everything else away too."

"I didn't mind."

"It's no insult. Your mother was pretty too."

"It must be terrible to be here," she said.

He smiled weakly. "It takes a long time to die," he said.

The incredible brownness of his eyes. Everything worldly in them was burned away: all vanity gone, all ambition, all disappointment.

"You helped me a lot. That day you told me not to be afraid — remember? I'll remember it always."

He smiled and closed his eyes, and she couldn't tell if he knew what she was talking about. She heard Booth's voice in the hall; he and her father were coming back.

She touched the pearls her father had given her. It might be nice to get more pearls for the necklace, not because two were not enough, but because if she had more of them she would have a secret symbol, known only to herself, of what she believed about life. She was thinking that she was foolish to hope that someday, if she found the right path, she would be continuously happy. No one is that fortunate. The moments of beauty, the moments when you feel blessed, are only moments; but memory and imagination, treasuring them, can string them together like the delicate glories on the necklace her father had given her. Everything else passes away; that which you love remains. She had to believe this, even if she wasn't sure it was true.

18

"I have to toddle along now," Ariel said. Evidently she had somewhere to go: a client to see, or a friend, or a boyfriend — Schiller didn't know. She kissed them all good-bye, and leaving, she took her magic with her. Now they were three old men in a hospital room.

He sat with his friends for another half hour. Levin was obviously tired, but Schiller was reluctant to say good-bye, and Booth seemed to feel the same way. It was hard to know when to leave.

It was comfortable to be with these men. Schiller felt deeply accepted by them, deeply known. He had nothing to prove here.

With people you've known all your life, you're not just the person you are today. Today, sitting next to Sol Booth, he wasn't just an old, semi-embittered man, with heart problems, arthritis, and several other chronic medical conditions; he was the boy who had taken a long walk with Booth on the night in 1939 when Booth, a politically hyper-developed fifteen-year-old, decided to leave the Communist party because of the Hitler-

Stalin Pact; and he was the young man who had given the toast at Booth's wedding, in 1947, to Florence, the woman who was still Booth's partner, still his love; and he was the not-so-young man who, with his wife and daughter, had huddled around the television set with the Booths during the Cuban Missile Crisis, waiting to see if the world was about to come to an end.

More. More than that. These friends were his anchor; they kept him from floating off into the uncharted realms of his own self-regard. Schiller was probably the most ambitious of the three, and certainly the most self-absorbed. Booth's cheerfulness might have had something to do with the fact that he was abidingly concerned with matters larger than himself: he was a political creature down to his bones. Levin was the kind of old-fashioned literary critic who believed that the act of criticism was secondary to the act of creation — that the work of critics like himself was less important than the work of poets and novelists. As a critic he was primarily an enthusiast: he wrote his essays in order to pay homage to the writers he loved. Schiller, compared to both of them, was an egomaniac. He was a muted egomaniac — he tried to keep his grandiosity under cover — but an egomaniac nonetheless. He probably had to be: in order to accomplish any-thing merely good, an artist probably *must* consider himself capable of greatness. But he needed friends like these, to tease him out of his depressions and his wilder flights of self-regard, and to remind him, through the example of their lives, of what mattered.

When Levin couldn't keep his eyes open any longer, Schiller and Booth finally took the hint. They left the hospital together and walked a little while, ending up in a coffee shop on Second Avenue.

"Do you remember what you said to me when Levin got married?" Schiller said. "He was having his wedding in — where the hell was it? Somewhere out in Jersey."

"Connecticut. That restaurant in Con-necticut."

"And we were driving there with Florence and Stella. I was complaining about having to go all the way up to Connecticut, and you said, 'Look at it this way: we have two obli-gations to our old friends. We have to go to their weddings and we have to go to their funerals. With George, we're halfway home.' "

Booth smiled at the joke that he'd made almost forty years ago. "I guess we're almost all the way home now."

★ ★ ★

Booth took a cab downtown; Schiller walked west. Hobbling down the street, he passed a man wearing a sweatshirt that read DON'T MEAN SHIT TO ME.

Why on earth would anyone wear a shirt like that?

He hurt too much to walk any longer, and anyway he'd had enough exercise for one day. He stopped near Lexington at a bus shelter, which wasn't much of a shelter at the moment: someone had smashed the glass, which lay scattered in fragments in the street.

A crowded bus stopped and wheezingly knelt so Schiller could get on. This was one of the nicer changes the city had seen in recent years: the buses knelt for you now if you needed it, in one of the few marks of respect that age and infirmity still received.

He squeezed toward the back of the bus and gripped one of the metal rings. He was crammed in between a nun and a baby-faced man with a Walkman, who was humming aggressively — something from *The Magic Flute* — and waving his hands around. Schiller had to tilt in the other direction to avoid getting clipped on the head. As the heavy bus shuddered back into the traffic, Schiller had a revelation. A theory of human

188

nature blossomed between the bus stop on Lexington and the bus stop on Park.

The primary human need, he decided — stronger than the need for food or sex or love — is the need for recognition, the need to make a mark in the world. One makes one's mark according to one's capacities. If you have talents, you exercise them: if you're Mozart you write *The Magic Flute*. And if you don't have any talents, you thrust yourself into the path of others in cruder ways: you wear stupid T-shirts or you become the impresario of the back of the bus. And if your life has been stunted from the first by violence and harsh surroundings, then you steal things or destroy things or hurt people: anything, anything, to leave an image of yourself in other people's minds.

Why was he coming up with crackpot theories? Because he was meeting Heather in a few hours, and he was so excited that his brain had started to overheat. All day long he'd been refreshed by a delicious current of anticipation, but now he was starting to feel feverish.

It was still hard to believe that someone so young found him interesting. But he was beginning to believe it.

And he was also beginning to believe in her abilities — beginning to think she really might be able to keep his name alive.

He got off at Broadway and waited at the bus shelter for a transfer. He took off his overcoat. The unexpected warmth of the day made him realize that spring was near.

He didn't really need the weather to remind him; the condition of his bones was enough to tell him what season it was. Spring was bursting into painful birth. Every joint in his body ached, from his toes to his knees to his knuckles. He felt at one, in his pain, with nature — with the pain of the natural world. The sparse young trees on Broadway were aching also, from the life tensing furiously inside them. Spring was approaching, and every living being must respond or die.

He wanted to respond. He wanted to open himself — open himself like some . . . He didn't know what simile to use. Everything that came to mind was a cliché. Maybe that's the problem: when you open yourself to life, you begin to think in clichés. It's better to be guarded.

But that *can't* be true. The thing is to let life assault you, make yourself as defenseless as you can. If it bruises you, don't protest. Love your fate.

He boarded a northbound bus and got off at 94th Street. He had to cross the street to get to his house. During the last year he'd lost the ability to get all the way across Broadway on one traffic light. When the sign said WALK he turtled his way painfully to the median; by the time he got there the DON'T WALK sign was blinking, and he waited for the light to begin another cycle before completing his trek across the street.

At home he started to remove his clothes. He thought he'd try to take a nap before seeing Heather. With his stiff arthritic hands, it hurt to undo each button. He hadn't seen her since their strange night.

For years all the people in his life had been people he'd known for a long time; it was strange, at this late date, to face the challenge of impressing someone new.

But why do you feel you have to impress her? He didn't know why, but he did. Often, when he was with her, he found that his desire to seem interesting took the form of an urge to make generalizations about himself. He didn't know why he thought generalizations would make him interesting — he *didn't* think so, on a rational level, but on some deep subconscious plane he was obviously convinced that the way to a woman's heart was to make statements that began with phrases like "I am a man who . . ." I am a man who works slowly. I am a man who rarely worries about success. I am a patient man. I am a man who has loved only a few people, but who has loved them deeply. He hadn't said any of these things, thank God, but he was always on the verge of saying them. Perhaps he wanted to prove how reliable he was, how consistent. But often the statements that came to his lips were merely ridiculous: two weeks ago he'd had to stop himself from telling her that he was a man who didn't like soup.

But he didn't *need* to do any of that; he didn't *need* to enthrall her with the revelation that he was a man who didn't like soup. She found him interesting *already*. She had given him an astonishing gift, the gift of her interest. If it weren't for the fact that he was seventy pounds overweight and staggered by two heart attacks and so hobbled by arthritis that he sometimes had trouble lifting himself up from the toilet seat, he could have danced. For Heather had accomplished the impossible: she had made him feel young.

For the first time in the seven years since he'd begun this latest book, he thought that maybe it *wouldn't* be his last.

He took his nap and woke with a new thought. He wanted to give her something.

He wanted to show his appreciation in some tangible way. His first idea was jewelry — earrings, maybe. She seemed to like to wear five or six of them at a time; she could always find room for a few more.

But he didn't really know her taste, and in any case he'd just given those pearls as a peace offering to Ariel; he didn't want to give jewelry to Heather on the same day. He rummaged around in a dresser drawer, not knowing what he was looking for. Until he found it.

He had one extra set of house keys there. The keys that used to be Stella's.

He picked them up, trying to feel, through the decades, the pressure of her touch. She had once used these casually, every day.

As soon as he thought about giving the keys to Heather, he knew it was what he wanted to do.

It wasn't as if he wanted her to replace Stella. The thought was absurd. No one could replace Stella. Stella was his person.

He would have to make it clear that he wasn't asking for anything. He wouldn't want her to think he was asking her to move in, or even to spend more time here. And he wouldn't want her to think he was asking to relive the other night: he was sure that that was a one-time-only miracle, like any miracle worthy of the name.

He simply wanted to show her that if she ever needed a place where she could come without explaining herself, without asking anyone's permission, she could come here. He wanted to show her that he trusted her.

It had been a long time since he'd trusted someone new.

Barefoot and bare-chested, dressed only in his boxer shorts, with his large breasts sagging and his enormous stomach bulging like a sack of fruit, he stood in front of the dresser drawer, holding the keys in his open hand. Stella used to say he had boyish hands. And now he was seventy-one years old. Could anyone ever think of him as boyish again? And yet he felt like a boy. Life!

19

Heather had a line of poetry stuck in her head. Usually when a phrase lodged in her head it was some idiotic thing from the radio, but today it was Yeats.

"Labour is blossoming or dancing where . . ."

She couldn't remember what came next; she couldn't remember *where* labor was supposed to be blossoming or dancing. She could have looked it up — she knew it was from "Among School Children" — but she didn't want to. She preferred to let it simmer in her mind without its context.

The reason the line had lodged in her head, she thought, was that she was still trying to puzzle out why Schiller's work had declined.

Was labor blossoming or dancing in Schiller's life? She didn't think so. Whenever she met Schiller after his workday, he looked gray and spent; he looked as if he'd just paid a visit to the casket of a friend.

She was meeting Schiller in the evening, but she had something else to do before that. The Knitting Factory was sponsoring a weeklong benefit series for a local musician who'd been paralyzed in a car accident and who didn't have health insurance. About forty acts were playing, and all the revenue was going toward his medical expenses.

There was a band playing tonight that she'd been wanting to see for a long time. Yo La Tengo, a three-piece rock band that mixed dreamy acoustic ballads with long feedback orgies, had been a favorite of hers since college. But that was only half the reason she was going. In an article in the *Voice* a year ago, Sandra Bennett had said that Yo La Tengo was one of the few bands she tried to see every time they played in New York. So Heather was hoping to bump into Sandra there — accidentally.

Heather got there just as the band was taking the stage. They opened with something very loud. She bought a beer and leaned against a wall and listened.

About fifteen minutes into the set, Sandra arrived. With her amazing cheekbones and her thick black hair pulled back, she looked imperious, Egyptian, eternal. Heather was delighted to see that she was alone.

Heather approached her, trying to look surprised. Sandra recognized her immediately — she even kissed her. This *was* surprising: Sandra looked so cool that you didn't expect her to be affectionate. She seemed too hip to be nice.

It was too loud to talk while Yo La Tengo was playing, and as soon as they left the stage another band came out and started tuning up. Heather had never heard of them, but she took Sandra's arm and said, "These people are no good. Why don't we go out and have a drink?"

Sandra seemed to be amused by Heather's aggressiveness; at any rate, she cheerfully agreed to leave.

Maybe it was because she was hungry. She suggested they go to a Chinese restaurant down the block.

"How's your work going?" Sandra said after they ordered. Which was the same thing Schiller had asked her the second time they'd met.

She was excited to be part of a world in which the most natural way to greet people was to ask them about their work.

"You're writing a biography, right?" Sandra said. "About your friend William Schiller."

"Leonard Schiller," Heather said. And then she had to make a decision. She could remind Sandra that she wasn't writing a book, only a thesis; or she could allow Sandra to persist in her misconception. It wouldn't be lying, really: she did hope to write a book about him someday.

But she didn't want to start this relationship off with a lie. So she admitted that it was only a thesis so far.

And she admitted that it wasn't going well. This wasn't easy either, because she would have liked Sandra to think that she was awesomely gifted. But there was something about Sandra that invited you to speak freely.

"I'm done with the part about his first two books," Heather said. "That was easy, because I love his first two books. But I don't know how to write about the last two. I've read both of them three times, but I just don't get them."

"You don't get them or you don't like them?"

"Maybe I don't like them."

"What don't you like about them?"

Their food arrived as they were talking; Heather ate, but paid no attention to what she was eating.

"I don't know," she said. "Maybe the first two books were about defining yourself, the last two were about defending yourself? Maybe the first two books were about freedom, the next two were about order? I'm not sure." She was finishing her second beer of the day. "I don't know what to do. I feel like, if I write honestly, I'll hurt him. So I'm trying to figure out how I can say nice things about the last two books without being completely dishonest."

Heather was surprised at herself: she was being much more open than she'd planned. Normally her self-revelations were strictly calculated; she didn't like to give too much away. But Sandra had an unusual air — a mixture of the motherly and the mysterious — that made you want to tell her things.

"You have to write honestly," Sandra said. She was leaning forward and speaking with a special intensity. "If you don't do it honestly it's not worth doing. You're not doing him any favors if you praise him in a dishonest way.

"Let's say you do end up writing a book about him. You'll just have to face the same problem all over again, so you might as well deal with it now.

"Think about it. If you write a book about him, and you say he's a great writer and all his books are masterpieces, the falseness will show through. No one will take you seriously. It won't help him, and it won't help you. If you think his first two books were good and his last two books were bad, then say so. You'll be speaking with conviction, and when you speak with conviction people

199

notice. They'll notice your book, and that may lead them to rediscover his first two books." Sandra examined Heather closely, as if trying to make sure she'd absorbed this.

"And two good books, by the way, is nothing to be ashamed of."

"I know that," Heather said, though in fact she didn't know it. From her point of view, two good books was a skimpy legacy. The more she'd thought about Schiller's career, the smaller his achievement seemed.

"I'm starting to feel like there's a question I have to deal with. If I'm right, and his last two books were bad, then *why? Why* was he written out by the time he was forty years old?"

"I don't know if it's such a mystery. It happens to a lot of people. Bob Dylan was brilliant until he was thirty-five. Rimbaud was finished by the age of nineteen."

"Those are poets. I thought novelists were supposed to grow into their gifts."

Sandra looked at a litchi nut at the end of her fork. "Maybe you should ask *him* why he went downhill."

"Have you read him?" Heather asked.

"No."

"Have you heard of him?"

"Yeah. But I was never very interested in that crowd. 'The New York Intellectuals.'

For me, the interesting writers from that period were the Beats. Or Paul Goodman, who had a foot in both worlds. Or James Baldwin. But the New York Intellectuals . . . I imagine them all as a bunch of white guys in suits, going to bed early."

It occurred to Heather that she'd never seen Schiller without a tie.

"But don't take what I'm saying too seriously," Sandra said. "I haven't read him. He might be the greatest writer of the century, for all I know."

With no preliminaries, Sandra was entering into Heather's questions as if they were important. Heather hadn't expected her to be this generous.

Sandra went to make a phone call, and it was only when Heather was alone that she was able to take the measure of her happiness. It felt wonderful to be taken so seriously by such an interesting person. When Sandra spoke to her, she clearly spoke from the point of view of someone who was older and more experienced, but there wasn't a trace of condescension in her manner.

When Sandra had urged her to be honest, she'd looked as if she were saying something it had taken her all her life to learn.

It was time to leave: time to meet Schiller.

She didn't want to see Schiller, not now; she was too revved up. But Sandra was leaving also: she was going back to the Knitting Factory to see Aimee Mann. On the subway uptown, clinging to a pole because she was too wired to sit down, Heather tried to figure out whether she could catch up with Sandra again later that night.

When Sandra talked there was an edgy intensity in her voice, as if she heard a clock ticking, or a bomb — as if this might be the last conversation she'd ever have.

There was no bomb ticking when you spoke with Schiller. For Schiller, the bomb had gone off years ago.

20

She met him at his apartment. She sat in the kitchen, a 105-pound jumping bean, while he opened a bottle of seltzer. He opened it with the same methodical care that had impressed her the day they'd met — but now she wanted to say, "Open the damn bottle already! So what if it sprays on you? What are you, the Wicked Witch of the West? You're gonna melt?"

She was shocked at how changeable she was.

She remembered what Sandra had suggested. Ask him about his books. Find out why the last two books were so different from the first two.

But she didn't want him to talk about that — not now. She didn't want him to talk about his years of decline. She wanted him to talk about the days when he was as young as she was now, the days when his labor was blossoming and dancing.

"Did you write anything before *Tenderness*?"

"Oh yes. I wrote three unpublished novels — two of them when I was still in my twenties. I had a tremendous amount of energy when I was young. But they were all pretty bad." He was moving around his kitchen; he wouldn't sit. Was he nervous? She couldn't tell, because she couldn't concentrate: most of her mind was still downtown, waiting on line at the Knitting Factory. "It's very hard to write a good novel when you're young. You're changing too fast. The central subject of a novel has to be something you care about deeply. And when you're young, it can be hard to care deeply about one thing for a long time. I started my first novel at twenty-four; by the time I finished it, three years later, I was a different person."

They went to get a bite at his usual coffee shop, the Argo. It was frustrating to walk with him — he was so slow. He was the only person on the island of Manhattan who wouldn't cross against the light.

At the Argo Heather ordered a glass of wine. She knew the wine would be terrible at a place like this, but she wanted to keep drinking. She would have preferred a beer, but somehow she couldn't see herself drinking beer around Schiller: it seemed too coarse. Schiller ordered a Sanka, an egg-white omelet, and whole-wheat toast without butter.

He was looking at her with an expression

of timid yearning. "There's something I'd like to give you," he said. He reached into his pocket and withdrew a pair of keys. "These are keys to my apartment. I thought since you spend so much time in the city, if there are some nights when you don't want to go all the way back to Hoboken, you can come over and stay in the guest room. Or if you need somewhere to read in the afternoons. I just want you to know that you can always have a place to stay."

"Please," she said. Her mind was blank. She felt herself shrinking away from him. It wasn't voluntary: it was a purely instinctual reaction. Schiller kept his arm extended, holding out the keys, and Heather couldn't think. She had a picture of herself being locked *inside* his apartment.

There was silence. She knew they shouldn't let it go on too long. If the silence went on too long, the refusal of the keys would seem momentous.

It seemed momentous already. The Refusal of the Keys: it seemed like something from mythology, from medieval legend. The lady refused the keys, and the old king cried out and rent his garment, and for seven generations the vines of the land would bear no fruit.

He was offering himself up to her, putting

all his trust in her. If this had happened three weeks ago, she would have been thrilled. But now that she'd been meditating on the problem of his decline, everything seemed different.

But then she had a memory — a memory of high school basketball, of all things. As small as she was, she'd been one of the best players on the girls' team. The reason was simply that most of the other girls used to fall apart in the clutch: near the end of a close game, they didn't want to be anywhere near the ball. They were afraid to take the shot. Heather was the only one who wanted the ball when the game was on the line, the only one who wanted to meet the moment.

Meet the moment then. She had set all this in motion, she wanted to see where it led. If he was going to offer her the keys, then she was going to take them.

"Thank you," she said, putting out her hand and cradling them. "This is an honor."

The look in his eyes made her happy about what she had done. For a moment she thought he was about to weep.

He must have been embarrassed by his own emotion; he put his head down and applied himself assiduously to his omelet. He used his knife and fork very carefully. It struck her that he was like Laurel and Hardy combined in one man: Laurel's sweet and tender fussiness and Hardy's girth.

He was dressed ridiculously in a suit and tie that seemed to have come from the 1950s: probably they'd gone in and out of style several times, with Schiller remaining oblivious of each cycle.

She was amazed that her mind was racing on at this level of trivial cattiness, when the man was before her like this: grave, respectful, and infatuated, all too willing to worship her.

He glanced up at her shyly while taking a sip of his Sanka. She could feel his desire for her. It was immense, breaking over her like a wave. In high school she used to watch reruns of *The Avengers*, and she loved the way Mr. Steed would look at Mrs. Peel: a gaze that was appreciative but not acquisitive, a gaze filled with desire but without vulgarity. Because Mrs. Peel's husband was not officially dead but missing somewhere in Africa, she and Mr. Steed, though they were mad about each other, never touched; they made love only with their eyes. And thinking about this now, she realized that Schiller would never ask for a repetition of their night together: he was content to be her Mr. Steed.

She felt crude in comparison — a creature of bare crude wanting, a creature who lunged after the things she desired and tossed them aside after she no longer desired them.

He began to tell her about a documentary about Mike Nichols and Elaine May that he'd seen on PBS the other day. There was something odd about his voice — it was too rich, too resonant. She realized that she'd heard this tone of voice from him before. It was his name-dropping voice. He was going to tell her that he used to know them.

She always found it sad when he tried to impress her this way, but she didn't have the heart to cut him off.

"It really brought me back," he said. "There was a period of about a year when I saw a great deal of them. When Mike was just beginning to do some directing, he even suggested I try my hand at writing a play for him. I was very flattered."

"Did you write one?"

"Of course not."

"Why of course not?"

"I was in the middle of a novel, for one thing. And in any case, Mike was thinking in terms of a collaboration. It wasn't for me. Oscar Wilde once said that the problem with socialism was that it would involve too many meetings. That's how I felt about writing a play."

"But didn't you think it might be exciting to learn a new craft?"

"The craft of writing novels was the only one I've ever wanted to master. I didn't have any time to waste."

Purity of heart, she had once read, is to desire one thing; if this was the case then Schiller was the purest person she had ever known. But it was disappointing all the same. Weeks ago, when he'd talked about having declined an offer to write an advertisement, she'd admired his integrity. But now she was beginning to think he'd refused too many things.

The characters in his early novels weren't this pure; they didn't guard their lives this closely. Part of their charm was that they didn't resist temptation. Schiller had always resisted temptation; his every waking hour was mapped by strict routines. It was sad to think that it may have been precisely his single-minded devotion to his art that had drained his art of its freshness.

After they left the coffee shop he walked her to the subway. She was still brooding on what she was going to write about the second half of his career; it was like a scab she couldn't stop picking.

"In your novels, have you ever written

about someone you care for in a way that you knew would hurt them?"

"Of course. I generally don't like to admit that I ever work from real-life models, but I can admit it to you. Sometimes I do. And sometimes I've drawn unflattering portraits of people who mean a great deal to me."

"How did you feel about it?"

"I regretted it. But it can't be avoided. A writer has to use everything he has. If you want to write, you have to be willing to be a son of a bitch sometimes."

He was still thinking about this when they reached the subway entrance. "The same thing is true for critics, you know. You should give that some thought, if you're really considering becoming a literary critic. You have to be prepared to say things that will hurt people's feelings."

He was giving her permission to write about him harshly. She wondered if he realized this. She didn't think so.

21

"Sorry I'm late," Ariel said, kissing Sam in an ambiguous location: half on the mouth, half off. They were in an Italian restaurant on Columbus. "It takes about a year to get here from my neighborhood."

"Actually, there's a reason for that," he said, and her heart sank. The word "actually" was the infallible signal that he was about to embark on one of his lectures.

Sam was a new man. Newish. They were on their second date.

There was only one thing wrong with Sam. He was a pontificator. He was the Village Explainer. But Ariel was trying to persuade herself, once again, that it was time to cut her losses, time to settle down with a man who, though uninspiring, was at least better than dreadful.

"Originally," he said, "the subways were run by private companies, with very little coordination between them. That's why they have those apparently meaningless names: the BMT, the IRT, and so on. The city government took over the system — actually, bought the system — when the owners realized that running the subways was a money-losing venture. It was really just a bailout of private industry: the taxpayers ended up subsidizing the capitalists' mistakes." He spoke about the subway system for the next ten minutes, providing a political and economic analysis of its origins, and finally broadening his lecture to embrace the theme of the structural limitations of the New Deal–era reforms.

He was a very knowledgeable man, and some of what he talked about was interesting. The problem was that he couldn't shut up. Often, she was beginning to notice, he would ask a question not because he wanted to hear your answer, but because he wanted to speak about the subject himself. On the night they met, he'd asked whether her family roots were German or Eastern European; the only reason he asked was because he wanted to deliver two lectures: one on the poet Schiller, another on his own complex family tree. Sometimes she felt like suggesting that he cut out the middleman: he should just ask himself a question and say, "That's an interesting question," and then proceed with his response.

She ordered some wine and braced herself for another learning experience. They were sitting near the glass wall of the restaurant and she could see people strolling past on Columbus.

He was now talking about Fiorello La Guardia. "One of his opponents accused him of being an anti-Semite, and La Guardia challenged him to debate the matter — in Yiddish." This made Ariel smile, and if he had stopped there she would have been charmed. But then he launched into a discussion of how La Guardia transformed coalition politics, complete with a demographic breakdown of changes in New York City voting patterns from the immigration wave of the 1840s through the influx of displaced rural African Americans in the 1920s and '30s.

He wasn't a bad guy. She just wasn't that interested in what he had to say.

She closed her eyes for a moment. When she opened them she looked out the window. Casey Davis was standing on the street — skinnier than he used to be, and with a lot less hair, but otherwise unchanged. He was standing with his hands in his pockets, looking at her with a bittersweet smile.

The waiter appeared at their table. "Are you ready to order, or do you need another minute?"

"I don't need any more time at all," she said. She was standing. "So long, Sam. It's been nice meeting you. You certainly have a lot of knowledge. Good luck." And then she left the restaurant and took Casey's arm.

22

"I thought you were in California," Casey said.

He was amazed by the coincidence. He'd been thinking of her just the other day — or maybe it was a week ago, or two weeks . . . at any rate, he'd been thinking of her recently, when he was browsing through his mental file of old girlfriends. He'd been thinking that, though all of them had been interesting women in one way or another, Ariel was the only one who'd actually been *fun*. Most of the rest of them had been clench-fisted leftist scholars. He'd been indicting himself for walking away from the only woman who could always make him laugh.

But here she was, in the flesh. Ariel Schiller.

"This is like a dream," she said.

Casey felt the same way. She had floated out of the restaurant as if the man sitting across from her didn't exist.

They were walking, and she was lightly touching his elbow, exactly as she used to do in the old days. That light perpetual contact always used to amuse him: he used to feel as if she were guarding him in basketball. He remembered how in the old days, because of this habit — they were a couple during the basketball heyday of Magic Johnson — he used to call her Magic.

He remembered that it was a good nickname for other reasons — for example, the way she used to show up, unexpected, on street corners. She had a way of appearing before your eyes a few minutes after you'd been thinking about her.

"Hello, Magic," he said.

They always used to share nicknames. "Hello, Magic," she said.

23

Whatever you do, don't sing. Walking down Columbus, touching Casey's arm, Ariel was telling herself not to engage in any operatic demonstrations of joy. But she *wanted* to sing.

She walked around him in a semicircle so he would be to her left. She did this almost unconsciously, out of ancient habit. Casey tended to speak softly, and she didn't hear well out of her right ear; in the old days, when she was outdoors with him, she would always keep him to her left.

"I was wondering about something," she said.

"Yes?"

"Should we have dinner first, or should we go bowling?"

He laughed. "What makes you think I have the time? What makes you think I'm not on my way to an important meeting?"

"Even if you are, I know you wouldn't want to pass up the chance to spend a few hours with a bowling genius."

He stopped walking and took a long look at her. "Christ," he said. "How long has it been? What have you been up to? What's new?"

"What's new?" she said. She couldn't think of what was new. The last five years of her life — since she had last seen him — all seemed to have vanished. Finally a sentence came rising up to her lips. "I joined a glee club," she said.

"When?"

"Just now."

Casey looked puzzled. "What do you mean?"

She didn't know what she meant. She thought about it for a moment, and then she knew.

"I just mean I'm happy to see you."

24

Heather had moved into a zone of brilliance. She was working harder than she'd ever worked in her life. And yet it didn't feel like work. She was completing her thesis in a state of creative frenzy; she slept only four or five hours a night and woke up every morning burning to get back to her desk.

She had decided to say frankly what she thought about Schiller's work, and after she'd made that simple decision, everything had begun to flow.

She wrote that Schiller had written two beautiful books. They were completely personal, yet completely in the American grain: they were books about people breaking away from their fates, making their own lives. They were books about freedom. She referred to Thoreau and Emerson and Whitman — not to say that Schiller belonged in their company, but that he breathed the same moral air.

His last two books, she said, were much weaker. He seemed to have lost his compass somewhere along the line. She cited something F. Scott Fitzgerald had said: Most good writers "line themselves up along a solid gold bar," like Hemingway's courage, or Joseph Conrad's art, or D. H. Lawrence's "intense cohabitations." Schiller, she said, had strayed from his solid gold bar: the theme of personal liberation.

His third novel, *Stories from the Lives of My Friends*, was a well-meaning attempt to make sense of the social problems of America in the sixties, but he had tried to extend his imagination into territory where it couldn't thrive. The central figure in the book was an earnest older man trying to make sense of the young, and in creating this neutral, camera-eye narrator, Schiller had deprived himself of his greatest resource: his skill at creating central characters who are willing to pay any price and break any bond in order to claim their freedom. His last book, *The Lost City*, was another honorable failure. A novel about Jewish immigrants on the Lower East Side in the 1920s, it was a careful act of historical reconstruction, but it was too careful, too reverent. It seemed imitative of *Call It Sleep*, but without the startling atmosphere of spiritual violence that made *Call It Sleep* unforgettable.

She wrote the second half of her thesis — the half that covered the works of his decline — with sadness. She kept this part short, because there was no point in dwelling on what he had failed to accomplish.

She started to write a more theoretical last chapter: an attempt to explore the mystery of creativity. She asked why someone who started so strong should have wandered so far off course.

She wrote it in the form of an imaginary dialogue between two writers: Henry James, whom Schiller loved, and D. H. Lawrence, whom she loved. James had cared for almost nothing except art. He never had a profession other than writing; he never married — he apparently never even had a lover; he allowed nothing to distract him from his novels and stories and plays. Lawrence, by contrast, had a fiery relationship with his strong-willed wife; he loved to paint almost as much as he loved to write; he wrote long tracts to announce the truth about sex, religion, psychoanalysis, and everything else; and he was filled with schemes for transforming the world — he was always dreaming of establishing communes where men and women could live in a more authentic way.

Her point was that although James may have been the greater craftsman, Lawrence was the greater artist, precisely because his passion for art competed with other passions.

The richness of his life enriched his art.

She worked on this chapter for a few days, and then she gave it up. She felt it would be presumptuous to write as if she knew exactly why Schiller's work had gone wrong. She wasn't his biographer; she was a student of his work, not of his life. And in any case, she wanted her thesis to end on a high note, celebrating the enduring value of his first two books.

She finished the thesis on a Saturday afternoon in early April. At almost 200 pages, it looked lean but substantial. She knew it was only a draft; she knew she had more work to do on it. But it was an accomplishment.

She had managed to finish it just a few days before her twenty-fifth birthday, which was the goal she'd set when she'd begun.

When she'd begun her project, she was so in love with Schiller's first two books that she felt confident that she'd eventually find a way to love his last two. But it hadn't happened, and the manuscript she'd produced would hurt him, which was the last thing she ever would have wanted to do. She believed in the worth of what she had written, but she was aching with a sense of her own disloyalty.

And now the hardest part was coming.

Weeks ago, she had told Schiller she'd show him the manuscript when it was done. He hadn't even asked to see it — she'd volunteered. And now she felt she had to show it to him.

She was afraid it would kill him.

Well, it wasn't all her fault. It was Schiller's fault too. Because he had changed. If he had kept the flame of his life alive, then she wouldn't have had to write about him like this.

She took out the photograph of Schiller that she'd stolen on the day they'd met. She studied it closely. The young Schiller: laughing, bright with youth, bright with arrogance.

"I love you," she said to the photograph. "Where are you?"

25

Schiller was packing his bag. He was heading off to Paris in a week, to keep a fool's appointment.

No: he was keeping an appointment that had been made by a man in love.

It made no sense for him to pack his bag this far in advance, since it meant packing away some of the things he'd normally wear during the week. But he was lit up with nervous energy and he needed to do something to work it off.

He was meeting Heather for dinner tonight, and she was giving him a copy of her thesis.

He wasn't looking forward to reading it. They had talked this afternoon, and when she told him she'd finished a draft of it, he knew it wasn't going to make him happy. He didn't know how he knew it, but he knew.

When you've been a writer for a long time, you develop an uncanny sensitivity to barely perceptible verbal signals of rejection. There was something a little off in Heather's voice, though he would have been hard-pressed to define it.

The memory of Edmund Wilson came into his mind, but he pushed it away. He didn't want to think about Edmund Wilson now.

Well, whatever it was, he wanted to be ready for the blow. He wanted to be perfectly warm to her, but perfectly armored.

He took a shower and shaved meticulously in front of the misty mirror. Normally he shaved with an ascetic briskness, as if it would be vain to do the job too carefully. Tonight he shaved so attentively that he felt as if he were seeing his own face clearly for the first time in years.

Not that that was such a good thing.

Tomorrow was her birthday: she was going to be twenty-five. He was taking her out for an early dinner and then to a Rembrandt exhibition at the Met.

The doorman, Jeff, buzzed up and told him that "Miss Wolfe" was waiting for him downstairs. He met her in the lobby; her face was tight. She was holding a cardboard box under her arm.

"Is this it?" he said.

She nodded stiffly. "I hope . . ."

"Don't say a word," he said. He said it to relieve her of the necessity of an apology. He handed the box to Jeff and asked him to keep it in the package room. "Take good care of this."

"You know I will, Professor," Jeff said. Jeff had worked in the building for ten years, and he had always done his job with an impeccable style: his uniform was always perfectly clean and pressed; when you were carrying heavy packages he always met you on the street and relieved you of your burden. No matter what was going on in his life — Schiller knew him well enough to know that his life wasn't easy: he had a large family to support — Jeff was always sunny and efficient. He was a professional, a craftsman, and for this reason Schiller had always felt a kinship with him. At this moment he felt that his bond with Jeff was more substantial than his bond with Heather. When he came home tonight Jeff would still be here, and they would say good night — one old pro to another.

As he walked toward the restaurant with Heather, he felt a lumpy unhappiness. He knew that their strange shared time had come to an end. This little period in which he'd had a young admirer, a young adorer, was over.

Well, there was no need to be bitter. There was nothing to be done but accept it gracefully. He would order a bottle of wine at dinner, wish her well, and bow gracefully out of her life.

He asked her how she was, and when she answered, he didn't listen. He was thinking about how astonishingly young she was. He was thinking that she would probably still be alive in the year 2050. Which meant that he would still be alive then, in her memory.

But what would she remember? He couldn't remember his own twenty-fifth birthday. He'd been living on Bleecker Street, working on his first novel, which was never published and which he later lost. He'd been seeing a woman named Molly, a cheerful mystic who liked to stay up late gossiping with her long-dead grandmother through the medium of a Ouija board. He assumed that he'd probably spent his birthday with Molly, but he couldn't remember it. Maybe he'd seen his parents that day?

He could only guess. He'd never kept a diary, so he couldn't check. His parents were dead, Molly was unfindable; so Schiller was alone. And since he couldn't remember that day, the day was gone, as if everyone who'd been alive in it, including himself, was dead.

And now, as he walked with Heather, leaning on his cane, knowing that she was walking as slowly as she could for him but wishing she would walk a little slower, he felt as if he weren't really there. He imagined her in the middle of the next century, thinking back on her own life. Would she remember this day? And if she didn't, then what was this moment now? This moment, with its whitened sky, with the wind bone-grippingly groping through their clothing, was already gone.

"Please remember this day," he said, and she looked at him quizzically.

"For how long?" she said.

"How about forever?"

"I think I can do that," she said. "That should be no problem."

That was a moment of peace, but by the time they reached the restaurant she seemed jittery again. She kept unclasping her little bag and searching around in there, for God knows what.

"I should remind you that it's only a draft," she said. "If there's anything that doesn't make sense, or anything that's just plain wrong, please tell me. I still want to do a lot more work on it."

"Don't worry so much," Schiller said.

The waiter came up, a bony boy in his twenties with a blond goatee. Reaching for his napkin, Schiller clumsily swept his fork to the floor. "No problemo," the young man said, and grabbed one from another table, holding it not by the stem but by the tines. Schiller was repulsed by this — not merely by the slovenliness but by the lack of professionalism. No matter what you do, try to do it well: this simple idea, for Schiller, summed up half of life's ethical obligations.

"What can I do you for?" the waiter said, with a kind of frat-house jocularity. "Get you something to drink?"

Schiller had intended to order a bottle of wine, but Heather asked the waiter what he had on tap, and he recited a long list of beers, and as he spoke he smiled at her, and she was smiling back, and there seemed to be a note of complicity between them, as if "Rolling Rock" and "Amstel Light" were coded phrases that gratified them both.

"Someone you know?" Schiller said after the waiter left, and she smiled guiltily. Of course he wasn't someone she knew, and the only complicity between them was the complicity between two people who are young and sexually alive. Schiller understood that Heather was withdrawing from him, had already withdrawn, and that she herself was so flustered by this that she felt driven to behave badly and make the situation even worse.

At least that was what he thought was going on.

He told himself to ignore it, to keep his moral armor on, to comport himself impeccably throughout the evening. Then, when he got home, he could collapse.

The waiter returned with Heather's beer and Schiller's wine. Schiller had never seen her drink beer; as she took her first gulp and then used her fingers to wipe a spot of foam off her lip, it struck him that she had a touch of vulgarity he'd never noticed before.

"Do you think you're going to write more critical studies?" he said.

"I'm not sure. I've been thinking about it. I've thought that I might like to write a critical biography of Tillie Olsen."

He had discreetly refrained from asking whether she still planned to write a book about him; nevertheless he was wounded by her response.

Tillie Olsen. A writer who made Schiller seem prolific by comparison. But no one held it against her, since she'd shrewdly turned her lifelong writing block into a badge of feminist honor.

"If you're going to make a career of literary criticism," he said, "I should lend you some books by the great critics of my era. I doubt if they're taught in the academy these days. Which is all to their credit: they weren't theorists, they were *readers*." He began to tell her about the literary critics he admired most: Wilson and Kazin and Howe and Trilling and Rahv. He thought he might be talking too much, but he also thought this was good for her: if she wanted to write about literature, she should know something about the best critics of our time, and much of what there was to know about them couldn't be found in books. He had met these men; he had interesting stories about them all.

But he knew he was talking too much. The older you get, the harder it is to be concise. It's no longer adequate merely to say what you know; it's urgent to explain *how* you came to know it.

She smiled politely as he spoke; at one point he thought she was suppressing a yawn; the waiter showed up all too often to refill her water glass; and Schiller could tell that he was boring her. Yet he kept talking. As if he thought that if he just kept talking, he might finally say something that would recapture her interest.

After dinner they took a cab to the museum. Turning into the Central Park Transverse the cab swerved wildly and they were thrown against each other in the backseat, and, because he thought he might never see her again, he took a deep but surreptitious breath in order to drink in her scent. But he smelled nothing. He didn't know whether to blame today's womanhood, because they don't believe in perfume, or to blame himself, because his sense of smell was gone; but in any case, if you can't even smell someone you probably shouldn't feel hurt about the fact that she doesn't love you. Even if the young women of today don't wear perfume, the young men of today can undoubtedly smell them. The young waiter, that bony goat, could probably smell Heather's scent when he'd leaned over to serve her her shark steak.

Schiller paid for Heather and himself at the museum. The suggested six-dollar admission charge is optional; you can pay what you wish. When he went there alone he usually gave a dollar, but tonight, because he wanted to be an urbane companion, he paid the full twelve. They proceeded up the central staircase. This is when Schiller became William James.

26

In his biography of Sigmund Freud, Ernest Jones recounts the story of Freud's only meeting with William James. It took place in 1908, when Freud was in America to give a lecture at Clark College. Freud was in his early fifties, and James — the father of American psychology, and the older brother of Henry James — was in his seventies. The two of them were walking up a hill when James felt a recurrence of the angina that had troubled him for several years. He handed Freud a bag he was carrying and told him to walk ahead, saying that he needed a moment to rest and that he'd join him shortly. James knew that he was a dying man, and Freud knew that he knew. James caught up with Freud a few minutes later, and they resumed their conversation, exploring their intellectual differences with energy and good humor. James didn't say a word about his illness. "I have always wished," Freud later wrote, "that I might be as fearless as he was in the face of approaching death."

As Schiller and Heather were walking up the long main staircase at the museum, he felt something go wrong in his chest. After two heart attacks, he knew what heart attacks felt like, and this was something milder. He felt reasonably certain that this was only angina: it was painful but it wouldn't kill him.

He touched Heather's arm. "I need to hold on for a moment," he said, and leaned against the wall.

John Berryman once wrote mordantly that in today's America it's possible to live your entire life without ever finding out whether or not you're a coward. Schiller had always thought this a childish idea. Every day, there are occasions when one can discover — when one is forced to discover — whether one is a hero or a coward.

Now, though the pain in his chest was alarming — maybe it *was* a heart attack — he felt triumphant. His time had come; his test had come; and he was meeting it as bravely as William James.

"Can I help you?" Heather said. "How can I help you?"

"Please." He put his hand over hers and clasped it tightly to reassure her. "I just need to rest for a minute. I'm fine. Go on ahead. Meet me at the Rembrandt exhibit. In ten minutes. I'll be fine."

As Schiller said this, he felt proud of himself, and thankful for his lifelong engagement with literature. He had read the anecdote about Freud and James many years ago, but it had always remained vivid in his mind. Now he *was* William James. He felt horrible, but he felt magnificent. Heather walked up the long staircase, and he hoped that she wouldn't look back; magnificently, she did not. She was also a hero.

The only question now was whether he should sit down on the steps or not. If he sat, the pain might be easier to endure. But to sit down on this polished staircase struck him as unseemly. Already people were looking at him strangely as they passed. He didn't want to make a scene. The thought crossed his mind that if greatness had eluded him as a writer, perhaps this was why: because he'd never wanted to make a scene. Subtlety and indirection are important tools, but you can't scale the highest peaks with these tools alone.

It would be very helpful to sit. Perhaps he could walk back down to the lobby and find a chair. But the journey down the staircase seemed too difficult. Looking all the way down, he wondered how he'd made it up so far.

27

She paced among the Rembrandts not knowing what to do. Maybe he was already lying dead on the steps.

She wildly threw her glance over the paintings, as if they could tell her something, but they were dark and unwelcoming.

Schiller had told her not to stay with him, but he didn't know what he needed. He might be dying. She should go back and get help for him. He was already dead, and it was because of her.

Apparently he wasn't dead. Here he was. Schiller was making his way toward her, leaning on his cane, smiling with stoical embarrassment; his head bobbing slightly with each painful step, he looked like some unprecedented turtle.

"Are you all right?" she said.

He assured her that he was fine.

"Do you want to sit down?" Against the wall was a bench where two kneesocked schoolgirls sat sketching.

"Thank you. I'm fine. I'd rather walk. I'd rather look."

They went through the exhibit slowly.

Schiller paused for a long time before the self-portraits, but Heather couldn't see a thing. She kept expecting him to collapse, and it was all because of her: because she'd been too guilty and unhappy and tense to pay attention to him in the restaurant, and above all because he knew somehow that she had written critically about his work.

When he was finished looking at the pictures, he asked if she wanted to get a cup of coffee with him. "I'm not ready to go home, but I wouldn't mind sitting down for a while," he said.

He took her to a coffee shop he knew on Madison Avenue. "This place always makes me mournful," he said after they sat down. "I used to have lunch with Irving Howe here sometimes."

Under the table, Heather's knees were jumping around madly. As she had all evening, she was finding it hard to concentrate. It was painful to be with him, knowing that her thesis was waiting for him back at his house.

"He was really the last of the New York Intellectuals," Schiller said. "He was the grumpiest, orneriest, busiest man I've ever known. But also one of the most impressive. You'd sit down to have lunch with him, and within five minutes he'd be looking at his watch. But if you knew him at all, you weren't offended. It was just that he had this compulsion to get back to work. And the work he did was important, so you didn't begrudge him. He was a serious man."

Schiller was in an expansive mode. "He was two years older than I was, and he was the wunderkind of that group — you know, the New York Intellectuals. That's one of the reasons I went to Paris. I felt I could never out-wunderkind him, and it seemed to me in any case that the New York literary scene was dying. What I didn't realize, of course, was that the expatriate literary scene in Paris had been dead for years. By the time I got there, Paris wasn't Paris anymore. The writers who'd made it such a thrilling place were long gone. That was my fate. I think that's why I called my first novel — my first unpublished novel — *Starting Out in the Evening*. At the time, I didn't even know what I meant by the phrase. But I think I understand it now. I think I was giving expression to this feeling of being historically late."

New York was dead by the time he was in his twenties, so he went to Paris; but Paris was dead too. She didn't believe a word of it. She had come here fifty years later and she didn't think New York was dead. She thought New York *was* Paris.

Starting out in the evening! It's only evening if you think it is. She was starting out fifty years later than he had, but the world was in its blinding morning dazzlingness to her.

Schiller was not only wrong, she thought: he was unfair to his own past. In his first two books he'd brought Paris and New York to life for her — he never could have written about those cities so vividly if he'd believed they were dying. The truth, she thought, was that the disappointments of old age lay so heavily on his mind that he couldn't even remember what he'd believed when he was young. The young man who had written those early books knew more about life than the man who was sitting before her.

Starting Out in the Evening. Whatever he'd meant by that title at the time, it was probably far different from the meaning he was giving to it now.

"I'm going to have another Sanka," he said. "Would you like another coffee? You still have some time tonight, don't you?"

She didn't want another coffee: she wanted to leave. But she made herself stay put. To leave too quickly would be brutal. He was still recovering from whatever had hit him in the museum, and he was about to return home to read a manuscript that would break his heart.

"Sure," she said. "I have time."

Later, after he paid their bill, she walked him to the bus stop. He was no longer the young man he'd been, but the young man was somewhere inside him. She had the sense that he was surprised by the fierceness with which she hugged him good night.

28

When Schiller got home, Jeff went into the package room and retrieved the cardboard box with Heather's manuscript. Schiller took it upstairs, put it on the coffee table, sat down on the couch and closed his eyes. When he felt strong enough, he opened the box, and he read the manuscript over the course of the next two hours.

It was fairly well written, it was intelligent, and it made large claims for his first two novels. The last two, she said, were not very good. She tried to say this tactfully — too tactfully, because in this part of her thesis the language was often unclear. It was as if she wouldn't allow herself to be as blunt as she wanted to be, so the second half of the manuscript seemed bloodless and indirect.

Parts of her manuscript were cracklingly intelligent — she made connections between his works that he himself had never made. And yet it finally wasn't very good. She simply didn't know enough. She was too young. Even when she praised him, her praise was excessive. She compared him to Whitman and Thoreau; she compared *Tenderness* to

Women in Love and *The Red and the Black*.
This of course was flattering, but it didn't
make much sense. If she'd compared his
work to the work of his contemporaries; if
she'd argued that he deserved a place beside
Bellow and Malamud — claims like this,
though more modest than the claims she'd
made, would have been more coherent, more
persuasive, and, to him at least, more satisfying. But she'd probably never read Bellow
and Malamud; she compared him to the
writers she knew.

So this was what these past two months
had come to. A bright but rather half-baked
master's thesis, which ended on a dismissive
note.

He knew that she'd never write a book
about him. He knew that his four novels
would never be disinterred.

It was ridiculous to have hoped that
Heather might transform his fate. What was
his fate? To keep writing. That was all that
mattered.

He closed his eyes, and when he opened
them he realized that there had been a
brownout in the building: the lights in his
apartment were dimmed; the walls looked
grayer; the room seemed to press in on him.
He waited for the lights to go back up to full
power, but they didn't. And then he realized

that there hadn't been a brownout at all. It was his disappointment that had made the room seem dim and small.

He wasn't going to be translated to another literary realm. There would be no brilliancy.

He laughed at himself. From Edmund Wilson to Heather Wolfe.

In 1968, at a party on Central Park West, he was introduced to Edmund Wilson, whom he considered the most formidable literary critic of the age. To his surprise, Wilson had heard of him; to his astonishment, Wilson told him that he'd enjoyed his second novel, and asked him to send him the first. He sent *Tenderness* to Wilson's house in Talcottville, and a few weeks later Wilson sent him a note telling him that it was a "gem."

About a month later someone passed on the word that Wilson was thinking of writing an article about Schiller's work for *The New York Review of Books*.

This was unbelievable news. Schiller had received some glowing reviews, but a review by someone like Wilson could put him on the literary map for good. For days he couldn't concentrate on his work: he kept writing and rewriting Wilson's review in his mind. Phrases like "the most interesting novelist alive" occurred with an unlikely frequency.

A month passed, and then another month, and then another. The review didn't appear. Other pieces by Wilson did appear: an attack on the Modern Languages Association, a brief review of a new biography of Hemingway. Schiller's second novel had been out for more than two years at that point, so it made sense that these more topical pieces had pushed aside the article about his books. He imagined that Wilson's piece about his work had already been submitted and was sitting on some shelf in the magazine's office. He kept haunting the newsstands, waiting for each new issue, which reached the streets a few days before it arrived in the mailboxes of subscribers.

A year passed; no review. By this time, Schiller understood that it would never appear, that it had never been written. Wilson had moved on to other things. But even so, with each new issue of the magazine he had a moment of hope, and then a brief silent tantrum — invisible, but as intense as the tantrum he threw when he was eight years old and his father reneged on a promise to take him to the Polo Grounds to see Carl Hubbell pitch against Dizzy Dean.

One day in the spring of 1972, Schiller

woke, showered, picked up *The New York Times* from his doormat, and sat down to breakfast. He liked to glance at the paper before getting to work. Wilson's obituary was on the front page.

Schiller read it slowly and carefully — it was a long article, treating Wilson's career in detail.

Years before this, he thought he had stopped hoping for anything from Wilson, but somehow all his fantasies — about fame, immortality, riches, and the love of beautiful women — seemed to have clustered around the never quite extinguished dream that the review might yet appear. And now, with Wilson gone, he lost the last lingering trace of hope that his books would ever kick off their tombstones, that the messages he had placed in those two bottles would reach anyone in any future time.

He was at a low point in his life and work. Stella had died two years earlier; his daughter was unhappy; he was groping blindly through the tenth draft of his third novel; his first two books had recently gone out of print.

Sitting in the kitchen that morning in 1972, it occurred to him that he could simply walk away.

The folklore of the writing life includes

many stories of people who walked away from their occupations in order to become writers. Sherwood Anderson, who worked as an advertising copywriter until well into his forties, supposedly put on his coat one afternoon, left the office, and never came back: he had decided to devote himself to art. Henry Miller did much the same: in middle age he sailed to Paris, cut his ties with America, and invented a new life.

Schiller knew of no stories celebrating the reverse journey. But this is what he was considering. In the lowness of that moment, sitting at his table with the *Times* in front of him, he made a mental balance sheet of his professional life and concluded that the frustrations had outnumbered the accomplishments by far. He had been writing devotedly for twenty years, and he had given the world two slim novels. He hadn't received much in return. Not that the world was under any obligation to appreciate the gifts he'd tried to give — but the question remained: if what you offer the world isn't needed, then why continue to bring it your offerings?

He decided to walk away. He closed the door of his study and kept it closed. He decided to see what life would be like without writing.

He found that it was wonderful. For the

first time in decades he felt free. Life seemed oddly . . . *easy*. There was no reason for him to spend most of his waking hours struggling to repair the broken-backed sentences of his early drafts — struggling not only to repair them, but to give them limberness and grace. All he needed to do was his wage-work — he was teaching literature at Hunter — and the rest of his time was his own. He could read as much as he wanted, go to movies, concerts, lectures, take long morning walks. He could enjoy himself.

Life went along this way for a week, two weeks. Then, one afternoon, an odd thing happened when he was sitting in the Hunter cafeteria with some other faculty members. One of them, a psychology teacher, was telling a long story . . . and Schiller couldn't understand what he was talking about. The words were familiar, but they didn't add up. At first he thought the man was conducting an experiment to see if people really listen — talking nonsense to see if anyone would notice. But the other people at the table were nodding and responding, and they couldn't all have been in on the joke.

The next day he was at the grocery store when a tiny man in a huge blue hat came up to him and said, "Magazine?"

"Beg pardon?" Schiller said.

"Magazine?" he repeated.

"What magazine?"

The man waggled his eyebrows disapprovingly and stalked away.

A few days after that he had a long conversation with a woman he was seeing, in which she told him how much she valued their friendship. She clasped his hand warmly, led him to the door, and kissed him good night.

He walked a few blocks toward home, and then he called her from a pay phone.

"Did you just break up with me?" he said.

Once, long before, he and Stella had smoked hashish. The drug scrambled up his categories of understanding: space and time spent the evening at war. A friend who was leaving the room disappeared down a hole; time, in certain parts of the room, blew backward, so that at midnight Stella was younger than she'd been at dusk.

During the weeks after he stopped writing, he felt the same way. There were moments in every day when his understanding gave out. He felt as if his mind had been drained of its power to grasp the significance of things.

While he was still in this disoriented state, he dreamed that someone in the next apartment was tapping out coded messages on the wall. When he woke he realized that the tapping was real: there was construction under way on 94th Street. And then he had a revelation. He understood why we dream. During the night the body shuts down, and the mind receives little information from the outside world; but the narrative function of the mind remains awake, laboring to make stories out of the little information it receives — out of hints and scents and glimmers and tapping sounds from fifteen floors below. The story-making organ never sleeps.

When he awoke from his dream, Schiller felt as if he'd seen into the structure of existence. The world, the human world, is bound together not by protons and electrons, but by stories. Nothing has meaning in itself: all the objects in the world would be shards of bare mute blankness, spinning wildly out of orbit, if we didn't bind them together with stories.

If he had felt intellectually dizzy during those last few weeks, it was because he'd been starving the narrative function of his mind. He'd spent the previous twenty years single-mindedly trying to make stories; now it was as if he were depriving himself of water, or air, or light.

He thought he'd feel better if he gave himself time. The problem was that he'd stopped writing too abruptly, like a deep-sea diver who gives himself the bends by coming too quickly to the surface.

But in the next few days, instead of getting better, he began to develop a new symptom. He began to be hit with enormous waves of loneliness.

He couldn't understand where the feeling came from. He spoke to his daughter regularly; his friends were all in touch. He missed Stella terribly — he'd never stopped mourning her — but this loneliness was something new.

He opened the door of his study. The several thousand pages of intractable manuscript, the book that hadn't cohered, was still on the table, where it had remained untouched for weeks.

The novel was a picture of life in the mad America of the late 1960s. It was confused, unwieldy, wild, altogether too ambitious. It had a large cast of characters. He had been struggling with them for seven years. He had come to hate them, almost, because they'd been unremittingly resistant to his wishes and unwilling to disclose their own. But he realized that it was they whom he missed.

He sat at his desk and looked through the manuscript again. He didn't have any sudden insights about what to do with the book

— but he knew that he couldn't leave these characters half-born. They were his people, his community. If he walked away from this writing life, no one else would take up their stories.

He went back to work. And in the days and weeks and months that followed, he found that he was no longer so troubled by the question of whether he was or ever would be a "successful writer." It was beside the point. He was a writer. He knew that he'd keep going even if he were sure that nothing he wrote would ever be published again. He couldn't understand the world, couldn't live, without putting stories on paper.

Over the decades since then, this feeling had remained with him. The craving for wider recognition never vanished: when he wasn't actually writing, it was almost always near. Wilson's unwritten review still ached sometimes, as a bone broken long ago will ache on a damp day. But these discontents rarely touched him when he was working. When he was at his writing table, the labor was its own reward.

At the heart of the greatest disappointment of his professional life, he had found a lesson in how to keep on. Heather's thesis, this fresh disappointment, was one that he would weather soon enough.

Though he thought it was off the mark, Heather's manuscript was certainly intelligent. She offered a clear interpretation of his work and vigorously argued her case. But the writing was not always as lucid or direct as it might be. It could use some help. Despite the lateness of the hour, he started to go through it again, slowly, with his pen in his hand.

29

Casey's grandmother once told him that if he ever wanted to figure out whether he was really in love, all he'd have to do was ask himself two questions: "Do we laugh a lot? Does she kiss good?"

These were fine questions, but he didn't need to ask them. For him it was easier than that. Every time he got together with Ariel, when he had his first glimpse of her — on the street, or entering a restaurant, or at her door — he had a feeling of lightness, a feeling that the fun was about to begin.

He was meeting her for a late dinner. When he saw her on Broadway, crossing against the light, with her graceful and nimble and somehow comic way of walking — she walked like a mime — he wondered how he had ever let her go, and he hoped that what had happened to them years ago wouldn't happen again.

"Hello, Happer," she said, meaninglessly, except that maybe the word was derived from the fact that he made her happy.

They went to a little place on Broadway — one of Ariel's seedy bars. She liked the place because it was dark and the booths in the back were secluded and most of the food they served there was deep-fried. "Can we share?" she said as she took a menu, her eyes glittering hopefully above the candle flame.

She always loved to share their meals. The pleasure she took in this was intense: as she speared a piece of his French toast in a diner on a Sunday morning, you would have thought from her expression that she had reached the summit of her life's ambitions.

More than anyone else he'd ever known, Ariel taught him the delights of everyday life. She was excited by the smallest things: sharing a meal; picking up catnip for Sancho; buying plastic earrings on the street. She had a way of making every occasion seem like a festival.

She ordered fried chicken, cole slaw, "Sexy Fries" — whatever they were — and a Caesar salad. Casey ordered a steak.

She eagerly laid into it all. It was wonderful to watch her eat. Alone among women, she'd never been on a diet in her life, she'd never had an eating disorder or a food hangup of any kind. He'd never even known her to step on a scale. If you asked her how much she weighed she'd give you a rough estimate. She was a full-bodied woman, a woman with meat on her bones, and she was beautiful.

She was talking about her father and some young babe who was writing about him.

"If he had money I'd think she was scheming to get put in his will. But he doesn't have money. Maybe she thinks he has money."

Casey listened poker-faced. He'd always thought she was way too tied up, psychically, with her father. Whom he'd always thought of as a loser. Imagine: a man who had spent his entire life writing something like three books! It was pathetic. Casey had read one of them — the first or the second or the third one, he wasn't sure. He finished it in one sitting — it was pretty light — and getting up he'd tossed it on the table and thought, Four people bothering each other. Who cares?

"I think he's actually having sex with her!" Ariel said. "It's unbelievable. I mean, I love my dad, but I can't understand how she could get naked with him. She's, like, twenty-*five*."

"You really think they're having fucking?" He'd meant to say "having sex," but changed it to "fucking," and it came out a little bit of both.

"I don't know if they were having fucking, Casey, but I know they were having something. I came over to his place one night and he was sitting in his bathrobe eating cookies and her little black booties were on the floor."

"So we don't really know they were having fucking. All we really know is that he was eating cookies when her shoes were in the room."

"That's bad enough," Ariel said.

They were silent for a moment. Casey felt oddly shy.

"It's incredible that we found each other again," he said after a little while.

"I know. I wasn't even supposed to be at that restaurant. I was supposed to be meeting Sam downtown, but at the last minute I called him and said I'd rather meet at Perretti's. I think God must have wanted us to find each other."

"God, eh? So you've finally learned to believe in God?"

"No. But I still think it would be nice."

God was their private joke. She was looking for God when he met her — in fact, he met her *because* she was looking for God.

They'd met eight or nine years ago, at a birthday party for a mutual friend in a chicken and ribs restaurant on West 57th Street. Life takes place in restaurants. The conversation that night was extraordinarily stupid: everyone was talking about "the yuppie murder case," in which a prep-school student had strangled his girlfriend while they were having what he described as "rough sex" in Central Park. Casey didn't have any interest in this kind of thing — he was a hard-news man. He was wondering how soon he could leave the party without being rude.

Ariel was sitting across from him, talking to two guys; in a high-spirited way, as if she weren't entirely serious, she said, "My yoga teacher says I'll never be happy until I let God into my life. Do you think you need God to be happy?"

Casey was an atheist, but her question, which sounded somehow both lighthearted and desperate, and which, unlike anything else that had been said at the party, was about something serious, captured his attention instantly. Sometimes he thought that it was at that moment that he'd begun to fall in love with her.

"I don't think you need God, no," he said. "But I do think everybody needs something to keep themselves going."

"What keeps you going?" she said, flirtatiously.

"What keeps me going," he said — and he trembled with the sense of his own pretentiousness before he even finished the sentence — "is justice."

"Justice," she said. "That sounds so . . . boring."

Maybe *that* was when he'd begun to fall in love with her.

They left the party together and went to a bar for a drink. He didn't ask her over to his place, because after a couple of lousy relationships in a row he was trying to be cautious.

While they were having their second drink she leaned over and kissed him. "Maybe we can go to the park," she said, "and you can strangle me."

She really did want to go to the park. When they left the bar she led him to a bench in Riverside Park and said, "Let's sit here and chat for a while." He scratched his face hesitantly. "You're not scared," she said. "Are you?"

"Scared, me?" It was about two in the morning, and the idea of sitting in the park didn't strike him as very relaxing.

"How can you be scared? You're a black man!"

She said this sweetly, with a drunken, innocent, and idiotic smile. Maybe this was when he fell in love with her.

They sat on the park bench and kissed until five in the morning, and in the gathering light they walked to a coffee shop and he watched in amazement as she downed two fried eggs, hash browns, sausages, two-and-a-half waffles, and three cups of coffee.

"I always have a good appetite after I take advantage of a guy on a park bench," she said.

And now, after all these years, here she was again, still looking for God, still polishing off enormous meals, and still beautiful. If he'd told her that he'd been thinking about her all these years, it would have been a lie. He'd thought about her often, but not all the time. He was too old to believe in true love, in the idea that there was one woman destined for him. But with Ariel, he could almost believe it.

Ariel went to the jukebox to try to find something by Van Morrison; when she came back to their booth she slid in beside him. "Cozytown," she said as she pressed her leg against his.

A man can grow, he was thinking, a man can grow. Because he himself had grown. When he'd known Ariel years ago, if she had said "Cozytown" it would have bothered him. Ariel, then and now and forever, was a child-woman: in the deepest part of her being she was still a child of nine. She was the most guileless person he knew, the most trusting, the most tender, the most innocent.

When he'd known her years ago he couldn't reconcile himself to the fact that he was in love with a child-woman. She wasn't the kind of woman he thought he *should* love. He thought he should be loving an activist, an intellectual, a crusader — some unholy combination of Rosa Luxemburg, Hannah Arendt, and Sojourner Truth.

After his mother met Ariel, a year or so before she died, she said to Casey, "She seems sweet, but you can't be serious about the girl. Do you really want to marry a flapper?"

His mother didn't really give a damn about whether Ariel was a flapper or not. She was in the last stages of her illness, shuttling around among a series of "alternative cancer specialists" who were subjecting her to barbarities far beyond the reach of mainstream medicine. She was in constant pain, and one of the few pleasures that remained to her was tearing down other people's. With an unerring ability to find Casey's weak spot, she knew just how to diminish his girlfriend in his eyes.

Casey always used to think that he wanted to end up with an intellectual — a woman with whom he could discuss the question of why manumission rates declined in post-imperial Athens. Now he'd come to think that what he really wanted was a woman who would slide in beside you in a restaurant and press her leg against yours and say "Cozytown." Cozytown had vanquished Athens.

What matters, finally, isn't finding the kind of person you think you *should* love. What matters is finding someone you feel more alive with. When he was with Ariel, he felt alive.

30

But. There's always a "but" in life, isn't there?

Finding her again had made him happy, but his mind kept turning over in fretfulness, because of the fear that what had happened before was going to happen again.

What happened before was that they'd had a wonderful year and a half, and then they'd started to fight about having kids. His position — that he already had a kid and didn't want another — was not negotiable, and Ariel was equally unbudgeable in her desire to have one. They fought about it all the time, and finally they reached a point where they couldn't talk about anything else. If he forgot to water the plants she told him he didn't know how to take care of anything except himself; if she snuggled with Sancho he thought she was engaging in a creepy display of make-believe motherhood. After six months of this they'd accomplished what he would have thought impossible: they had destroyed their affection for each other.

Though not permanently. Because here she was.

Here, tonight, in the restaurant, he half-listened as she talked about Sancho's world-view. "If there's a fly in the apartment something major is happening. It's a big day."

He was thinking: Don't hurt her again.

It wasn't only that he cared for her; it wasn't only that she was the tenderest soul in the world. It was that he thought she *did* need to have children. It was her telos, as Aristotle might have put it if he'd known her: it was the destination of her being. There weren't many women of whom he believed this, but he believed it of Ariel.

They'd talked about all this, of course, in these last few weeks of rediscovering each other. Ariel kept telling him not to worry. "I'm just using you for a while," she'd said. "After I've toyed with you for a couple of months, I'll leave you by the wayside. Let's just keep things like they are right now. Hot and light."

But he knew it was easy to talk about hot and light, harder to keep things that way.

Ariel had a spot of ketchup on her cheek; as Casey reached out with his napkin to dab it off she closed her eyes and brought her face forward trustingly. Most people, if you go to wipe something off their face, will draw back slightly, flinch. But Ariel offered herself up to you, trusting that you would treat her well. Don't hurt her, he told himself. Don't hurt her again.

31

Heather received a large brown package in the mail. Schiller had returned her thesis.

She wasn't sure she wanted to open it. She assumed there was a note inside, and she assumed it would be unpleasant to read. She thought it would be a howl of outrage.

She thought of just dumping the package in the trash. She was still unhappy about having hurt him, and she didn't want to read his howl of betrayed trust.

She opened the envelope. It was one of those padded envelopes, thickly stuffed with gray clumps of weirdness that pour out of the lining when you open it up. The gray junk spilled all over her jeans.

Schiller had enclosed a note. It had been typewritten, on his old manual.

I can't say that your study filled me with elation, but I appreciate your honesty, your kind remarks about the first two books, and, especially, the seriousness with which you've thought about my work.

I'm grateful that you looked for a

common thread in my work, a figure in the carpet, although I do wonder whether it was precisely your conclusion that my true theme is "freedom" that left you unable to appreciate the two most recent books. But I suppose it's not for me to say: a writer isn't the best judge of his own work. There's room enough in the world for both of us to be wrong.

I once knew a literary critic who, when asked to characterize his critical "method," said that he simply tried to read the hell out of a book. You've read the hell out of mine, and that's all that a writer can ask.

Yours,
Leonard

P.S. Your prose is good, but here and there it could be more direct. I made a few suggestions on the manuscript.

She looked through the thesis. He had edited it closely: there were suggestions — mostly suggestions for cuts — on every page. He had strengthened her arguments, eliminating most of the qualifiers, the bland attempts to be nice. He hadn't tried to rewrite her prose; he'd merely scraped away the fuzz that blurred her judgments. He had made it stronger — and he had made it much more clearly critical of his work.

She'd never been more impressed by him than she was now.

It was a Saturday afternoon in the middle of April. She didn't know what to do. She decided to go into the city. She was thinking about visiting Schiller. She didn't know if he'd left for France yet.

She couldn't make up her mind. His note seemed friendly enough, but she didn't know if he would want to see her.

She took a train into New York, wandered east, and then took the subway uptown. She was near the Metropolitan Museum. She decided to go in and have another look at the Rembrandts.

Somehow they seemed more arresting than they had the other day. The colors he favored — browns and blacks and grays — had struck her, the other day, as drab, washed-out, dead. Today they seemed beautifully somber.

Schiller had seemed to have a special fondness for the self-portraits, so she examined them closely now. She saw an interesting progression. In the early self-portraits he looked like a red-faced fool: a ruddy, puffy master of good cheer. He

266

seemed like someone you'd see at a fraternity beer blast, hanging around the keg and bellowing "Party!" — a sort of late-Renaissance John Belushi.

In the later self-portraits, she could see a change. When he was old he had the face of a man whose life had been marked by tragedy.

She was especially stuck by a self-portrait from 1667. He's at his easel, but he's looking away from it, toward the viewer; he looks as if a visitor has momentarily distracted him from his work. He doesn't appear to be happy about the interruption. With his eyes he seems to be asking, "Well, what is it?" He can't attend to you now; he has work to do.

She was struck by the objectivity of the portrait. He doesn't make himself out to be physically handsome: he pitilessly records the way his face has been ravaged by time. Neither does he make himself out to be morally better than he is. We see him as a man of complexity, sympathy, and deep feeling; but we also see him as impatient, curt, capable of harshness.

Something about his expression reminded her of Schiller. Schiller was no Rembrandt, but like Rembrandt, he was a serious man. She remembered that he had described

Irving Howe in that way: as a "serious man." The simple phrase seemed to mean a lot to him; from his tone, it sounded like the highest praise he could bestow. She wondered whether he would refer to her as a serious woman.

She wanted to see him. She called his apartment, but got his machine. That didn't mean anything, though: she knew he left it on when he was working. She decided to go over and ring on his doorbell.

She took a taxi to the West Side; she was excited to see him. But when she got there, Jeff, the doorman, told her that she was half an hour too late. Schiller was already gone.

32

Ariel was accompanying her father to the airport.

"I can't believe you're only taking one bag. You're like a Zen master, Dad."

She knew why he was taking this trip, and she wanted to be part of it, at least to the extent of escorting him to the airport. She wondered if she should have gone along all the way to Paris. He had asked her if she wanted to, but she'd told him that this was his trip. This was his reunion, not hers.

He was moving more slowly than ever, depending more than ever on his cane. He told her that both his legs felt stiff and that when he came home he might start using a walker.

Not a walker, she thought. I don't want to see my father struggling along half-collapsed over a walker.

He looked so terribly fragile: with his bloated torso and his tiny little feet, he looked as if he was going to keel over. Walking beside him, Ariel, as she had a hundred times in the past six months, began thinking up an exercise regimen that would restore

269

him to health. If he walked just half an hour every day, and worked out three times a week with some free weights — not monster weights, just some light weights to increase his upper-body strength . . .

He'd do no such thing, and she knew it, but she couldn't let go of the longing. She wanted to see him become a supple old man, radiant with well-being, like those eighty-year-old yoga guys she sometimes saw at the Whole Life Expo, sitting on little throw pillows in the lotus position. She clung to the dream that her father might grow young again.

They had a little time before his flight, so they went to get something to eat. The cafeteria was crowded; he claimed the only vacant table and Ariel went to get food.

For herself she bought Swedish meatballs, an apple crumb cake, and a glass of milk; she got a salad with low-fat cottage cheese and a Diet Coke for him. Standing on line, she looked over at him; he was immersed in a novel he'd pulled from his carry-on bag.

She could make out the title from here. *The Ambassadors*, by Henry James.

When she was little, about eight or nine, she had a big reputation in her family as the girl with the eagle eyes. If her mother or father lost their keys, she would always find them. She could still remember how good it felt to hear her mother praise her.

Her father looked content, serenely absorbed in the book. He *was* a Zen master, she thought: not because he'd only brought one bag, but because he lived in a kingdom of purely spiritual struggles and purely spiritual rewards. He didn't care that he was sitting at a table in the smoking section, and that two nerdy guys next to him were chortling like goats. He didn't care that his body was falling apart. He was somewhere far away, taking a walk with Henry James.

As she brought the tray of food to the table, she looked out to watch a plane taking off, and she caught an alarming glimpse of herself in the glass.

"My hair's in trouble," she said, sitting down.

He laughed. "My dear," he said, "your hair is fine, but in fact you're such a lovely young woman that you'd be beautiful even if you had no hair at all. So I really don't think you need to worry about your hair so much."

She loved it when he was gentle with her like this.

She sensed, without having asked him, that the miniskirted scholar had dumped him. A certain lightness that he'd had for a while was gone. She'd noticed it last week, and, in spite of herself, she was glad.

But today he seemed to have recovered; he seemed excited about his trip.

"Did you see the paper this morning?" he said.

"No. I didn't get a chance." The truth was that she hadn't looked at a newspaper in about three months.

"There was a story about a comet that'll be visible in July. Russell's Comet. It was discovered by a woman astronomer, so it's a feminist comet. It comes close to the earth every sixty-four years. I saw it with my mother when I was seven years old — she took me out to New Jersey to have a look. And I remember my grandmother saying she saw it when she was a girl in Russia. You should try to see it this summer. You can tell your children about it, and when it comes around again, in the year two thousand and something, they can see it themselves."

My children, she thought. That was sweet of him to say.

He was still holding *The Ambassadors.* She took it from his hands and opened it near the middle. "It was the first time Chad had, to that extent, given this personage 'away'; and Strether found himself wondering of what it was symptomatic. He made out in a moment that the youth was in earnest as he had not yet seen him; which, in its turn, threw a ray perhaps a trifle startling on what they had each, up to that time, been treating as earnestness."

"Is it possible to get an English translation of this?" she said.

Her father laughed. "It's not so difficult once you get the hang of it." She thought that was all he was going to say about it, but after a moment she could see he was thinking, and she knew that his teacherly impulses were coming into play. "During his last years," he said, "James used to *dictate* his work. He would pace around the room, talking, and his faithful secretary, Miss Bosanquet, would take it all down. Some people think that's the reason his late style became so indirect. James always denied that had anything to do with it, though: he thought he was simply growing more precise. In any case, there's a lot of feeling hidden inside the coils of those sentences."

They talked a little more about Henry James — he reminded her that she had loved *The Heiress*, the movie based on *Washington Square*. "That might be a good place to start with James. That, or *The Portrait of a Lady*." She was no more likely to read Henry James than to translate him into Dutch, and he knew it, but she appreciated the kindly way he told her about this writer he loved. He never made her feel bad about the fact that she was more of a TV person than a reader.

She wanted to tell him that she was seeing Casey again — Casey was all she could think about lately — but she couldn't.

Why not? She wasn't sure.

Maybe, she thought, it was because it was still too new. It's foolish to speak of your happiness before you're sure you have it.

Or it might have been because she wasn't quite sure how he'd take it. Though he'd been friendly enough to Casey when she'd gone out with him years ago, she'd sensed that he was relieved when she and Casey broke up. As if he'd expected her to go back to white guys, where she belonged. If she did end up with Casey for keeps, she was sure her father would give them his blessing, but it might not be easy for him.

The funny thing was that the two men had a great deal in common. Beneath the differences of age and skin color, both men were passionately serious in a modest, unshowy way.

"Have you been thinking about Mom a lot these days?" she said.

"I think about her every day," he said. "It's funny. When she died, all I was aware of was the loss. But as the years have worn on, she seems more present to me than ever."

To Ariel, as the years wore on, her mother seemed more and more distant. Her ghost, which had once been so powerful, had dwindled to a small white light.

It was time for him to board the plane. He kissed her and told her he loved her. It wasn't something he said often; she knew he'd said it because he wanted it to be the last thing he said to her if the plane went down. He joined the crowd at the gate, and then he disappeared.

In the waiting room, for some reason, there was a TV monitor where you could see the passengers going through the metal detectors; she saw her father, dragging along slowly with his cane.

She sat staring blankly at the monitor long after he was gone, and suddenly she felt weak with relief. It was only now that he was gone that she realized how much she worried about him, every moment of the day. It was as if the two of them made a trade-off: he worried about her emotional health and she worried about his physical health.

Her emotional radar didn't extend to

France. He'd be out of her range of worry for a while.

She left the terminal and boarded a bus — one of those one-stop buses that take you straight to Grand Central. She was still turning over the question of why she hadn't told her father about Casey.

She found a seat in the back and closed her eyes. She could nap if she wanted to — the driver would wake her when they got to New York.

It felt good to be borne along, safe, in the darkness. And this feeling, the pleasure of letting go her hold, gave her the clue she needed. She hadn't told her father about Casey because if he knew she was happy with a man, he might feel that his task — the task of taking care of her — was over. He might let go his hold on life. She didn't want him to let go his hold.

33

Casey decided that if this part of his life had a chapter title, it would be "Getting to Know Your Penis."

He examined the base of his cock, for the twelfth time that day.

In college he'd gone out with an ardent feminist who spent a good deal of her time peering into her vagina with the aid of a mirror and a speculum — a plastic instrument resembling one of those two-in-one salad spoons, with which she propped herself open. Her thesis was that women have to understand their bodies intimately if they are to liberate themselves from patriarchal oppression.

Too bad she wasn't around now. They could have kept each other company, interrogating their sexual organs together.

A few months ago he'd gone out with a woman named Liz. A very nice woman with herpes. And now he was worried that he had herpes too.

When she'd told him she had it, he had shrugged heroically and said, "What's a little herpes between friends?"

He was sincere. She gave him so much pleasure in bed that he didn't care about herpes.

No: it wasn't just pleasure in bed. She gave him pleasure in many of the realms of life. She was an interesting, moody woman, and he loved to listen to her think out loud.

Sometimes, it was true, she could be a bit much. She was one of those overearnest left-wing white women who seek out black boyfriends as tokens of their own high ideals, and whenever they discussed some political question she would ask Casey what the black community thought about it. "I don't know," he said at one point. "What does the white community think?" But despite his belief that she was too dogmatic, and despite her belief that, politically speaking, he wasn't black enough, they found each other stimulating, and they were enjoying each other a great deal until they got to the inevitable discussion about children.

It was a hard conversation. Liz kept giving him opportunities to say he wasn't sure about whether he wanted to have kids: opportunities to lie a little, so they could go on. But he wouldn't avail himself of them. It was hard for him to insist, because it hurt her, and because he knew it would drive her away. But he couldn't string a woman along anymore. He felt like a rat, but a rat at peace with itself.

She was furious, and she had a right to be. Actually, she didn't have a right to be: he'd never lied to her; but he understood why she was furious all the same. She called him a bastard; she even called him an Oreo — an insult he hadn't heard in years; she threw something at him — it was a copy of Perry Anderson's *Arguments Within English Marxism*; and they ended up making love. And then, later, as he was leaving her apartment for what they both knew would be the last time, she smiled wickedly and said, "I hope I didn't give you anything. I've been feeling tingly this week. But I don't think I'm contagious yet."

It was wicked because she knew he was a hypochondriac.

And now he was sitting on his toilet seat examining his penis with a mirror.

The amazing thing is how little you know your own sexual organs. A year or so ago he'd gone for a checkup and his doctor had asked him routinely whether there were any new lumps or bulges in his testicles. "How the hell should I know?" Casey had said. His testicles consisted *entirely* of lumps and bulges; who kept track of them all? Now he had to keep track. For three or four days after his final evening with Liz, his balls had itched madly, but there were no eruptions, and he'd concluded that the itching was psychosomatic; and when it finally passed, he'd congratulated himself on his refusal to panic. But earlier this week, sitting in his robe after a shower, talking on the phone with one of his ex-students and idly scratching his crotch as he made a point about the intellectual origins of the French Revolution, he had noticed a little red bump at the base of his penis that he'd never noticed before.

He knew, in the rational part of his mind, that it wasn't herpes. Liz was angry at him, so she'd left him with a little zinger, but she was basically a good person, and there was no way she would actually put him at risk.

The thing was, he already had a kid. He'd fucked up at fatherhood once already, and he felt that having fucked up once, you don't deserve a second chance.

That was putting it too harshly. He hadn't fucked up at fatherhood, he'd fucked up at marriage. After they broke up, Yvonne moved back to Chicago and of course took William with her. Casey faithfully paid his alimony and his child support; he talked to William once a week, saw him several times a year, and wished he could see him more often. But he didn't want to have another kid. That time of his life — the time when you can give your best energies to the needs of a tiny child — was over.

He had other things to worry about.

He had reached a dangerous age. He was at an age when you either advance in the direction of your dreams or else succumb to the creeping blight of Scott Carter's Disease.

Scott Carter was Casey's former mentor. He had been a young professor, a brilliant guy with seemingly unlimited promise, when Casey was studying political science at Columbia. Scott had eventually taken a job at Boston University, and he and Casey lost touch.

A few years later Casey ran into him on the street and they had a drink. The first thing he noticed was that Scott was fat. He was fat, and he was relaxed. At Columbia, Scott had been nervous — physically and intellectually intense. Now, pudgy, bland, listless, Scott had the aspect of a neutered cat.

As they talked, Casey discovered that Scott had grown spiritually listless as well. Remembering the three-hour discussions they used to have at the West End Gate, he was eager to put some of his new ideas to the test of Scott's skepticism. Casey kept trying to get a conversation started; Scott kept having nothing to say. "You know," Scott finally said, "I'm not proud of it, but I haven't been reading much lately. At this point in life, when I come home at night I'm not in the mood to strain my brain. I'd rather drink a couple of brews and watch a hockey game."

This was Casey's glimpse into the horrors of aging. This is what can happen to you after tenure. Scott, at that time, was hardly over forty, but, intellectually speaking, he'd checked out.

That was a few years ago. And now Casey was alarmed to find symptoms of Scott Carter's Disease in himself.

His was a more benign form of the disease. He wasn't dying intellectually. His problem was that he found teaching so challenging, and so exhausting, that he didn't have much room for anything else.

There was a part of him that was fulfilled by the life he was living now. But he wanted to be more than a little professor; he wanted to make a contribution in the wider world.

In the last year he'd started thinking about how he might make one. He'd been talking with a few friends about starting a small-circulation political magazine. There was certainly room for a smart new magazine of the left. *The Nation* was maddeningly glib:

there was no conceivable question it didn't have an answer for. *Dissent* was stifled by its own sobriety: always intelligent, never exciting, it was a finger-wagging grandfather of the left. *Monthly Review*, now past its fiftieth year of existence, was still laboring tirelessly to prove that Marx's theory of the falling rate of profit had relevance to the modern age.

He thought he could be a good editor: he had a nose for what was interesting, and he didn't have a huge ego. As a teacher, he'd always been good at helping people clarify their own thoughts. And what he liked to do best in his spare time, after all, was read magazines. Sometimes he thought about putting together a graduate course whose syllabus would consist exclusively of selections from magazines: from *The Westminster Review* and *The Edinburgh Review* to *The Liberator* to *The Masses* and *The Crisis* to *Partisan Review* to *Studies on the Left* and *The New Left Review* to *Transition*. Civilization, he sometimes thought, advances through its magazines.

It was almost time to meet Ariel. He took one last look at the bump at the base of his penis. He had a medical book around the house, in which he'd read that the herpes virus "causes a genital sore that weeps colorless fluid." Could this thing be described as a "sore"? He wasn't sure.

He peered at the red bump closely. "Are you weeping colorless fluid?" he said.

He had been to his shrink that morning, and his shrink, an irrepressibly upbeat woman who reminded him of a cross between Mary Tyler Moore and Minnie Mouse, had suggested that he was freaking out about herpes because he was afraid of infecting Ariel — not with herpes, which he knew he didn't actually have, but with unhappiness.

34

Ariel arrived in Manhattan near Grand Central and took a train downtown. She was meeting Casey for a movie at the Film Forum.

She was thinking that sometimes life can be generous. Meeting up again with him like this, they had the best of both worlds: the comfort of an old love and the intensity of a new one.

It was a cool night, but he was waiting outside in just a sport jacket and corduroys and a white shirt. He always wore white shirts. He had sort of a perpetually preppie look.

"Hello, Man from Glad," she said — the hero of a series of commercials from the sixties, who was always popping up in the nick of time when somebody needed to wrap a sandwich.

The Film Forum was having a retrospective of movies by the English director Michael Apted. They were going to see *35 Up*, a movie they'd both missed when it was originally released.

In the early sixties Apted made a documentary for British television, *7 Up*, in which he interviewed a racially and socially diverse group of seven-year-olds. Every seven years after that, he'd interviewed the same subjects and made a new film, incorporating footage from the earlier ones. So you watched these people grow.

They held hands during the movie, and Casey, in an idle moment, gently undid her watch — she'd bought a new watch — and put it in his breast pocket.

She thought it was a very sexy gesture.

Afterward they went to a Middle Eastern restaurant. They ordered drinks and looked at the menu, but when she asked him what he was in the mood for, he said he hadn't thought about it yet.

"I found the movie a little depressing," he said. "In *28 Up*, life seemed so full of possibilities — for most of them at least. Now they all seemed defeated."

She'd noticed it too: at thirty-five, the people in the movie seemed to have put away their dreams; the most they dared hope for was that their children would have better lives than theirs.

"Is that the way it really is?" he said.

"That's the way it is in England," Ariel said. "In America you can keep starting over again."

"That's true," Casey said, brightening.

She was happy that her sociocultural insight had impressed him.

"America is the land of second chances," she said, pushing her luck.

She was also, of course, speaking about them.

He sipped his beer. "I guess that's what this magazine is for me," he said. "A second chance."

It bothered her that he wasn't thinking what she was thinking.

"Sometimes," he said, "I think of myself as being in the second phase of life. In the first phase you have these grand ideas about all the things you want to accomplish, and you get a day job to support yourself in the meantime. But after ten years, fifteen years, you haven't accomplished the grand things, and you start to realize that what you've been doing in the meantime might be all you'll ever do. And then you have to decide — do you really want to go for the grand things, or do you just accept the life you've already made?"

"So what's the answer?"

"For me the answer is the magazine."

"The magazine is your grand idea? You never used to talk about starting a magazine."

"That's true. I used to think I'd be a political activist. But I don't see any political community that I want to be a part of right now. So I thought I could try to create one. A place where people on the left can argue with each other."

"But why a magazine? Why not a community of people who are *doing* things?"

Chewing his bread slowly, he thought about this.

She watched him as he thought, and she was happy. She loved the fact that he was introspective. She loved the fact that he *talked.*

Most men, in her experience, didn't know how to talk. They lectured you, or else they didn't talk at all.

"I feel like I have more questions than answers. It's hard to build a movement around questions. So that's why a magazine. I thought it might be possible to start building a community around people who have enough in common to be asking the same questions."

"Can't we be our own community? You and me?" She was editing herself: her ideal community wouldn't be just the two of them — it would include one or two little ones.

"I think people need to be part of something larger."

She didn't want to take this conversation further. She wanted him to know she was glad to have him back in her life, but she didn't want him to know *how* glad. She didn't want him to know, for example, that her ambitions had flown out the window the moment she got back together with him, and that her only ambition for the moment was to make sure that this thing grew. If he knew this it would scare him away. A man can't understand how a woman feels — how she can offer up her entire life to him. The man thinks she's bringing him a burden. He doesn't understand that she's trying to give him a gift.

It alarmed her a little, how much he meant to her. Having Casey in her life had the effect that you're supposed to get from Prozac. Everything seemed easier; she felt more confident, more intelligent, more serene. But why did it take a man to make her feel like this? What would her role models of yesteryear have said about that — her women's studies teachers, for example? "A woman without a man is like a fish without a bicycle" — that was the slogan her feminist-minded classmates used to scrawl on the toilet stalls in college. You weren't supposed to need a man to complete you. Yet here she was, a tender little grouper, happy at last because she had a bicycle she could call her own.

She knew that this relationship wasn't as important to him as it was to her. If he was being honest he'd probably admit that she was the second most important thing in his life right now. The first most important thing was this fledgling magazine.

When she knew him years ago he was still reeling from his divorce, and though he used to talk a lot about how he wanted to make some larger contribution, it was all talk. Now he was absorbed by the effort to get this magazine off the ground. When they got together they usually got together late, because he was trying to wheedle an article out of someone or following up some tip about getting hold of a used computer.

Sometimes she fantasized about falling for some easygoing guy, a guy who forgot all about his work when he got home. But if she'd really wanted that she would have stuck with Victor Mature. She liked a man who was living a passion, even if it meant she had to compete with it.

They finished dinner and walked up Seventh Avenue, holding hands and laughing. A police car slowed down as it passed, and the cop in the passenger seat looked them over closely. Ariel could feel Casey tightening — a subtle inner flinch.

Ariel never really thought about the racial thing except at times like this — when strangers gave them the evil eye. It wasn't an issue for her, and she knew that Casey felt the same way. Years ago, when everything was falling apart between them, she once overheard him talking on the phone with his ex-wife. She heard him saying, "You want me to tell you it's because she's white? You're looking for a drama about how racial differences make it hard for two people to love each other? I'm sorry, but you'll have to look somewhere else for that. Ariel and I have our problems, but that's not one of them. That's not our story."

It might have been different if Casey had had a less complicated family background. But his mother was white — not only that, she was Jewish; she was closer to the stereotype of the Jewish mother than Ariel's mother had ever been. Casey knew more Yiddish words than Ariel did.

Blackness and whiteness was their story only when the outside world made it their story. It was their story, for instance, when Ariel talked about visiting friends in Boston together. Casey never wanted to. When he was in graduate school he'd had a girlfriend in Boston; he used to borrow his parents' car and drive up there on weekends, and not once or twice but three times he was stopped on the Massachusetts Turnpike and hassled by state troopers, apparently for the crime of Driving While Black. Ever since then he'd been allergic to Massachusetts.

Back in her apartment, they made love. She loved the way he made love — with a rare combination of passion and patience. There was just one thing wrong with him in bed: he didn't know how to kiss. Never did. In the old days she'd managed to teach him a little — tactfully, by example — but he'd forgotten most of what he'd learned. She'd have to start over again. His kisses were too rote; they were assembly-line kisses. She wanted complex kisses; she wanted each kiss to be a conversation.

He knows nothing of kissing theory, she thought.

That was a small sad thing. But there was also a big sad thing, which kept her up worrying after Casey had fallen asleep. The big sad thing was that she knew they weren't going to last. On the morning after their first night together, a month ago, Casey had let her know that he hadn't changed his mind about having kids. She'd told him not to worry about it, it wasn't a problem. But of course she was lying.

35

Schiller installed himself in his hotel room slowly and carefully. He laid out his clothing in the drawer, with an inward shiver of distaste at the thought of how many other people had put their clothes there. He took a shower, and was displeased by the lukewarm water. These were things that never bothered him when he was young. He had grown too old for Paris.

He went to bed in the afternoon, with the sun burning in through the blinds. Every object in the room was painful to look at, shatteringly bright. Jet-lagged, he fell into a heavy, drugged sleep, and woke twelve hours later in the chilly dark with a stiff neck, aching joints, and an aching spine. Why was it the *bones* that hurt? He wished he could be deboned like a chicken, and make his way through the world in the form of pain-free meat.

He showered again, left the hotel, and took a walk in the cold spring day. It was morning; people were hurrying to work. But they seemed to be hurrying in slow motion.

When you leave New York you realize

you're a New Yorker. On the sidewalks of New York he always felt that everyone was whizzing past him; he felt in danger of getting knocked over. But in Paris, he felt as if he was part of the pace: *everyone* in Paris walked slowly. Somehow, instead of making him comfortable, this annoyed him.

He took a seat in a café and ordered a croissant and *"du café"* — some coffee. The waiter came back with a croissant and two cups of coffee — *deux cafés*. Schiller decided that he should stick to English.

The café was crowded; he drank his two coffees and listened to the conversations around him, which he could only half understand. Two heavyset, rough-looking men were arguing about politics, and he was struck anew by a thought he used to have often when he lived here: there is no such thing as a French tough guy. A French tough guy, even if he's tough as nails, speaks French, and therefore isn't very tough at all. These men looked like boxers, but they were speaking a feminine language and sipping daintily from tiny espresso cups. Schiller, six-foot-something and wide, always felt terribly manly in France, the land of fragile men.

He walked much of the day. Paris seemed smaller, more provincial than he'd remembered it.

It grew warmer in the afternoon. He sat on a bench in the Luxembourg Garden, watching children put little wooden boats in the pond.

Sometimes he used to have lunch here with Stella.

He and Stella had spent the first two years of their marriage in Paris. They weren't children: he was in his early thirties and she was just a few years younger. The freedom and the foreignness were all the sweeter precisely because they *weren't* young: they both knew what it was to be nailed to desks in unfulfilling jobs.

Every morning they worked side by side at the long table in their apartment — she was writing her dissertation and he was working on what was to become his third unpublished novel. Around noon they would leave for their jobs — she was giving English lessons to French businessmen and he was working as a copy editor for an English-language tourist magazine. They would meet in the early evening and take long walks, getting to know the city street by street.

For two years they had a perfect life. It was hard to say why they felt so free here. If they'd lived in New York they would have been doing the same things: she would have been working on her dissertation, he would have been writing his novel; they'd both have been working at day jobs to pay the bills. But somehow Paris made everything different. Being in a new place and speaking a new language made every encounter more interesting. A trip to the market in the morning to buy bread, an afternoon spent reading in a café — nothing was routine; a strange place helped you find the poetry in everyday life.

Now, almost forty years later, he had spent the day visiting their personal landmarks. Most of the things he remembered were still here: Paris preserves its past. But his mind was too stunned to contemplate persistence and change: all he could think about was that she was alive then and she was no longer alive. That once they were young, and now he was old, and now she was gone.

How could it be?

In *The Ambassadors*, when Lambert Strether, a sheltered, middle-aged American, pays a visit to France, he is rejuvenated by its broader moral atmosphere, and he realizes that he has never really lived. In the central scene of the novel, he sits with a young friend in a quiet garden in the Faubourg-Saint-Germain and implores the young man to *live* while he's still young, to live all he can.

Schiller didn't have the same regret. He and Stella had valued their youthfulness —

they *had* lived, they'd lived intensely. But no matter how deeply you live, it comes to this in the end: one of you will be gone and the other will be in mourning.

He had no doubt that if he had died and she were still alive, Stella would be mourning him with an equal intensity. Stella would be keeping this appointment.

They should have been keeping it together. Stella had died an absurd death. She'd died in a fire in a hotel in Pittsburgh, where she'd been attending a conference of the American Philosophical Association. She hadn't even been sure she wanted to go; she'd made up her mind at the last minute, because it didn't seem that important either way.

Sitting in the Luxembourg Garden, he thought of Heather's manuscript, and her view that he had lost his literary compass after the second book. He didn't quite see it that way, but she might have been right. It was hard to say. Certainly his work changed after Stella died. He wrote less nakedly; he became more guarded — or maybe it was simply that his own life began to interest him less. The third book, the book about the sixties, was rather impersonal; it was his first, his only, attempt to work on a large social canvas. Writing it was a ten-year struggle; he had high hopes for it after it was done, but it had the bad fortune to be published not too long after *Mr. Sammler's Planet*. He still liked to think that his was the better novel, but Bellow's reputation was an ocean liner that capsized his own small craft. The fourth book, the one about his parents, was filled with passion — he thought it was, at any rate — but it was a passion to preserve the memory of their lives and their time; he was no longer exploring his own personal life as he had in the first two books, and evidently that was what Heather had loved.

Some people had told him they liked his last two books the most.

Maybe Heather would look more favorably on his next book, if he managed to complete it.

He was near the end of it — of the book he thought of simply as the Stella book. It was six hundred pages long, and it was a mess: he wasn't sure if the parts fit together, and he'd written about some of the events they had lived through in five different ways, finally deciding to leave in all the alternative versions and hope that his readers — if he ever had readers — would at least find the novel an interesting mess. But interesting or not, the important thing was that it was almost done. He had just one more appointment to keep, and all he wanted to do was transcribe the feelings he had when he kept it, and then the book would be over, and his life's task would be complete.

After resting, he continued his walk, and in the late afternoon he found himself near the Rodin Museum.

When they'd lived here, he'd go to the museum once a month or so to look at Rodin's sculptures of Balzac. There was one in particular that he always paid his respects to. Balzac used to write in a huge robe that resembled a monk's cowl, and one of Rodin's statues depicted Balzac in this robe: fat, arrogant, gifted, grinning, wholly at ease.

When Schiller was young, he drew inspiration from the thought of Balzac. Perhaps he valued the idea of Balzac more than he valued Balzac's books. In a career that lasted only twenty years, Balzac wrote more than forty novels; with a feverish desire to put "all of France" into his books, he crowded them with representative figures and made sure to include portraits of every region and every sector of society. He was a passionate monarchist — he mourned the death of the old regime — and yet he kept a bust of Napoleon on his mantel, for he admired Napoleon's world-conquering ambitions: he sought to become the Napoleon of literature. Schiller hadn't had such grand desires — he'd never sought to become the Napoleon of literature — but he'd cherished the example of Balzac's dedication and his immersion in his creative world. When Balzac was on his deathbed he supposedly cried out for a doctor who existed only in his books — one of his recurring characters, Bianchon.

When Schiller paid those monthly visits to the Rodin Museum, he came full of hope and anxiety. In his middle thirties, with two unpublished novels behind him, he had no idea whether he would become a novelist at all. He wasn't sure how long he could keep going.

And how had it turned out? With his four published books, he hadn't exactly matched the master: Balzac once wrote five books in a single year. At seventy-one, he was as fat as Balzac, but that was the only realm in which he rivaled him. But he had certainly kept going. Schiller had no illusions about the scale of his own achievement, but he had tried, through art, to bring a little more beauty, a little more tolerance, a little more coherence into the world, and now he felt he had earned the right to look back at the statue with an unembarrassed eye.

36

Casey got to Penn Station a few minutes before the train was due, bought a papaya drink, and started pacing around the waiting area. He was tapping the bottom of the cup to get the last few pieces of ice into his mouth when he saw William coming up the stairway. He watched the boy for a moment, without trying to get his attention. William had grown taller in the last six months, but not much else had changed: he was still pudgy, awkward-looking, sincere-looking — he looked like a person who bore the world no ill.

"Hello, young man," Casey said as his son approached. Casey wanted to give him a hug, but instead he squeezed him on the shoulder; and in that momentary touch, the love and the guilt and the sadness and the distance came together in such a confused flood that he could hardly think.

He took one of William's bags, and as they walked toward the subway he realized that his son was quite a bit bigger than he was. This wasn't saying much — Casey was five-eight — but it was new.

Casey was amused at the way people — that is, white people — were getting out of their path. Apparently the fact that William bore the world no ill was obvious only to his father. On the subway platform, people gave them a great deal of space, which wasn't true when Casey stood by himself in a jacket and tie with his nose in a copy of *The Last Intellectuals.* He was often shadowed by security guards in bookstores and record stores; he often saw white women cross the street to avoid him after dark; but he'd forgotten what it was like to see white people of all descriptions scurry out of your path in broad daylight, and he'd forgotten the mixed feelings it engendered: anger, because people were making assumptions about you, and pleasure, because you had the power to inspire fear.

"I should keep you around as a bodyguard," Casey said.

He might not have been a bad one. William was a strapping boy, and he walked with that badass slouch, that shitkicker limp, that young black males had favored since the beginning of time. Casey used to walk that walk himself. When he was growing up he heard a rumor that there was one original kid somewhere, Badleg John, who was the baddest kid in the world, who dragged one leg behind him because he had polio, and that everybody else who walked like that was unwittingly imitating the polio-stricken gait of Badleg John.

William walked the walk, and William wore the uniform. With his huge baggy sweatshirt and his huge baggy jeans, he looked as if he was in training to become a dirigible.

"How's your mother?" Casey said.

William looked at his father as if this were a stupid question. "She's the picture of health," he said.

"Mason?"

William smiled — slightly. His smile was like a shrug. "He's Mason."

"Are you hungry?" Casey said.

"I could eat." This was how it was going to be. Nothing had changed. William never told you anything about anything. He provided information on a strict need-to-know basis, and as far as he was concerned, nobody needed to know.

When they got home Casey ordered some food from a Chinese restaurant and William started putting his things away. He hauled his bags to the living-room closet, half of which was always reserved for him, and began to hang up his stuff. He was only staying here for a couple of days, but he'd brought a lot of clothes for his trip. He was visiting colleges across the East Coast.

Evidently he knew enough not to wear the uniform on his interviews: he was hanging up button-down shirts and nice wool trousers.

As William took things out of his bag, Casey noticed that he'd brought a bow tie.

"Is that to make you look like Louis Farrakhan," Casey said, "or to make you look like Arthur Schlesinger Jr.?"

Stupid attempt at a joke, Casey thought. He's probably never heard of Arthur Schlesinger Jr. Don't make jokes that require research.

"You really sold me a woof ticket," William said. Casey didn't know what this meant, and that was the point: his son was showing him that he too could command an incomprehensible dialect, if that was Casey's game.

William was the most guarded person Casey knew. Sometimes Casey wanted to tackle him and not let him up until he had uttered one true thought. You never knew what he was thinking. Never. He was no longer the boy who used to wake you up in the morning to tell you what he had dreamed.

Maybe there was nothing to be done but

wait out his adolescence, and hope that at the end of it all he might be a person who would want to talk to you.

Yvonne had assured Casey that he acted the same way with her. She said it didn't bother her. "He's a good kid. He does his homework, or some of his homework. He has friends. He has a girlfriend. What else do you want?"

"Would you like something to drink?" Casey said. "Juice, water, milk, soda?"

"Fruit juice is for faggots," William said. "Milk is for kitty cats. Water — fish fuck in it."

"You'd like some soda, I take it?"

"I could have a sip. As long as it's not diet soda, which is . . ." Apparently he couldn't think of who diet soda was for.

When he came back from the refrigerator, Casey noticed something new.

"What's that thing on your ear?" he said.

William fingered it self-consciously and, for the first time this evening, he smiled a genuine smile. A half-guilty smile.

"It's called an earring," he said.

"What is the meaning of this?"

"Does it have to have a meaning? It's beyond meaning. It is what it is."

Casey understood the sentiment. An earring on a guy no longer meant what it meant

305

fifteen years ago. Barry Bonds wore an earring. Springsteen wore earrings. Half the guys in Casey's classes wore earrings these days. But still, it gave him the creeps to see one on his son.

Nose rings on young women, earrings on guys, let alone nipple and navel rings: he was baffled by contemporary tastes in self-mutilation. But every generation makes itself ridiculous in its own way. When he himself was in high school he had a mile-wide Afro, so big he couldn't wear a hat.

But he still didn't like to see an earring on his son's ear.

"Are you making a statement?"

William seemed amused. "What kind of statement would that be?"

"I don't know. An earring and a bow tie. Are you tweaking the sensibilities of the bourgeoisie?"

"You tell me. You know more about the sensibilities of the bourgeoisie than I do."

Forget the earring. After all, they'd been here already. They'd already had a few dead-end discussions about the way William dressed. A few years ago William had shown up wearing an X cap, and Casey had subjected him to a lecture about Malcolm X.

Whom he had never been impressed by. The early nonsense about Yacub, the mad

306

scientist who'd caused the world's problems by inventing whites in the first place; the tardy revelation that hey, white folks are people too — politically and intellectually, he had always considered Malcolm a lightweight.

In black intellectual life there were certain people, scattered all across the ideological spectrum, who, when the name of Malcolm X came up, exchanged ironic points of light. Stanley Crouch, Jerry Watts, Julius Lester, Adolph Reed — Casey admired the courage of these people, all of whom had written witheringly about the sanctification of Malcolm, no two of whom, probably, agreed with each other about anything else.

So when William showed up wearing an X hat, Casey delivered a long lecture in which he had dealt not only with Malcolm's career but with the simplicities of Afrocentrism, arguing that Afrocentric ideas were both historically and theoretically naive, and that rather than searching for some authentic black identity in our African roots, African Americans should recognize that we have created our culture *here*, and that the authentic black cultural identity is a diaspora identity. Casey had spoken about this at great length, trying to render these complicated ideas in accessible language. This was when he felt most alive: trying to explain a difficult idea to a young person. He often felt alive like this with his students, but very rarely with his son.

After he finished his little lecture, he asked William what *he* thought. It turned out that William had a much more practical view of the Afrocentrism question. "I've heard a lot of stuff about how Africans, you know, invented math. But I don't really care who invented math. It's boring to me no matter who invented it."

More than once, Casey had vowed to stop delivering political-intellectual lectures to his son. But it was a hard habit to break. He worried about his son's political education. And providing a political education was what parents did for children, wasn't it? It was what his parents had done for him.

Casey was the product of one of the classical mixed marriages of the old left: a black labor lawyer for a father, a Jewish social worker for a mother. Casey's grandfather had been the patriarch of Philadelphia's oldest, most respectable Negro law firm; Henry, Casey's father, became a lawyer too, but, radicalized as a young man during the 1930s, he specialized in labor law and eventually joined a small left-wing group ("the Johnson Forest tendency"), where he met Ruth, Casey's mother.

Simply by virtue of loving them he'd been delivered from the simplicities of ethnocentric thinking. His parents were true-blue internationalists: they'd really believed in the brotherhood of man, and he'd inherited that belief. The family heroes were Paul Robeson and Rosa Luxemburg and Eugene V. Debs, and those still seemed like pretty good heroes to him.

Growing up as he had — the child of a mixed marriage, the child of socialists — had left him with a lifelong feeling of alienation, of being an outsider even among his fellow outsiders. Near the turn of the century, W.E.B. Du Bois had written of the "double consciousness," the sense of "twoness," imposed on those who were black and American. For Casey, fiveness or sixness was more like it. Twoness would have been a relief.

William planted himself on the couch, picked up the remote control, and started clicking aimlessly among the seventy-six stations on cable.

"Your mother tells me you have a girlfriend." William's girlfriend, according to Yvonne, was his true soul mate: intelligent, watchful, and as silent as a thief. Yvonne had reported that once, thinking William was

309

out, she'd opened the door to his room to borrow his boombox and found the two of them sitting on the floor a few feet away from each other, not talking. "They were sitting side by side like a couple of cats," Yvonne said. "I think they spent the whole evening like that."

"Diane," William said. "She may be referring to Diane."

"Is she nice?"

"Nice," said William. "Nice." He pronounced the word experimentally. "I've read that word in books, but I don't believe I've ever heard it used in conversation."

"Would you shut up and answer me? Is she a nice girl?"

"She's angel food cake," William said. "She's the life of the party."

"Well I just hope you keep your party hat on." This was an attempt at a streetwise reminder to wear condoms.

"The tragic rise of out-of-wedlock births," William said. "I saw something about that on *Oprah*." He leaned back on the couch, large, smug as an owl. He was fifteen years old, and there was no way you could touch him.

Children must avenge themselves upon their parents. Yvonne was a fiery achiever — a woman who wanted to make it in the world. Casey was an intellectual who, despite the political befuddlements of recent years, still wanted to make the world over. William's revenge was to be neither a joiner nor a reformer. He looked upon all enthusiasms with scorn.

But he's only a boy, Casey reminded himself. Every teenage boy looks upon all enthusiasms with scorn.

He remembered the gullible boy William used to be, the boy who was always stunned by his good fortune. On Christmas morning of William's sixth year — Yvonne and Casey's last year together — after tearing the wrapping off his presents — his swords and his football helmet and his baseball bat and his baseball books and his dinosaur books and his Batman costume and his team of little robots — William had opened his mouth in comic-book astonishment and cried out, "Santa Claus not only brought me what I asked for, he brought me extras!" Casey and Yvonne were in the bitterest days of their battling, but they were trying hard to keep it all offstage, trying to shield him. When William said that, Casey had thought, Christ, it's so easy to be good to someone. As he sat there that morning, already sloshed on eggnog, William's remark inspired in him a half-baked philosophy of life. Despite Marx and despite Freud, each of whom, in his own way, had devoted his career to refuting this proposition, people do know what they want in life. And the trick to making anyone happy, and making yourself happy in the bargain, is to bring them not only what they ask for, but to bring them extras.

Well, that was a long time ago. Casey didn't know how to be good to him anymore — because it *isn't* always so easy to bring extras to your loved ones. To bring someone more than what he asks for, he has to ask for something in the first place. And that was something William wouldn't do.

37

The Eiffel Tower has the distinction of being the world's tallest cliché. During Schiller and Stella's first year in Paris, they felt smug about the fact that they never visited the thing. They were too sophisticated to stand in a crowd of tourists, gawking slackjawed at that graceless immensity.

But even if you don't visit it, you can't avoid it either. Walking in a distant, unfamiliar neighborhood, hemmed in by little buildings, feeling lost, you would turn a corner and see the tower in the distance. No matter where you were, it was always nearby.

Coming to know it was like coming to know a person: someone who strikes you as vulgar at first, but who, little by little, day by day, begins to reveal unexpected qualities of subtlety, steadiness, tact.

Finally, taking a long walk one day from the Louvre to the Arc de Triomphe, they decided to extend the tour by walking to the Eiffel Tower.

Standing close to it for the first time, they were surprised by its magnificence. It was a different creature from the thing you see at a distance: it was impossibly graceful, with all its heaviness flung up into the air so that it seemed to defy gravity.

At dinner that evening, Stella remarked that it was already hard to remember what it looked like from up close: all the trite representations that she'd seen over the years — the photos and the postcards, the book-ends and the paperweights — had crept back into her mind, covering up the memory of the tower as it actually was. "We'll have to go back," she said. "So we can remind ourselves of what it really looks like."

"Of course we'll go back."

"I want to make a date. I want to meet you there on this date — forty years from today. I want to meet here again near the end of our lives and hold your hand."

"The men in my family don't generally make it to seventy."

"This will be an incentive. And if you're dead I'll come here anyway, and I'll expect your ghost to visit me. And I want you to do the same. If I'm a ghost I'll do my best to get here."

He liked the idea of meeting her here in forty years. He liked the idea that they would come together to review their lives and re-affirm their choices — their choice of vocation, and their choice of each other.

He believed that their choice of each other was permanent. He was sure that they would wake up in the same bed that morning and walk to the tower together.

On the morning of their appointment, Schiller woke alone, with a howling backache from the too-soft mattress of his hotel room. He dressed slowly and went out into the bright cool day.

He took the Métro to the Champ de Mars, walked up the long row of stone steps, and emerged on the large bright plaza, with the tower in the middle distance to the west.

The tower was resplendent in the clear day. He sat on a low stone wall a few feet from a group of German tourists who were taking pictures of one another and clowning for the camera.

He sat there, an old man in a breeze, in the quiet of the spring afternoon.

Nothing is foreordained. If a few things had gone differently, Stella would still be alive.

It was astonishing that she couldn't join him here.

When most of the people you've loved are gone, you begin to let go.

Once, when he was five years old, he asked his mother why people have to die. She told him that when people get old they get tired, and they want to die, because it's like going to sleep. When she said this he was sure she was lying: she was just trying to make him think that things always worked out for the best.

But now, sixty-six years later, he felt that there was a kind of truth in what she had said. With the death of so many of the people he loved, the world had become a strange place, and leaving it would mean less than he had ever thought it could.

It was a cool blue breezy day; thick clouds were hurrying along low in the sky. For forty years, he had wondered what the weather would be like on this day. He'd hoped it would be a nice day, so that he and Stella — as he'd pictured it during the first fifteen years of his anticipation — would be able to sit outside. He had worried that the day, when it finally came, might be marred by rain or by a freak April snowstorm. But it was pleasant and cool.

He sat huddled up in his raincoat; the few hairs he had were stirring in the breeze.

Of course he had considered not coming. The money he'd spent on this trip — more than a thousand dollars, what with the airfare and the hotel and the meals — could have been spent in much more intelligent ways. He could have just given it to Ariel, and he probably should have.

But he had to come. He had to come, to keep faith with the young woman and the young man who had made the appointment.

He didn't look like a romantic figure, this tall fat man in his battered raincoat. If you had seen him there, you would have thought he was sitting on the little wall only because he was out of breath. You wouldn't have thought him a romantic hero, and Schiller certainly wasn't thinking of himself that way. But perhaps that is what he was. As mild a man as he seemed, he had lived steadily in the service of his passion; and if he had come to honor an impossible appointment, then it was only another gesture in keeping with this way of life, this need to live out his passions, even if they were futile passions, to the end.

He could still remember what it was like to walk these streets with her when it seemed as if the possibilities of life were endless. It was a time when, out of necessity, they kept everything simple — they had few possessions; there was nothing in their lives but love and work. But they had everything they wanted.

They had two years of it. Sometimes they talked about living there permanently; but when Stella became pregnant within a month of finishing her dissertation, she took it as a signal that they should go home.

He resisted for a while; he thought they could make a life in Paris. But he knew his position was doomed. He could never hold his own in arguments with Stella: she had spent the better part of her adult life immersed in the Western philosophical tradition, and whenever he tried to engage her in debate she made short work of him. They got ready to go home.

On the eve of their departure, she was seized with worry that they'd made the wrong choice. She suggested that they cancel their flight and stay on for a few more months. He didn't take her seriously — they'd paid for the tickets and it was too late to get a refund — and they left Paris the next day as planned.

Forty years later, he still wondered whether everything might have turned out differently if he had listened to her that night.

He had thought about this for years. If they'd stayed here only six months longer, only six weeks longer, everything that followed would have been subtly changed, and she might be alive today.

But now he realized that it didn't really matter. She was gone, and he would follow soon enough, and it would be as if neither of them had ever been.

Sitting on the little stone wall, he waited for her ghost to come, but it didn't. He couldn't feel her presence at all.

He had thought about this odd appointment so many times over the years that in a part of his mind, the part that doesn't believe in the laws of nature or in any laws at all, he had come to believe that perhaps her ghost would somehow show him a sign. In the irrational part of his mind there had survived the hope that she would find a way to show him that some slip of a glimmer of a trace of a hint of her still survived.

There was nothing, of course. She hadn't made the journey. But even so, it seemed to him that the air where he sat was charged, alive. He had been looking forward to this appointment so deeply, for so long, that the spot itself seemed to have been affected by his longing. It was hard to understand how the tourists bustling around him could fail to notice that there was something different about this patch of space: that it was charged, that it was saturated with love.

The mind cannot sustain itself for long at a great pitch of reverence and yearning, especially a tired mind in a tired body, and after a few minutes he noticed that his foot was asleep. This felt like a betrayal; but he knew that it wasn't really a betrayal. He could never betray her now. Not merely because she wasn't alive to be hurt by him, but for a deeper reason. He would never leave her. He might be driven to move now by the need to restore the circulation in his foot and by simple distraction, but he would never leave her. She was his person; and this was the way it would be until he died.

It seemed right that they had arranged to meet at this spot, near this monument, this huge and beautiful cliché. It seemed right because of what they had discovered about it many years ago: when you were in this city, you could never lose it. You could be wandering around through narrow winding streets in some unfamiliar district, utterly disoriented, and suddenly, when you turned a corner, you'd see it in the distance, glittering in the smokeless air. You could never lose it. It was always near. Exactly like you, my love. Exactly like you.

38

Heather had never seen Sandra in daylight before. She was dressed in a T-shirt and jeans — all black. Her skin was very pale.

They were sitting under a tree at the edge of the Great Lawn in Central Park, watching a baseball game: *The Village Voice* against the National Writers Union.

Now that her thesis was done, Heather had called Sandra to find out if she could write something for the *Voice*. In the course of the conversation Sandra had invited her to the game.

"So you finished it," Sandra said. "You must be thrilled."

"I guess." Heather shrugged and tore a clump of grass from the earth.

"Postpartum depression?"

"Maybe. I'm not happy about what I said about Leonard. I meant what I said, but I'm not happy that I said it. I'm sure I must have hurt him."

Sandra smiled in an affectionate, almost maternal way. "Sidney Hook," she said, and paused for a second to check for a sign of recognition. Not getting one, she said, "Sidney Hook — a philosopher about whom your friend Leonard Schiller undoubtedly has strong feelings, one way or the other — used to say that most of the difficult decisions in life don't involve right against wrong, but right against right. That's why life is tragic. It was right for you to write about him honestly, but it also would have been right for you to write something that would have spared his feelings. I can understand why you have mixed emotions."

They watched the softball game for a while. The *Voice* was going through hard times lately; there were rumors that it was going to close down. But the writers and editors and photographers who were here today, making jokes that you needed a graduate degree in semiotics to understand, didn't seem like people who were troubled about their future; they seemed like the smartest, most self-confident group of people she'd ever seen.

When she'd come to New York a few months ago, Heather had thought she was coming to Schiller's New York. But Schiller's New York didn't exist anymore. It was Sandra's New York now.

Heather didn't think that was such a bad thing. She was happy to be on good terms with this curious person, who was successful enough to be a mentor to ambitious younger people, but who behaved with none of the self-importance that one usually sees in people who assign themselves that role.

The ball rolled their way and the third baseman, a ponytailed Writers Union guy, said, "A little help?" Sandra scooped up the ball and threw it to him. It reached him on a bounce.

"Do you still write poetry?" Heather said after Sandra sat down.

"Poetry?" Sandra was looking at her with suspicion — almost with alarm.

"What I'm asking," Heather said, "is why you never published another book of poetry after *Misplacing Marlene*."

"What are you? A detective?"

Misplacing Marlene was a book of poetry that Sandra had published with a small press in 1971, when she was still in college.

"I thought that title had been obliterated from the historical record," Sandra said. "At least I hoped so."

"I've looked for it," Heather said. "I've never been able to find a copy."

"Thank God for small favors," Sandra said.

"Should I infer that you don't think it was very good?"

"The heartfelt effusions of a twenty-year-old with a highly developed sense of self-pity. How good could it have been?"

"So you stopped writing poetry when you stopped pitying yourself?"

"Not quite. I did stop writing poetry, though."

"Why?"

"I stopped when I realized that it wasn't going to lead to an exciting life."

"An exciting life?"

Sandra walked over to a plastic cooler and got two cans of beer. "Now you get to hear the story of my life, you lucky girl."

She tossed a can to Heather and sat down. "For a long time, my sole ambition was to become a poet. When I published that book I thought I had everything I wanted in life. I thought all I had to do to be perfectly happy was keep doing what I was already doing. I thought I was going to go on writing poetry, and find a teaching job in some MFA program somewhere, and spend the summers in writers' colonies, and become a grand old literary lady. I thought I was going to become Marianne Moore.

"In the summer of . . . 1972, I guess it was, I visited a friend in Ecuador, and a few days after I got back I came down with a fever of a hundred and three. It didn't go away, and I ended up in St. Vincent's with what the doctors called a 'fever of undetermined origin.'

"I ended up spending two months there. I was too weak to write, too weak to read, too weak to do anything except lie there and watch TV. I missed my life. But I was surprised to find that it wasn't poetry I missed, or going to poetry readings. I missed movies. I missed music. I missed going to clubs and dancing and listening to music so loud that my ears would still be ringing the next morning. When my friends would visit me and talk about what was going on in the world, I noticed that none of them talked about books. They were talking about *Mean Streets* and *The Godfather*; they were talking about Bob Dylan and Patti Smith and that primal-scream album John Lennon made when the Beatles broke up. And even when they talked about the written word, they talked about a Joan Didion article in *The New York Review of Books* or a Tom Wolfe article in *Esquire* or a Hunter Thompson article in *Rolling Stone*. They weren't talking about Robert Lowell and Elizabeth Bishop. And they weren't talking about Leonard Schiller either, I might add.

"But the point isn't that my friends were talking about these things. It's that these were the things I wanted to *hear* about. I didn't want to know whether Muriel Rukeyser had published a new poem somewhere; I wanted to know whether Lou Reed was putting out a new record. I'd been going through life with the idea that I wanted to be a poet, but that wasn't really where my passion was.

"During those two months in bed, I made a vow. I told myself that if I ever got out of there, whatever I was going to do in life, I was going to do it only as long as it was fun.

"That's how I found my way into the work I do now. And now I'm having all the fun I can handle. And even in terms of adding something to the cultural conversation, if there is such a thing, I think I'm doing more as a journalist and an editor for the *Voice* than I ever would have done as a poet."

An old-time *Voice* writer, a woman who looked like someone who had traveled to Nicaragua in the 1980s to help the Sandinistas gather the coffee harvest, picked up a bat and waved ineffectually at three pitches; the inning was over.

"It's time," Sandra said, "for me to strike out a couple of labor lawyers."

The *Voice* people were going out on the field again; Sandra took over from the guy who'd pitched the previous inning. Heather was struck by Sandra's physical awkwardness. She wasn't much of an athlete. She would lob the ball toward the batter and then skitter backward, covering her face.

After fouling off two pitches, the batter hit a looping line drive toward shallow left field. As the shortstop, running with his back to home plate, made a graceful over-the-shoulder catch, Sandra, on the pitcher's mound, jumped up and down with delight.

Heather sat on the grass, watching the game and thinking about Sandra's theory of fun. Sandra had found a way to make sure that her labor was blossoming and dancing. It seemed to work for her: she was vital, happy, generous, interesting, and interested in life. But Heather didn't think she could structure her own life that way.

She was still thinking about it when Sandra came back and sat down. "You say you're just out to have fun, but in fact you've made sacrifices for what you believe in. You quit *The New Yorker* when they got rid of William Shawn."

"You *are* with the FBI," Sandra said. "You know more about me than I do." She seemed embarrassed to be reminded of her good deed. "I still just file it under the category of fun. I couldn't have enjoyed myself there after they canned the person who gave me my first break."

Heather didn't quite believe her. It was as if she wanted to appear less serious than she was.

But she didn't really care, finally, about figuring out Sandra's reason for living. She cared about figuring out her own.

It was good to search for "an exciting life." But is that enough? Don't you have to have something that sustains you through periods when excitement is nowhere to be found? Don't you have to have some guiding principle, some center?

What's *your* center? She didn't know.

It was maddening to be so unformed.

She wanted to keep talking about all this, but she no longer had Sandra to herself. A young man had arrived, a man about Heather's age.

"Jedd!" Sandra hugged him. "I thought you were still in Mexico." She looked happy to see him. As happy as she'd looked when Heather showed up? Not quite as happy? Happier?

Jedd started telling Sandra about his travels. Heather, sitting a few feet off, couldn't quite hear the words, but it was clear, somehow, that the main element of his conversational style was knowingness: he had the style of connoisseurship. This was a man who knew which wines to choose, which obscure poets to read and which to condescend to.

He was knowing, but he was humble too. He was taller than Sandra, but when he spoke to her he managed to bend over so much that he had to look up at her. He looked, Heather thought, like a dog granting dominance to a more important dog.

They talked for a few minutes; Heather, thoroughly ignored, studied them. His eyes were lively — with flirtatiousness, with ambition, with the desire to please. Sandra said something — Heather didn't catch it — and he burst into a belly laugh.

Heather thought of a research project: measuring the decibel level of laughter in social hierarchies. When Jedd made a joke, Sandra, the top dog, smiled; when Sandra made a joke, Jedd, the little dog, howled with laughter.

He was another young striver, pasting together his own act — part Don Juan, part doormat. There was something repulsive about the routine when you saw it from the outside, performed by someone other than yourself.

After the game a cluster of people headed over to Columbus Avenue for dinner. It would have been easy enough to drift along with them, but Heather didn't want to.

She hugged Sandra good-bye, perhaps too

passionately. She was always hugging people too passionately. "Are you going away or something?" Sandra said.

She felt that something was finished here. She still admired Sandra; she still wanted to get to know her; but she didn't want to become her protégée.

It wasn't that the spectacle of Jedd had transformed her. He was just the finishing touch.

Heather walked through the park, furiously thinking. Not quite thinking, really: it was more like a train wreck in her mind. Sandra, Schiller, this Jedd person . . .

Ever since she'd met her, Heather had been thinking, in the back of her mind, that she could glide from Schiller to Sandra without a hitch. For years she'd gone from mentor to mentor, like someone who crosses a stream by stepping from rock to rock. But she didn't want a mentor anymore.

She stopped at the pond near the statues of Alice and the Mad Hatter. She watched three ducks making their way across the pond: calm, matronly, inane. A gaggle of schoolgirls in uniforms — blazers, pleated skirts — passed by. They were threatening one another with ice cream cones, happily trying to push their cones into one another's faces.

Heather sat on a bench and thought of how far she had come. She remembered herself as she was at fourteen, talking to herself in front of the mirror. "Freedom has always been my theme in life." She had her freedom . . . but what came next? For the first time in her life, she had no idea.

39

Schiller took the A train from the airport back to Manhattan. He was very tired. It was three in the afternoon, but it felt like three in the morning, and in his state of jet-lagged stupidity he kept wondering why so many children were riding the train so late.

The train was crowded, not with airport commuters, but with people going about their normal lives. Most of them were black people. There was a great deal of activity here. A family was traveling with its belongings — was this what people did now instead of using moving vans? To Schiller's left, a scary-looking teenager was smoking. No one said a word to him. In Paris he had seen a shriveled old lady admonish a young man for smoking on the Métro platform, and the young man had obediently tossed the cigarette away.

A little Asian man hustled into the car carrying a box filled with trinkets: he placed a wind-up toy on the floor — a drum-major monkey — and it strutted merrily around, banging on its drum. "Five dollars! Five dollars!" Then he put down three yellow birds, battery-powered chickadees, and they flapped their wings.

A gangly teenager scooped up the closest chicken and dropped it down his shirt. The toy seller, a small man in his fifties, started yelling at the boy in fractured English. The boy smirked and tossed the chicken behind his back to one of his friends. The boys were in full glee; the toy man looked unintimidated, ready to fight for his rights; Schiller had no sense of whether this was a conflict that could lead to violence, or whether it was a more innocuous form of urban friction, a ritual familiar to each of the parties involved.

Examining the people in the subway car — people with black skin, people with brown skin — he was thinking about the fact that he couldn't imagine anything about their lives. This thought wasn't new to him: it often occurred to him when he rode the subways or walked around New York. He could never write about these lives; they were beyond the reach of his imagination.

This used to disturb him. But it didn't disturb him now — now that he was so close to the end. He had been put on earth to tell a few stories, and he was almost finished with the last of them.

He had a strange feeling in his arm. It felt empty and somehow sloshy, as if it were hollow and filled with water. Maybe he had a cold in his arm. Can there be such a thing as a cold in your arm? He had slept for a long time on the plane; maybe he'd slept on his arm.

When he got home, he dropped his bag in the hall with relief. He felt as if he could sleep for a week. He glanced through his mail and played back his messages. There was one from Ariel, and one — this surprised him — from Heather. She sounded sweet. She thanked him for his comments about her thesis and asked him to call her.

He ran a bath and eased himself in. He didn't know why he was in the mood for a bath; he hadn't had one in years.

He should have had a blissful feeling of completion. He'd kept his appointment, and now he could finish his book.

He closed his eyes, and he saw his wife's face. Not as she was in life, but as she was the last time he saw her.

Stella had died in a fire, but her body had been untouched by flames; she died of smoke inhalation. Her body was brought back to New York, and before she was cremated, he had asked to see her one last time. In the damp basement of a funeral home on the Lower East Side, he had stood over the body of the woman he loved.

Stella's beauty, when she lived, was marred by a terribly crooked row of lower teeth. One of her teeth in particular jutted up above the others; she used to refer to it as her "renegade tooth," and in moments of nervous self-assessment — when they were dressing for a party, for example — the sight of it in the mirror would make her frantically unhappy. She was always talking about having it pulled out or ground down, but somehow she never got around to doing it.

In the morgue Schiller maintained his grip on himself until he noticed that, with her mouth slightly open, he could see the tooth. Her renegade tooth had outlived her. The occasion for so many jokes, the focus of so much pointless worry — it meant nothing now.

Tonight, in the bath, her face kept floating in front of him when he closed his eyes.

He told himself it was only jet lag. He would feel better in a few days.

40

For the next few days Schiller rested. He sat in front of his typewriter each morning, but he didn't get much done. Maybe he had mixed feelings about bringing his book to an end. What would he do, who would he be, when it was finished?

He didn't return Heather's call — he was too tired — but she called him again. This surprised him. She sounded friendly and eager to see him, which surprised him still more. They arranged to have coffee on Saturday evening.

He didn't feel up to it, actually. He still had jet lag; waves of dizziness came over him whenever he stood up.

On Saturday morning he tried to work for a few hours, but he still found it hard to concentrate. In the early afternoon he took a short walk, and then he came home and read for a few hours. After a brief nap he got ready to see Heather.

His preparations were elaborate. He clipped his fingernails and toenails, cleaned out his ears with a Q-Tip, and took a shower.

Then he flossed and brushed his teeth, brushed his tongue for bad breath, and gargled with mouthwash. Then he applied deodorant, and after that he ran a comb through his hair, pretending he had enough hair to comb. He found a pair of scissors and trimmed the hairs that grew like tusks from his nostrils and sprouted luxuriantly from his earlobes. Only after all this did he take up a razor and begin to shave his face.

He was getting tired. "It's hard work to keep yourself beautiful," he said to the pale, doughy, multi-chinned face in the glass.

He'd been standing at the mirror, examining himself, for almost fifteen minutes. In the same way that your name will seem unfamiliar if you repeat it over and over, his face began to seem strange to him now.

He knew that if he looked away for just a minute, he could bring it back to its everyday shape. But he couldn't look away.

Stella's face, once again, came floating before his eyes: Stella's face as it had looked in the morgue, vacated of intelligence and wit and tenderness and anger. He closed his eyes, and when he opened them he saw only his own face. Looking at his own face, he was aware, as he had not previously been aware in other than a theoretical way, that before too many years were through, this face too would be vacated. This body, this face, would remain after his consciousness was gone. It was the kind of thought that stuns you when you're a child, and that ceases to stun you only because as you age you lose your capacity for wonder.

The vividness of the realization, and his tiredness, and the undercurrent of futility that he had felt during this afternoon's effort to make himself something like handsome, gave rise to the thought that all he'd been doing during the last half hour was dressing the corpse.

He had an odd feeling in the back of his head, as if something were pressing from inside, trying to get out. He put down the razor and sat on the lid of the toilet seat. The water was running in the sink. He would meet her, of course, but there was something else to think about first. He had a sudden tightness in his arm — that damnable feeling of water in his arm, where did it come from? — and then a tightness in his neck. There was something to think about here. There was something about getting Tolstoy out of the shoe box so he could write the postcard over again, which might not be fair. What? Things were swaying. Things were swaying very dear.

41

Heather made a point of getting to the Argo a few minutes early. She was looking forward to seeing him. His absence from New York, she thought, had been like a punctuation mark, bringing an end to the period when she had been his worshiper and, finally, his betrayer. Now she hoped they could start afresh, on a calmer note. He was important to her, and she hoped that she could continue to see him from time to time.

By about ten after six, when he still hadn't shown up, she realized that he was deliberately making her wait. He had never been late before.

She didn't mind. It would have been better if he'd found a less passive-aggressive way to show that he was hurt by what she'd written about him, but if this was how he wanted to do it, she could handle it.

By twenty after six, she was annoyed. She called him and got his phone machine. She left a message.

By six-thirty, she was worried. She walked to his building. It was a windy day; scraps of paper were skittering over the sidewalk.

Keep this in your head. She had a sudden feeling that she should try to remember everything about this day.

Jeff, the doorman she liked, was on duty. She asked him if Schiller had gone out.

"He took a little walk around two, but he came home over an hour ago. He hasn't been down since then. I would have seen him if he had." He delivered this report with an air of professional pride.

She told him there might be a problem. He came with her to the fifteenth floor. She opened Schiller's door with the keys he had given her. There was water in the hall.

"Maybe you'd better stay here," Jeff said. She ignored this and walked ahead of him. She walked quickly to the bathroom, where Schiller, dressed in his robe, was sitting on the floor.

He seemed preoccupied with something in his mouth. He kept opening and closing his mouth, with a look of worry.

"Leonard?" she said. He looked up at her; there was an expression of urgency in his eyes.

"Are you all right?" she said.

He didn't answer her; he just kept looking urgently into her eyes.

"Let me help you up," Jeff said. He came into the room and kneeled and tried to put

340

his arm around Schiller's body.

"You're very ambitious," Schiller murmured.

This remark gave Heather hope. Maybe he was all right after all.

Jeff, a small man, couldn't get Schiller off the floor. Schiller didn't seem concerned; he sat in the water moving his tongue around his mouth in an exploratory way. Heather went to help, and together she and Jeff lifted him onto the toilet seat.

She left the bathroom and called 911. When she returned Jeff had turned off the water in the sink and was trying to calm Schiller down. "We're getting an ambulance for you, Professor," he said.

Schiller looked confused. His fingers — his long, soft, white fingers — kept fluttering on Jeff's sleeve.

The paramedics arrived quickly. One of them, a scholarly-looking young man, shined a pencil flashlight into Schiller's eyes and asked him to count backward from ten. "I'm too old for that," Schiller said. "That's a young man's game."

The other one, a man with his hair combed back slickly — he looked like Pat Riley — asked Heather a series of questions about Schiller's medical condition, few of which she was able to answer.

They put him on a gurney and took him out of the room. He was staring at the ceiling; he didn't seem aware of Heather as he was wheeled past her.

"Where are you taking him?" she said, at the last minute. They said they were taking him to Roosevelt Hospital.

They wheeled him out of the apartment; he had a breathing mask on his face and little suction cups attached to his chest.

"Don't worry too much, Miss Wolfe," Jeff said. "The professor's a tough old bird." Then he went back downstairs and she was left alone.

She went to the kitchen, found a mop, and spent the next ten minutes cleaning up the water in his bathroom and hall. She needed to do something that didn't require thought.

She had an urge just to go home and pretend all this hadn't happened. She didn't want to follow him to the hospital; she didn't want to sit by his bedside while he died. She didn't want to see him in a devastated state, like some meal left out in the sun. She had a mental picture of a Mexican dinner on a picnic table in August: the guacamole turning sour, the cheese going globby and rancid, the refried beans looking like farts would look if farts had bodies.

Schiller as a Mexican dinner. She wished

she could scoop her mind out of her head and replace it with another mind, a mind more worthy of tragedy.

She tried to organize herself. What did she need to do? She needed to call Ariel and she needed to go to the hospital.

She called information but Ariel wasn't listed. Heather thought she might be listed under her exercise business, but she couldn't remember the business's name.

She found Schiller's address book in his bedroom. Ariel was listed under *S* rather than under *A*, which Heather for some reason found surprising. She made an effort to compose herself before she picked up the phone.

She called, got Ariel's machine, and left a clear, calm message; when she hung up she was proud of herself. I'm cool in a crisis, she thought. I'm omni-competent. Then she remembered that she hadn't mentioned which hospital Schiller was in. So she had to call again.

She had never had to deal with the death or serious illness of anyone she loved. She sat on Schiller's bed, and she tried to gather strength for what was ahead of her.

42

Heather was in the waiting room. Don't die, don't die, don't die.

He was in intensive care. That was all she knew.

Their last encounter had been so miserable — when he had his attack in the museum, and they went to the coffee shop together, and she went half out of her mind with impatience as he told her about the great critics he had known. It was intolerable to think that that might turn out to have been the last time they'd ever see each other — after all that respect, all that learning, all that . . . love.

She wanted to break into the intensive care unit and find him and say, "You can't die now, damn it! Not after I hurt you like that!"

She was on her fifth cup of vending-machine coffee when Ariel came in. She was dressed in flowered tights and sneakers and a torn sweatshirt. She looked like an off-duty clown.

She walked up rapidly and, to Heather's surprise, gave her a big hug.

"How is he?"

"I don't know."

"What happened to him? Did they tell you what happened?"

"They said they can't be sure yet. They think it was a stroke."

"Can I see him?"

"I don't know. You have to find his doctor."

Ariel was a generation older than Heather, but with her patterned leggings, with her hair all agog, with her purple knapsack and her thick white socks and her cross-training sneakers, she seemed, in Heather's eyes, to be a child. She had an expression of five-year-old disbelief: she looked like a child who had just found out there was no Tooth Fairy.

"If my father dies before I've had a baby, I don't know what I'll do," she said.

Heather pressed her hand and smiled with an air, she hoped, of sympathy. She was thinking: What a jerk. She supposed she should feel touched that this woman was speaking to her in such an unguarded way, but she couldn't help wondering what having a *baby* had to do with anything. Your father is *dying,* for God's sake.

"You don't know the doctor's name?" Ariel said.

Heather shook her head.

Ariel walked off in search of the doctor. Heather put her head back and closed her eyes, and when she closed her eyes she saw Schiller sitting in the water on his bathroom floor.

Everything would be all right if she could just erase the memory of those ten minutes from her head.

She started to wonder what would happen to her thesis if Schiller died. She wondered if she'd have to revise it.

She wondered briefly whether she should feel guilty for thinking about this. She decided that she shouldn't. You can care about somebody's illness and still be worrying about your own career.

It made her think more charitably of Ariel, though. Worrying about having a baby might be stupid at a time like this, but worrying about your career was even worse.

43

When Casey got the call from Ariel, he was sitting at home browsing idly through the latest issue of *Salmagundi*.

"Case?" she said. "My daddy's in the hospital."

He would never forget that: "My daddy."

"What happened?"

"I don't know. I mean, he had a stroke. But I don't really know what happened. They found him in the tub."

She asked him to come to the hospital. When he got off the phone he thought that things were suddenly different between them — different than they'd been the day before. A relationship that was still new — in this incarnation at least — was suddenly going to have to bear up under a great new weight.

He thought of how good Ariel had been to him on the day he found out his mother was dying.

He changed his clothes and got ready to go. As he was changing into a respectable pair of pants and a sport jacket — he had the feeling that situations of crisis had to be met with dignity — he felt as if he were preparing for battle.

He took a cab up to Roosevelt and made his way to the ICU. Ariel was pacing in front of the nurses' station; when she saw him she ran up to him and flew into his arms; but her embrace, which he'd expected would be whole-souled, was curiously distracted and insubstantial. She'd barely put her arms around him before she stepped back and said, "I'm so scared."

"How is he?"

"They don't know. He had a stroke. They don't know what's going to happen."

A young woman was sitting near the coffee machine, looking at him. At first he thought it was one of his old students; then he wondered if it was just some stranger who found him attractive. Then she came forward and said, "Hi, I'm Heather Wolfe. I'm a friend of Leonard's." This was the woman Ariel had told him about, the woman who was writing something about Ariel's father.

He'd heard so much about this girl from Ariel, who always spoke about her with spikiness and envy, that he'd desired her without ever having met her. You desire the woman who intimidates the woman you desire.

The young woman had an air of confidence and purpose. It seemed, perhaps, excessive — what seemed excessive was that she had come up to introduce herself while he and Ariel were having a private moment — but it was attractive too.

Ariel, by contrast, looked haggard, ragged, old. He never would have used these words to describe her before, but her grief made her face red and blotchy; there were clingy clumps of cat hair all over her leotard; and the younger woman beside her was so vivid — just glancing at her made you feel as if you'd inhaled a hit of pure oxygen — that Ariel looked blurred around the edges.

This was an annoyance. He wished the young woman wasn't here. He didn't like having a foxy young thing around when he wanted to be giving all his attention to Ariel.

Ariel took Casey's arm and deposited it on her shoulder and led him a few steps away from Heather so they could talk.

"I'm so scared," she said again.

No matter what happened to her father now, their lives were going to be changed. His guess was that her father wasn't coming back from this one. Love, during the middle years, is in great part a matter of accompanying your beloved through life's disasters.

"If I fall apart," she said, "will you take care of me?"

"I would if you did, but you won't."

Please don't, he thought. Please don't fall apart.

This isn't precisely what I'd bargained for, he thought.

And then he thought: This isn't precisely what I'd bargained for, but I'll take it.

He had no right to be surprised by her question. This was who she was: a woman who falls apart. He knew this; he had always known it. He had known about her college breakdown, and as soon as they got back together she'd told him about her California breakdown of a year ago. This is a woman who needs to be taken care of. During these last two months together she'd been perpetually buoyant — all laughter, lightness, and lust — but he should have known that that couldn't last forever.

"They're calling it a stroke," Ariel said, "but I wonder if they really know. I'm wondering if it might just be stress. I know he's been having a hard time finishing his book. Sometimes you can have too much stress and it's like you just snap, but it's not necessarily a bad thing. You kind of snap just to get the pressure off yourself, but it can be like . . . it can be like going on a vacation."

A little vacation, which leaves the man unconscious and on life support. Casey drew his breath in slowly, not knowing what to say. He was astonished at her powers of self-deception.

44

Who was this little black guy, so proper and perfect, with his carefully pressed chinos and his tasteful tweeds? Obviously he was Ariel's boyfriend, but what was his story? Heather couldn't figure out his body language; she couldn't figure out what he was. He looked like the kind of black guy you might see in an L.L. Bean catalog, modeling some corny plaid shirt. He looked as if he were impersonating a professor. He looked, she thought, like a black guy imitating a white guy imitating a black guy.

She had nothing better to think about because for the last two hours she had been breaking her brain on the thought that Schiller was going to die. Her mind had gone mute; there was nothing more to think about the subject.

So maybe it was time to leave. Clearly these two didn't want her here. Ariel had steered her boyfriend into the corner, as smoothly as if he had wheels, and now the two of them were huddled together and he was comforting her.

She felt lonely. There was no one to comfort *her*.

She wanted to talk to them. She'd had a strange ride with Schiller this winter and spring, but he was still an important person in her life. These two were the only other people she knew who cared about him, and she wished that they would let her in.

She drifted up to them again, which took an effort, because it would be humiliating if they ran away again.

She stood awkwardly near them, but they stayed in their huddle. She sensed that the guy was aware of her, that he was sympathetic — she didn't know how she knew this — but Ariel kept her head close to his and seemed to tighten her grip on the guy's arms. Heather had forgotten his name.

I'm hurting too, she wanted to say. But she couldn't say it. It was too corny, for one thing, and for another thing, she wasn't the star of this show. Ariel was the man's daughter. Compared to that bond, Heather was just passing through.

"I guess I'll go," Heather said. She wanted them to tell her not to, but Ariel nodded distractedly and the man didn't react at all.

Out on the street she was surprised to find that it was only nine o'clock. It was nine o'clock on a Saturday. She felt as if it were about three o'clock in the morning, and it certainly didn't feel like a Saturday. It felt like a day they didn't have a name for.

She didn't want to go back to Hoboken. It was too lonely there. She didn't know where to go. She walked to Ninth Avenue and went into a bar, but everybody was laughing and shouting. How can these people act like this? she thought.

She took the IRT up to 96th Street. There was a different doorman in the lobby — she didn't recognize him, but she must have met him before: he asked her how "the professor" was doing.

She let herself in to his apartment and double-locked the door. She didn't know why; she didn't know who she was double-locking it against. She didn't even know why she had come, except that it was the closest she could get to being with him.

His apartment seemed quieter than other people's apartments somehow.

Except for the one dim light in the hallway, she didn't turn on any lights. She tried to walk very lightly. He would probably never come back here. She felt the chill of how little a life might mean.

She stood in his living room looking at his bookshelves. All these thousands of books were waiting for him. What would all these books do if he never came back?

She looked out the window. You could see a slice of the river, although at this hour all you could see was the darkness where you knew the river was.

She went into his bedroom and lay on his bed, remembering their night together. Then she went into his study and sat at his writing table.

Here she could feel him. She could feel the force of his character: she could feel the years of labor, the years of patience, the years of frustration, the years of devotion.

What surprised her was that it felt calm.

It was so strange to be here, with all of his things waiting for him, not knowing whether he would ever return. Maybe he'd be back here in a week, working at this desk, or maybe he'd never be back here again.

The room was very bare. There was the writing table, there were the boxes of manuscript, and there was the big manual typewriter. Nothing else.

She thought that it was time to read the book he had been writing.

Would it be better *not* to read it? Would it be more respectful? His novel was still unfinished; she felt sure that he wouldn't have wanted anyone to read it in this state.

But if she didn't read it, who would? Probably no one. His daughter hadn't even read all the books he'd published. And Heather found it hard to imagine that publishers would be falling over themselves to get a look at Leonard Schiller's unfinished last novel.

She began to read the manuscript, which was apparently still untitled. The subject matter was familiar: the first part of the book, at least, was about the early years of his marriage. She was glad that he'd returned to this part of his life — in Heather's mind, it was probably his one true subject.

He wasn't remembering the past through a haze of nostalgia. His point of view was, if anything, drier and more disillusioned than it used to be.

In the first chapter, the wife — named Elizabeth in this book — is carrying on an affair with a French philosopher, and the husband, Stanley, is tamely, lamely putting up with it. In an early scene, just after Stanley and Elizabeth have finished making love, the phone rings, and, still naked, she answers it and chats calmly with her lover while her husband sits on the bed in despair.

It was a sharp and not very flattering portrait of his wife. But Schiller wasn't sparing himself either. In the third chapter, Elizabeth has been away for days, and Stanley is at home writing. Their daughter, Eve, sixteen months old, who has been cranky for days, is crying in her room. Stanley keeps on working, annoyed with her, assuming that she's merely afraid of the dark. After ignoring her for hours, he finally looks in on her, and finds that she has a blisteringly high fever. He takes her to the hospital, enduring a nightmarish ride with a deranged taxi driver through the rain-swept night. Stanley's negligence, his self-absorption, turn out to have serious consequences: Eve is suffering from an ear infection which, because he waited so long to get help, has left her with permanently damaged hearing in one ear.

Heather had no idea whether any of this was true.

The novel, or this part of it, didn't seem to be a portrait of moral monsters. Rather, Schiller seemed to be trying to write in an unvarnished way about two complicated people — strong-willed and blundering people intent on living their lives.

She read the first part of the novel with a mounting joy. She forgot that Schiller was in a hospital room, probably dying. All she could think about was that he had done it, he'd actually done it: at the end of his life, he had written his strongest book.

This feeling didn't last. She'd been reading

for less than an hour when she started to realize that the book was fading. The problem, she thought, was simple: he was too damned old.

The book was written in what she thought of as an old man's style. For a few pages, a few chapters, this wasn't a problem, but it grew to be a problem as the book wore on. When he reached passages that required force, strength, intensity, he couldn't quite rise to the occasion.

And the book was poorly organized. He would return to the same scenes in chapter after chapter, writing about them in a slightly different way. She couldn't understand why he was doing this. All too often, the second and third versions of a scene had less power than the first. Why had he included the weaker versions? It was as if he'd lost his ability to discriminate between what was best and what was worst in his work.

After a hundred and fifty pages, she couldn't bring herself to read on. It made her too sad. She had the feeling that this could have been Schiller's best book, because it was the least sentimental — he now approached his subject matter with the coldness of a surgeon — but that he simply lacked the physical strength to carry it off. He had begun it too late.

★ ★ ★

She had once read that an artist is someone who stands outside in rainstorms hoping
to be struck by lightning. Schiller had been
struck by lightning twice in his life, with
those first two books. He had spent the rest
of his life waiting, but the lightning had never
struck him again.

She was sure that this was the truth about
him, but she didn't know what it added up
to. She didn't know if he was a hero or if he
had wasted his life.

45

At about ten o'clock a doctor finally appeared. He told Ariel that her father had suffered a stroke, and that he was still unconscious. He wasn't in a coma, which the doctor said was a good sign, but it was impossible to know how extensive the damage was. "It'll be twenty-four hours or so before we really know where we are."

In the hours since she had arrived there, this was the first time she'd talked with someone her own age. Everyone else was much younger, as if high school students had taken over the hospital for a class play.

Dr. Rubin seemed serious and sympathetic, so she could believe her father was in good hands.

"Can I see him?" she said.

"It wouldn't be advisable for you to see him anytime soon."

"But I want to."

"You wouldn't be doing him any good. He wouldn't know you're there."

She couldn't bear the thought that some man who didn't know her father, who didn't love him, had the power to keep her away from him.

"You can't know that," Ariel said. "I know you're trying to do your job. Maybe you're even trying to be nice to me. You don't want me to be upset by what he looks like. But he's my father. I'm scared for him, and I want to see him again. This may be the last chance I can get to see him alive. Isn't that right?"

He didn't answer.

"Isn't that right?"

"I can't make any promises," he said.

"So I'd like to see him now please."

Dr. Rubin brought her to Schiller's room in the intensive care unit. Her father was lying under a thin sheet. When she entered, she couldn't see his face; she recognized him by his feet — his oddly small and delicate white feet.

He had a tube down his throat and another in his arm and another that went under the sheet, God knows where. His soft fat face was laboring. He was half-shaved: parts of his face were clean-shaven and other parts bore a two-day growth of beard.

He was attached to a machine of some sort, which was softly working away in the corner.

Despite the labor of the machine and the tube down his throat and the terror that was clouding her thinking, she nevertheless believed that she could sense the activity of his soul. She felt that his soul was hesitating about whether to leave the room, and she believed that if he was reluctant it was because he was concerned about her: he didn't want to leave her unguarded.

She drew closer; she put her hands on his chest, very lightly. And with this touch her perception of him changed. Somehow she knew now that whether he struggled back to life or let go of life would not depend on her. He had his own soul's journey. She would have liked to believe that his primary mission on earth was to take care of her, but she knew that that had never been true. She understood that her father, who had painfully learned tenderness toward her in the years since her mother died, was still radically alone in the world, and that his soul had its own itinerary.

What could she say to him, in what might be their last moment together? She wished she could invent a new language: "I love you" seemed so inadequate. But she didn't have a new language, so she said the old words to him, the inadequate words; she whispered them over and over and over.

46

Schiller could hear her.

He would have liked to tell her that he loved her, but he was too far under. He thought he had written it down somewhere, maybe in his will, but he wasn't sure.

After a while she was gone, and other people were in the room with him, taking care of the tubes that were attached to his body. *Skilled attendants have been ministering faithfully to his medical needs.*

Who said that?

He tried to lift his head, but he couldn't.

Our own concerns lie elsewhere. We find ourselves called upon to comment on the aesthetic and "personal" achievements of the estimable personage who lies before us in this humbled state.

Who was speaking? Who was that? Who? Schiller was alone in the hospital room, but someone was speaking — a man with a half-baked English accent. He tried to raise himself up, but he couldn't.

The desire to serve as a midwife to beauty, to bring forth works of high and lasting merit, has been, for Schiller, that which superseded all oth-

ers. It has been an interesting effort, an interesting lifelong effort, and although we must sadly note that he has failed to leave behind the magnificent literary monuments of which, in the dear bright days of untested youth, he dreamed, he can nevertheless count himself among the ranks of the distinguished, simply in having been a votary, even if a not wholly competent votary, of a humane and transcendent ideal.

There was this strange voice, and there was also an annoying clacking sound. With the greatest effort, Schiller managed to turn his head. Two figures were in the corner: an old man, standing, dressed with ridiculous formality in an antique three-piece suit, and a young woman, seated at a small desk, pounding effortfully at an ancient typewriter.

To the eye of the unsympathetic observer, his may have seemed singularly devoid of the qualities that make a life "worth" living, but to Schiller and to others of our little tribe, a life like his, almost wholly consecrated to the art of the difficult, is rich in the subtlest and most valuable remunerations. In this there is experience, in this there are the deepest and most abiding joys!

Schiller finally recognized the man. It was Henry James. Henry James was writing a letter about him. He was dictating it to his faithful secretary — what was her name?

Miss Bosanquet? Henry James and Miss Bosanquet — still together after all this time! The thought almost made Schiller weep.

But why is he speaking about me in the past tense?

When speaking of the consecration of one's life to the pursuit of the beneficent complexities of art, we do not of course intend to imply that this pursuit can honorably take pride of place before those cherished "natural ties" that can be said to lie near the heart of any disposition in which the qualities of tenderness and nobility of soul are prominent. The affection of the writer in question for his daughter has been a vivid and beautiful fixture in a life marked in the main by disappointment and uncertainty.

I should go so far as to hazard that if, at the end of the journey upon which he seems fated, on no very distant day, to embark, he were to be informed by the receiving angel that although his accomplishments in the realm of art have been viewed from that height as lamentably insignificant, closer in kind to the scribblings in the sand of a child than to the sublime productions of a Bach or a Tolstoy — productions which sound their notes of deep unceasing felicity not merely in mortal domains but even through the high bright vaults of the eternal — he was nevertheless to be fondly welcomed into the reposeful and blessed hereafter, having been judged to merit that distinction by virtue of the shining solidity of his affection for his daughter and wife, then he should be glad to be admitted on those terms, and would rest content with the knowledge that a life spent loving these two had been a life eminently well spent.

Henry James was in the corner, dictating Schiller's letter of recommendation to heaven. But it was so difficult to make sense of James's late style! His sentences always made sense after you read them a few times, but when you heard them spoken they were almost impossible to follow. What had Ariel said when she'd read that passage from James at the airport? He couldn't remember.

Schiller got the impression that James was trying to set up a double argument: Schiller should be admitted to heaven because he was an artist; but if his art was maybe not good enough to qualify, then he should be admitted anyway, because he had loved Stella and Ariel.

Again he wanted to lift himself up — this time in protest: How dare you say that my art wasn't good enough! "The not wholly competent votary of a humane and transcendent ideal." Fuck you!

And who the hell are you to speak about me in the past tense — you're the one who's dead!

But he couldn't rise, and he couldn't speak.

Anyway, it was impossible to stay angry for long. That was just the way James was — he never gave false praise. And even so, with all that, James had spoken of Schiller as a member of "our little tribe" — that in itself was a grander compliment than he ever could have hoped for.

Another thing that got in the way of his anger was his interest in the fact that James had apparently changed his mind about Tolstoy. . . .

It was all very interesting . . . but it was too difficult to think about it all now. It was too much of a strain. Schiller lapsed back — he would have lapsed back if he could move — and tried to think of what he had to do.

47

Casey and Ariel took a taxi down to her place. They stopped at the deli, as they often did. Usually Ariel bought snacks for herself and treats for Sancho, but tonight she just hung back by the door. Casey hadn't eaten anything since lunch; he got two roast beef sandwiches on sesame rolls with cole slaw, tomato, and Russian dressing, and two bottles of beer.

They walked up to her apartment in silence. Sancho greeted them at the door, smoothing his flank against their shins as they tried to pass. Ariel dumped her backpack on the floor, fell on the couch, grabbed the remote control and turned on the TV. A rerun of *Sisters* was on Lifetime; Swoosie Kurtz's daughter had joined the Moonies and Swoosie didn't know what to do. Ariel stared blankly at the screen; Sancho jumped on her lap and she pushed him away.

Casey sat at her table eating his dinner. He felt guilty to be eating. That he could eat two sandwiches while her father was dying, that he could polish off a beer, condemned him in his own eyes as a brute. Into his mind strayed a phrase from nowhere: "Absence of grief eats."

He wasn't, in fact, a brute; he wasn't absent of grief. He cared about her, and he cared about her father. But he didn't know how to help.

She touched her clicker again and the TV went off. She lay back and closed her eyes.

He wasn't even sure she wanted him here. She was ignoring him. He felt hurt by this, even as he realized the feeling was ridiculous.

"I don't know what to do," she said. "I don't even know what to want. Do I want him to get better? But how much better is he ever gonna get? Do I want him to die, so he won't have to suffer anymore? Anything that happens from now on will be bad."

"You don't know that," he said. "I think you should want him to get better. He's still got a lot of life left in him, your old man." Casey didn't quite believe this, but it seemed like a good thing to say.

"I can accept it that he's going to die," Ariel said. "But I can't accept it that he's going to be dead forever."

He didn't understand this, and he didn't try to. There are certain situations in which you can't convey what you mean. Words don't always work.

She had helped him in a comparable time.

Years ago, after he and Ariel had broken up but before they'd lost touch with each other, he'd received word one day that his mother's cancer had returned. It had metastasized in her liver, which meant that she only had a few months to live. It was a frigid afternoon in December when he got the news; he was in his office at the Graduate Center on 42nd Street, grading papers. He booked a seat on a flight to Florida for the next morning, and when he got off the phone he sat there looking out the window. There was nothing you could do to slow life down. His mother was alive, and in a few months she wouldn't be alive, and there was nothing he could do about it. And though he told himself that when he went to see her he would cherish every moment, cherish it so fiercely that time would come to a halt, he knew that that wouldn't happen, and that just as surely as he was sitting there in his office at that moment he would be sitting there in a week, having returned from his trip, and he'd be sitting there in a few months, having returned from putting her in the ground.

He'd put an end to these profitless musings and tried to reach Ariel. She wasn't in, so he left a message on her machine. He left his office and walked downtown toward home, along a route that took him past her place, and he kept stopping at pay phones along the way to see if she'd come home yet.

He was on the corner of 24th and Third, making his fifth and probably last try — he still had the receiver to his ear — when he saw her. She was walking down Third Avenue, wearing an orange beret. He knew she'd picked up his message because her face expressed everything: her joy on coming across him and her sorrow about his mother. "I was looking for you," she said. "I wanted to make you a tuna casserole."

They went to the supermarket and bought tuna, peas, mushroom soup, and macaroni; after they took their place on the checkout line she dashed off and returned with a bag of potato chips. "It's the finishing touch," she said. "We need this for the crust." They went up to her place, and he sat, drained, on her couch, while Ariel made the casserole, this meal from some mythical American childhood, and kept up a steady stream of jokes — jokes that were gentle enough to fit the moment, that didn't seem tactless or disrespectful of his unhappiness — and while Sancho, who was only a kitten then, acted like a show-off, leaping from the top of the refrigerator to the top of the bookcase and balancing precariously as the fragile bookcase swayed. Ariel's warmth — which was

filled with humor, not drippily solicitous —
comforted him as much as he could be comforted that night.

When he remembered that day, he could
still feel the pain of it. But he could also feel
the sudden shock of joy that had risen in him
when he spotted her, sauntering down the
block in her beret, a vision of color and life
and lightness in the gray day.

He didn't feel he had anything comparable
to give to her now. He didn't have the same
intuitive knowledge of what she needed. He
didn't quite think that a tuna casserole would
do the trick. If she asked him for anything,
he could try to provide it; but she wasn't
asking.

He slept for a while, waking at about one
in the morning. She was still dressed, walking back and forth by the foot of the bed.

"All I can do is pace," she said.

He got up and embraced her, but he could
sense that she didn't want to be embraced.
He let her go, and stood there lamely next
to her.

"I don't know what to do," she said.

It was a strange feeling: to care about her
as much as he could care about anyone, but
to be unable to share her experience.

Her father would be dead soon; she was
an orphan now. For most people her age,

the word would be inappropriate, but for Ariel it fit.

Casey thought of a phrase he'd once read in some collection of letters — he couldn't remember whose. It was some great man of our age — Marx or Freud or someone like that. One of the founders. Writing to a friend whose father had died, the great man had said, "It will revolutionize your soul." The death of Casey's parents had revolutionized his soul. He had loved his parents, and he'd suffered deeply when each of them died; but in the years after they died, he came to feel he breathed a freer air.

He knew that Ariel was at the beginning of the great and terrible journey, the journey into the experience of death. But everyone's journey is different, and there was no way he could accompany her on hers. How lonely everyone is!

"I don't know what to do," she said. She sat in a little easy chair, a chair she had bought with great pride recently in an effort to make her apartment nicer.

He wanted to say: "I'll protect you." But he kept silent, because he knew that he couldn't protect her.

48

In the middle of the night, when the only light to see by was the thin dim line thrown from the nurses' station, Schiller was awake.

He was almost free.

It had been hours since Ariel had come to tell him that she loved him. But time had no meaning in the realms through which he now moved, and she had visited him often during the night to repeat her message.

He knew, somehow, that she feared that her words were inadequate. He wished he could have let her know that her fear was unfounded. In his new condition, the language had been swept clean, and it was as if the words she had spoken had never been spoken before. They glistened with the purity of her feelings.

He wished he could tell her about all the things he had discovered in his new state.

We are more than our bodies; we are other than our bodies. Schiller understood this now.

He understood that we are not merely bodies and minds; each of us is, or has, a bundle of light. In and around the body, we are bundles of light. If you had to describe this light, you could say that it is warm, wet, blue; that it nourishes us, and is nourished by us; and that it is a sort of repository for our memories and our visions. Nothing of what we are is ever lost, for it is stored in the intelligence of the body's light.

He understood now why his arm, during the last week, had felt as if it were filled with water. It wasn't water, it was the wet blue light. Without quite realizing it, he had been gradually becoming aware of this substance that protects us, contains us, and survives us.

Schiller was floating somewhere above the bed. He looked down at his body: the hulking bulk of the torso, the gnarled, disappointed mouth, the nose as thick and twisted as a tree root. His body was worn out; he was ready to cast it off.

He — his consciousness, his being — was attached to that body only by glowing threads of light.

He understood that his task was to undo those threads. It was the finest, the noblest task he had ever undertaken — it was his true life's work. And to think that it was only this evening that he had discovered it! For many years he had considered himself too old to learn anything new, yet now he was engaged in the most momentous learning of his life — more important, more surprising, more strange, than his discovery, at the age of two, of his power of speech.

He remembered what it was to be an infant and to learn to speak. He had never realized that he could remember this, but now he remembered it clearly. He was under the kitchen table, lying on his stomach, in the apartment on Cruger Avenue. There were sounds, and after the sounds his mother picked him up. When she was lifting him, he realized . . . he realized everything. He realized that he had made the sounds, and that she wasn't just picking him up *after* the sounds, but *because* of them. The birth of his understanding of language was also the birth of his understanding of the laws of cause and effect, and it was also the birth of his understanding of time. It was everything.

That moment of comprehension was wonderful, but this one was incomparably richer. The understanding he was gaining now was at least as vast, and now he could *appreciate* what he was learning, as he could not when he was a child. Now he understood that our birth into the world of the body is only our first birth, and by no means the most important. He was laboring — this beautiful labor — on his second birth. He was undoing the threads that kept him bound to the body. To dissolve them was to become a creature of light. He thought about one of the threads, and it dissolved. He never knew that liberation could be so simple, so full of joy. This was the work he was made for, the work we are all made for.

He labored at this — if it could be called labor, it was so pleasant — all through the night. You think about each thread, each blue stream of glowing light, and you take the light into you.

Death was so easy, so pleasant, and it involved so much learning, such beautiful learning. He wondered if everyone's death was like this. Had it been like this for his father? Had it been like this for Stella? He had the sense that he shouldn't be thinking about any of this now — it was a distraction from his work — but now that he'd started he couldn't stop.

He thought that death might have been like this, all those years ago, for his father — comfortable in his hospital bed, dying sweetly in the night. But for Stella, in the burning hotel room in Pittsburgh, it could not have brought such pleasure. Death must greet each of us differently.

The thought of Stella interrupted his progress. The blistering heat, the confusion, the terror: it couldn't have been joyful. Stella had been cheated of a joyful death. It was unfair, and he wouldn't stand for it.

What was happening to him? Suddenly he didn't know whether the experience of the last few hours had happened at all. It could have been delirium, mirage. He didn't know where he was. He *thought* he was still hovering above his body, but he couldn't be sure.

The last stream of light that bound him to his body was still glowing wetly, glowing blue. It originated in a spot just below the navel of the man on the bed. He didn't want to undo it; he didn't want to dissolve that last stream. *Not without Stella,* he thought. He had the wild thought that he could rescue her from that burning building in Pittsburgh. But that was more than twenty years ago!

He felt utterly confused, and he wanted to cry.

He had reached the point in his labor at which the stream was dissolving by itself. In order to die, all he had to do was let it happen. But he *couldn't* let it happen; he had to hold on. He had to stay alive. He had work to do; he had that book to finish. It was his last tribute to Stella, damn it, and he'd be damned if he was going to let go of it now. He felt himself sinking back toward his body. The body exerted a gravitational force; the closer he sank toward it, the more fiercely it pulled him in. He began to lose the knowledge of what he was doing in the air; he fell back toward the body sickeningly, with anguish, and his mind began to shut down, because he had seen too much to be allowed to keep the vision. As his being — that vast and warm and liquid blue intelligence — poured back into the limited, stricken, pain-wracked body, he realized he was forgetting everything he had just learned.

49

Ariel wheeled her father out the big automatic doors and onto the sidewalk near Ninth Avenue. It was a beautiful day in June. The warm spring wind blew a few long strands of his hair over his eyes. To Ariel, it looked enjoyable, but she had no idea whether he was enjoying it at all.

Casey hailed a cab; he and Ariel helped Schiller into the backseat and Ariel slid in beside him while Casey folded up the wheelchair and put it in the trunk.

As they turned the corner Schiller tilted heavily against her. He felt extraordinarily heavy. He'd lost a little weight in the hospital; why did he feel so heavy now?

Maybe it wasn't just heaviness: it was that there was a new, peculiarly inert quality to his weight.

You can know everything. If you're sensitive enough, alert enough, you can know everything about everyone. The feel of her father's body was enough to tell her that much of his life force had fled.

When they got to 94th Street, Casey took the wheelchair out of the trunk and Jeff came out of the building and the three of them helped Schiller back into the wheelchair.

"Great to have you back, Professor," Jeff said.

Casey was prepared to wheel Schiller in, but Schiller took Jeff's hand and squeezed it. Casey and Ariel waited. Schiller didn't let go. Ariel began to feel embarrassed — enough already — but Jeff didn't try to take away his hand.

Ariel had visited her father in the hospital every day, and she'd stayed at his apartment, alone or with Casey, on the weekends. Every Friday night she had put Sancho in his traveling box, taken a cab uptown, and camped out here until Sunday. She was trying to give the apartment a lived-in feeling, trying to keep it warm for her father's return.

Probably it hadn't mattered. If the place had been left shuttered and airless, Schiller probably wouldn't have cared. But it mattered to Ariel. It mattered intensely to be able to believe, as she sat in the living room with Sancho in her lap, crying through a Bette Davis movie, that she was doing something to help her father get well.

Ariel and Casey wheeled Schiller out of the elevator and toward his door. She was about to insert the key in the lock but he put out his hand: he wanted to do it himself.

She pushed the wheelchair down the hall and into the living room, which was filled with spring light. Schiller looked around the room: the thousands of books, the couch and the chairs and the tables that he had lived with for decades.

She brought him into the kitchen. "Can I get you something to drink? Would you like some tea?"

He shook his head heavily, as if she had asked him a tragic question, a question of Shakespearean resonance. No tea.

Casey was standing awkwardly near the door.

"I should get back to work," he said. His school year was over, but he was working day and night on his magazine. "Take care now," he said to Schiller. "Good to have you back home."

Schiller made a low sound in his throat and attempted a smile.

Ariel walked Casey to the door and they kissed good-bye in the hall.

"How does he seem to you?" she said.

"Well, he's home. That's the important thing," Casey said, and the elevator came, and without answering her question he was gone.

Back in the kitchen her father was trying

to open a jar of jelly. He was giving it all he had. She reached out to help him, but he turned away from her, bringing the jar closer to his body.

She made a phone call to one of her clients. When she came back to the kitchen he was intently spreading jelly over a piece of toast. The toaster was overturned on the counter. She watched him as, concentrating hard, he manipulated the blunt butter knife, and she finally understood what he was doing. When he was finished with his snack he would laboriously and methodically wash the dishes, and then he would apply himself, with the same grim intentness, to setting the toaster right. He was training himself to be self-sufficient again.

He said "Thank you," in a loud, barking voice, with all the consonants mangled. He was a quiet man, normally, and this shout was unlike him. She didn't know what he was thanking her for.

After he had cleaned up, he asked for his walker. At his doctor's suggestion, she had bought a walker for him. She carried it into the kitchen and he haltingly made his way into the living room with it. She helped him down into his easy chair; he pointed to the newspaper and she gave it to him. He put it on his lap.

He hadn't read anything in the last month, and he didn't read the newspaper now. He just wanted to have it in his lap, apparently, to remind himself who he was.

Then he put his head back against the chair and closed his eyes. His efforts in the kitchen had exhausted him.

He slept for two hours; when he woke she made him a pasta salad and they ate together. He gripped the fork tightly with his left hand — his bad hand — and brought it to his mouth with a laborious effort. Then he chewed. It was as if he had to instruct his mouth to chew.

Because he had difficulty guiding his fork, by the time he was through he had food on his chin and his shirt.

Ariel wasn't neat herself and she didn't care about other people's personal habits. But seeing her father eat disturbed her, because she thought it must be disturbing to him. He was normally a fastidious man.

They talked a little at lunch. She asked if there was anything she could get him — books or magazines or some special food or something for the house — and he said that maybe she could take him to the bookstore later in the week. She asked him if he'd like to go to the park for a while that afternoon, and he said he would.

The stroke had almost completely immobilized the left side of his body. When he smiled, the right side of his face looked happy, but the left side was dead.

He braced himself against his walker and moved slowly to his bedroom for another nap. When he had reached his door, he turned around as much as he could, and, in a thick, slurred voice, as if there were a rag in his mouth, he said, "My daughter."

After he woke from his nap, they went to the park. He wanted to take his walker, but she convinced him it was too soon for anything that ambitious — the park was two blocks away — and he let her wheel him there.

Ariel locked the wheels in place and sat on a bench beside him at the top of the grassy hill that led down to the park. Two toddlers were tossing a Nerf ball around while their mothers sat on another bench, and when the ball rolled away from them, Schiller, with great difficulty, bent over in his seat and picked it up. One of the children, a boy of about two with a Prince Valiant haircut — a gorgeous little kid, a future heartthrob — wobbled up on legs that he was not yet fully in control of and looked at Schiller with friendliness and interest. "Baw," he said, reaching out with both arms.

His mother, tall and elegant, a long thin line of a woman — she was simply dressed but she radiated moneyed satisfaction — snatched up her son and took the ball roughly from Schiller's hands. "Don't bother the man," she said to her son — but she looked as if she were afraid that Schiller, or the mere sight of Schiller, would damage the boy.

It happened so quickly that Ariel's feelings didn't catch up with her until the women and children were halfway down the hill toward the playground.

Let it go, she said to herself. Let it go.

She couldn't let it go. "I'll be back in a second," she said to her father. She walked quickly down the path. The women were walking about ten feet behind the two children. When Ariel caught up to them she said, "Why did you look at my father that way?"

"I don't know what you're talking about," the woman said.

"You walk around with your kid and everyone smiles at you. Why do we smile at children? Because they're helpless, and we want to protect them. Well *he's* helpless too." She threw her arm back toward her father. "Why didn't you smile at *him?* You looked like he was going to infect your kid with some disease. What disease did you have in mind? Old age? Your kid is going to be old someday too, I hope, and I hope when he's old people don't look at him like you looked at my father."

The woman looked regally untroubled. "I still don't know what you're talking about," she said.

Ariel trudged back to her father and sat near him on the bench. He was calm, smiling, happy to be out in the warm daylight.

She pushed him slowly back to his apartment. As soon as she had installed him in his easy chair, she went to his bedroom to check the phone machine for messages. There weren't any. She was hoping Casey had called. She was also expecting to hear from a home-care agency: she was trying to arrange for someone to stay with her father a few hours a day.

She also needed to call the hospital about a physical therapist. She kept forgetting to make the call.

All of this was overwhelming her. She lay, exhausted, on her father's bed. Blowing up at a stranger merely because she'd given her father a funny look — it wasn't a good sign.

She felt as if she were at a fork in the road, where you have to choose between becoming a grown-up or remaining a child.

It was pretty late in life to be facing such a choice.

When she was little, her father, just before he went to bed, used to check his watch and ask in surprise, "How did it get so late so early?"

How *did* it get so late so early?

50

Lying in bed the next morning just after dawn, she heard something in the hall. It was her father, making his way slowly with his walker. Her impulse was to jump out of bed and ask him what he needed, but she thought better of it. What he needed was exactly this: to do things by himself; to become independent again. So she stayed in bed and listened.

Slowly and effortfully — she could hear how heavily he was breathing — he made his way down the hall to his study. She heard something fall to the floor. Again she wanted to rush out and help; but it was only some object that had fallen — *he* hadn't fallen — and she knew it would be wiser to leave him alone.

After a few minutes she heard a new sound: the slow, weak, hesitant clacking of his typewriter.

After his stroke, she had felt sure that it would have been easier for him to die, and that he had kept himself alive through sheer will. It was only now that she understood why he had kept himself alive.

51

Heather made her way through the weight of a July afternoon to the Upper West Side. She hadn't seen Schiller in more than a month.

She'd spoken to Ariel several times on the phone. Schiller never wanted to talk, but then he'd never been an enthusiast of the telephone. She supposed it was a generational thing.

Ariel had told her not to expect too much from him. "He gets tired after about a half hour. And sometimes it's still a little hard to understand him. He's a lot better than he was a month ago, but he doesn't have full control of his speech."

Thus warned, Heather went up to the apartment. Ariel let her in, and the two of them stood there, uncomfortable, in the hall.

"He's really looking forward to seeing you," Ariel said. "Your visits have always meant a lot to him."

It seemed to Heather that there was a hint of triumph in Ariel's eyes. She, Ariel, was the one who had stood by him.

Schiller came out of his study, hanging over a walker. He had lost a great deal of weight, but it hadn't improved his looks. The skin of his face was hanging down loosely; it looked as if you could pull his face off and find another, a trim face, underneath.

He was wearing a suit and tie, but the tie was knotted about two inches below where it should have been knotted, and one of the tabs of his collar was unbuttoned.

She didn't know whether to be impressed by his effort to pull himself together or disturbed by the signs that he wasn't all there.

He said her name, sort of — it sounded like "Header" — and awkwardly grasped her hand.

"Your snack is ready, Dad," Ariel said. She was on her way out to visit a client. "I'll be back in about an hour."

One of the kitchen chairs had been replaced by a big easy chair, into which Schiller now lowered himself. A mug of steaming coffee and two pieces of toast with apple butter were waiting for him on the table. He gestured with his head toward the refrigerator, and Heather, as in the old days — the old days of a few months ago — helped herself to some juice and sat across from him.

The afternoon light streamed through the

window, and didn't help. She didn't know whether he did his own shaving, but whoever was doing it was doing it badly: some parts of his face were smooth, but there were patches of unmowed hair on his chin and his cheekbone, and a long red gash on his neck.

The left side of his face sagged yellowly — it was a different color than the right. When he lifted his coffee cup and slurped from it the steam gave him a runny nose; large droplets of wetness glistened on the bushy tufts that protruded from his nostrils.

She didn't want to be revolted by his decrepitude. He was still the man she knew. Heather looked steadily at his nose, at his deadened flesh, until the sight of him no longer had the power to disturb her.

There was no air-conditioning in Schiller's apartment; the room was oppressively humid. Outside the sky was filled with thick clouds that intermittently blocked the sun. Every few minutes the room was plunged into darkness.

"How are you?" she said.

"Hanging on." He looked away, as if he were searching for the perfect phrase, but he didn't say anything else.

"Ariel tells me you're working again."

He smiled dismissively — or at least that was how it appeared to her. With one side of his face frozen, it was hard to interpret his expressions.

"I sit," he said. "I look for the typewriter keys. Sometimes I can find them."

Each of these sentences took a long time for him to say.

"Well I'm glad you're working. I'm glad you're going to finish your book."

Slowly, he turned his head and stared at her; beneath his drooping lids, his eyes had a lizardlike intensity.

"Maybe I'll finish it," he said, "and maybe it'll finish me."

He began to cough, violently and protractedly; he reached into his back pocket — it was a long, slow labor — and retrieved a much-used handkerchief, mottled with brown and yellow and gray. He brought it up to his face, released some sputum into it, folded it carefully, and put it back in his pocket. At a certain time of life, she thought, a man is no more than the sum of his discharges.

He broke off a slice of toast and brought it toward his mouth, but his hand was trembling so badly that he had to bring his mouth toward the toast to meet it halfway.

It was too sad to bear, and she felt herself detaching from the scene. She began to feel as if she were in a movie, a movie about an old man and a young woman. The man, of course, was Schiller, but the woman — the woman was someone a little different from herself.

During the rest of this visit, she decided, she wouldn't exactly be herself: she would be someone a little more considerate, a little purer of heart.

She started to talk, with the intention of filling up the room with good cheer, and once she got started she couldn't stop. She chattered on brightly about her life; she told him that she was papering the town with résumés, and that she'd lined up interviews for entry-level positions at *Harper's* and *Lingua Franca*. She told him some gossip: a story she'd heard about a feud between Gore Vidal and George Plimpton; an anecdote about a woman who'd spent the night in bed with Camille Paglia — the woman had been hoping for hot, "transgressive" sex, but instead Paglia spent the night lecturing her about the inanities of French poststructuralism. Telling these stories, Heather found herself delightfully entertaining, and she was sure that Schiller felt the same way.

It wasn't enough to be entertaining. She also wanted to massage Schiller's ego a bit. He must be so demoralized; she wanted to lift his spirits. "I wanted to tell you that my thesis advisor, James Bonner, really loved *Two Marriages*. He said it was an American classic." He hadn't quite said this, but he *had* liked the book. "I was thinking that after you're done with your new book you might be able to get the other ones published. I was reading about how Rosellen Brown got all her early books back in print after she hit it big with *Before and After*. I think that could happen for you."

Schiller didn't say anything. He was still negotiating with his toast.

"It's really wonderful that you're going on. I have a good feeling about this new book. I have a feeling that this is going to be your best." She realized that she was going overboard, but once you get started in this vein it's hard to stop.

If I can just make it through this afternoon, she thought, I'll deserve an Academy Award. Maybe I should actually be an actress. Maybe that's my true career.

Schiller, obviously, was deeply moved. He looked at her for a long time. Then he reached out toward her. She was touched by this. He was going to caress her face, or perhaps, as on the unusual night they had spent together, he was going to caress the air around her face. The wheel, she thought, has come full circle.

Lost in this reverie, she was unprepared when Schiller, using the meaty center of his palm, slapped her full on the mouth.

It wasn't hard enough to hurt her, but it was hard enough to sting. In his effort he'd had to lean on the table, and when he sat back down his cup and saucer rattled and his butter knife fell to the floor. But he seemed quite composed now; he seemed satisfied.

"I didn't deserve that," she said. "I was trying to be nice."

Schiller didn't look at her. She didn't know what to do. She wanted to hit him back, but that wouldn't be fair. She thought of maybe just getting up and leaving. The one thing she *wasn't* going to do was cry. She wouldn't give him that satisfaction. And yet somehow, with all this, she was crying.

She felt perfectly stoical, perfectly composed, and she wasn't making a sound, but the tears were coming steadily down her face.

Schiller took up his coffee cup and drew it unsteadily toward his mouth. He made no move to comfort her; he didn't seem to be taking any notice of her at all.

He placed his cup carefully in the saucer. She had the taste of salt on her lips. Neither of them said a word. She watched him through the wetness, noticing how he had to exert himself for every breath. She was all stuffed up from crying, and she had to take a deep breath through her mouth; at the moment when she did so, Schiller too was struggling for a breath. The room, again, was plunged for a moment into a humid purple darkness — she felt as if she were on board a ship. Something about the convergences of this moment — the two of them at the climax of a difficult indrawn breath; the brightness dropping a notch, so that they both were cast into shadow — made her feel as if they were joined; made her feel, for a fraction of a second, as if the boundaries of her individuality were melting away. Not melting away, but wavering. She was herself, she was Heather Wolfe, but she was also Leonard Schiller. It was unlike anything she'd ever experienced. She had never lost herself in life: even at the wildest heights of sex or drugs or reading, she'd never misplaced the compass of self-regard, reminding her of who she was and what she was out for. But now, for just a moment, she was no longer a young woman with more energy than she knew what to do with and decades to make a life for herself — or she *was* all that, but she was also a huge, wheezing, time-addled, sorrow-darkened, stroke-stunned, and unbreakably tenacious old man.

The feeling passed quickly, and then she was herself again.

"I'm sorry everything got so fucked up," she said.

"You gave an old man some excitement." Schiller looked at her searchingly, and she knew that he was taking her in as fully as he could because they would never see each other again.

"It's been good knowing you."

"I got the best of the bargain," she said. This time, she meant what she said.

Was there anything else to say? No, there wasn't. The only thing left was to leave. She found, however, that she couldn't do it. She had always thought of herself as a virtuoso of leaving, but now she couldn't quite leave.

Schiller, after a minute, realized that she wasn't leaving. "Strange girl," he murmured. He adjusted his pillow, leaned back in his easy chair, and closed his eyes.

She sat across from him and drank her juice, and this was the best part of her visit. She no longer felt the need to humor him, or cheer him, or judge him. She kept him company, for five minutes, ten minutes, without saying a word.

He didn't open his eyes. Finally she realized that he was sleeping.

The madness of art was sleeping, dressed in a suit and tie.

She took out the keys he'd given her and put them on the kitchen table. Good-bye, Schiller. She walked through the living room. Good-bye, Schiller's books. Jeff wasn't on duty, so she didn't get to say good-bye to him. Out on the street she decided to say good-bye to their old meeting place, the Argo.

She sat at the booth where they had first met — where she'd told him that if he gave her a chance, he might fall in love with her.

She had an iced coffee and put on some lipstick, and her mood began to lift. For months she'd been burdened by the thought that she'd betrayed him. But now it occurred to her that that might not be true. She had written about his work, after all, as seriously as she knew how. And wasn't that the highest word of praise in Schiller's vocabulary — "seriousness"? The decision to write critically about his books hadn't been easy for her — it might have been the hardest choice she'd ever had to make. If those characters in Schiller's early novels were heroes and heroines because of the difficult choices they'd made, she supposed she was a heroine too.

She thought it would have been nice if someone else had said this to her — Sandra, perhaps, or Schiller himself. But on second thought, she decided it was probably better that she had discovered it for herself.

52

Ariel tried to keep up a life. She taught her dance-exercise class five nights a week and saw her private clients during the day. Through Medicare and a Jewish home-care agency she arranged to have someone visit her father seven days a week, but she continued to see him almost every day herself. She did his shopping and his laundry and she cooked for him, and sometimes, when he was feeling very weak, she shaved him. Her father was getting better — slowly, slowly. He could speak well enough to be understood. He was doing his exercises faithfully, and beginning to regain some mobility on his left side. She knew he'd never be the same as he used to be — the smallest tasks were strugglesome, and he slept more than ten hours a day. But he was fighting steadily to get better.

A few old friends and former students visited him once in a while. His friend Levin, miraculously, had been released from the hospital. He looked like a wreck, and he wasn't expected to live long — his cancer was still spreading — but for a few weeks he was back in the world. One day he and Schiller ventured out on a two-block trip to Riverside Park; Ariel, heading back to her place, accompanied them out of the apartment. She watched them making their way across West End Avenue — very cautiously, like two small boys who had only recently learned how to cross the street on their own.

During these weeks, she found herself giving more thought to her future. She began to send away for applications to masters programs in dance therapy. But that wasn't the important thing.

She and Casey went to the Brooklyn Botanical Garden one Sunday morning; on their way back to Manhattan, they waited in the Grand Army Plaza station for the 3 train. They waited for five minutes, ten, fifteen. Finally, all the way down the dark tunnel, she saw the faint white glow.

She watched the light growing brighter and larger as it approached.

She would turn forty in a few months, and she had to have a child soon or forget about having one at all.

"I can't wait forever, you know," she said.

Casey didn't say anything. But she was sure he knew what she was referring to.

Ariel got off the train at 14th Street and

walked home alone. Casey was spending the afternoon with a few friends who were working with him on the magazine. Their first issue was coming out in September.

At home she fed Sancho and sat down to pay some bills. Sancho was pacing and meowing, trying to get his ideas across. "Sancho," she murmured, "don't you know I don't like noise from a cat? I like a quiet cat."

She made a few phone calls, tidied up the house, lay down on the couch and watched a rerun of *Star Trek*. She half-dozed as she watched. Jean-Luc Picard, the tragic, stoic, noble, bald-headed captain, had been given a chance by some omnipotent being to relive his youth and make different choices.

She knew she had to do some serious thinking.

She tried to examine her soul, but instead she found herself thinking about *Star Trek*. In every few episodes, because of transporter accidents, "spatial anomalies," or some other reason, someone gets hurled into a parallel universe. According to *Star Trek*, you and I — or rather, our slightly different counterparts — are alive in many parallel universes, living the lives we would have had if things had turned out differently.

Beaming down to the planet Rigel 12 to

set up an exercise program for the Romulan colony there, Ariel Schiller, the lovely though slightly weathered fitness instructor of the Starship *Enterprise*, is caught in a time-space anomaly, and finds herself tumbling from one universe to another.

She imagined a life in which she had a child on her own. She saw herself raising the child in a spirit of grim fortitude. She'd be a heartwarming inspiration for feminists from coast to coast, and she'd be unhappy.

That wasn't what she wanted. She wanted to be in love with a man, and to bring forth a child from that love.

She imagined a life in which she set off again in search of another guy to fall in love with. The future stretched ahead of her: years of bad dates. And even if she imagined a happy ending to her story, the happy ending meant finding a guy like Casey.

She imagined a life in which she came back to Casey and said, "Having a child isn't the important thing: the important thing is to be with you." She saw herself alone with Casey, childless. Childless at fifty, at sixty.

She started to tidy up the kitchen. Languidly squeezing liquid soap on a dish, she composed her own elegy. Here lies Ariel, who died womb-withered, wind-weathered, womb-blighted, mother of nothing, mother of none.

She tried to evaluate her situation politically, from a feminist point of view. Leaving a man to pursue the dream of having a child; putting aside the dream of having a child to be with a man — either way, from a feminist point of view she was a washout.

A friend had advised her just to throw her diaphragm away. "You'll get pregnant, and he'll do the right thing. You know he will."

She wished she could do what her friend advised, but she didn't think she could. She was incapable of duplicity, even in a good cause.

There was no way to decide. Ariel tripped from one parallel universe to another, and in each of them she was unhappy.

53

Casey and his friends spent the afternoon trying to make a final decision about the name of their magazine. They went through *Politics and Letters*, *American Pages*, and five or ten other possibilities before settling on *Arguments*, which satisfied everyone.

He was still on a high when he met Ariel for dinner; he couldn't stop thinking about the magazine. "I feel like this was what I was made for," he said.

Ariel raised one eyebrow and didn't say anything.

"He said pretentiously," Casey finally added.

After dinner they went to play indoor miniature golf on 18th Street. She built up a huge lead and then handicapped herself by hitting left-handed or behind her back. She was a much better athlete than he was.

"This is what *I* was made for," she said. "Miniature golf is my life."

She carefully putted the ball up a ramp and through the eye of a Cyclops. "The only thing more fun than playing miniature golf," she said, "would be playing miniature golf with the kiddies. Don't you think?"

A little while later: "It kind of makes you want to have kids, doesn't it?"

She was joking, but she wasn't.

"Don't start," he said.

"I've been giving this a great deal of thought since this afternoon," she said, "and it's an open-and-shut case. With my physical gifts, and your intellectual gifts, we could have the most amazing children! They could be in the Olympics! They could win big money on *Jeopardy!* Casey, it's our responsibility to the world!" Looking directly at him, not at the ball, she swung her club one-handed and somehow sent the ball smoothly through the open mouth of the grinning gargoyle on the seventh hole.

"We could have such beautiful coffee-colored babies!" she said.

He couldn't help smiling at all this, but he shook his head.

"You know," she said, "I think you're a fool."

He considered this, and decided that she was probably right. Because the feelings he had for her, he hadn't had for anyone since . . . her.

During the last week, not once but twice, he'd picked up the phone to call her and found that she was already on the line: she was calling *him,* and he'd picked it up before the first ring.

Coincidence. But the eagerness to find meaning in such coincidences is love.

His admiration for her had only grown over these past weeks. The way she took care of her father, steadily and without complaint, betraying no irritation, as if it weren't a chore for her — apparently she didn't find it a chore — amazed him. Her ability to keep her sense of humor, to take care of her father lovingly, but with a touch of roughness — a loving roughness, a healing roughness, as if she refused to see his condition as something that called for weepy protectiveness — was more than he'd expected. When this ordeal began, he'd half expected her to collapse. But she hadn't collapsed. She'd become stronger.

He was thinking of all this as he leaned on his golf club and watched her line up her next shot. She glanced up at him and saw something in his look. "You're getting all googly-eyed," she said. "You've never known what it is to be with a golfing genius."

When they went outside, the moon, low in the sky and nearly full, was enormous and pink. They walked across town to her apartment, stopping at the deli on the corner so she could buy Oreos for herself and cat food for Sancho. "He likes beef, cause he's still a growing boy. Beastie Feast," she said, and these words, so commonplace, were inexplicably touching to him. A million women care about their cats; a million women would tell you that their cats are partial to beef or chicken or whatever. Why was it that when Ariel said something like this, he was filled with tenderness and longing — longing for a life with her — and with the intuition that if he were to put anything above her, if he allowed his feeling for her to be less than the central fact of his life, it would be a mistake that he'd regret forever?

She wanted to get a last glimpse of the moon before they went inside. But it was hidden. "Where's that moon of ours?" she said, taking Casey's arm and leading him to the end of the block so they could find it again.

Back at her place, she fell asleep quickly; he couldn't sleep at all. He prowled restlessly around her little studio. He spent a minute looking through her medicine cabinet: NyQuil; aspirin; condoms; her diaphragm case; spermicidal jelly; Valium; "ouchless" Band-Aids; Flintstones chewable vitamins. He couldn't help smiling when he came across the Flintstones vitamins.

He looked through her bookcase, took down one of her father's books, went back into the bathroom, and sat on the floor. Her bathroom was the only place where he could read at night without waking her.

This was her father's third novel, *Stories from the Lives of My Friends.* It was about the alarms and disorders of the 1960s. He read the first forty-five pages, and found it much more interesting than the one he'd read years ago. That other one, his first or his second, was a trite little book about a couple trying to deal with their personal problems during a year in Paris. This later book was messier, but it took on larger subjects; it had more guts. He read until he felt tired; then he put it back on Ariel's bookcase, intending to return to it another day.

He went back out and lay down beside her. She was snoring softly. She hadn't snored in the old days.

Listening to a lover snore was a new experience. He knew that he had rattled the rafters for years — women had told him this often enough, with indulgence or exasperation, each according to her nature — but he'd never had a snoring girlfriend before.

It was hard to believe it, but they were traveling into middle age.

He was starting to feel drowsy, but he

couldn't sleep. This was nothing new: getting a good night's sleep in her apartment was near-impossible. For one thing, there was the cat. Sancho was up half the night, and he liked to keep busy: he would hone his hunting skills by going after your feet, and then he might make a trip to the bathtub, where Ariel's faucet was perpetually drizzling, and take a little shower — he was an eccentric among cats in that he liked to get wet — and then he'd come and lie down next to you in the dark, purring, and push his soaking fur against your face. This was his way of telling you he liked you.

Ariel always woke up several times during the night, and she would wake him to tell him her dreams. "I dreamt Paula" — an old teacher — "was a dentist. I wanted her to be my dentist." "I dreamt my father wrote a book called *American Smells*. He sampled the smells of all the different regions."

This morning he woke at about five; Ariel was tossing about in bed. "I can't sleep," she said. "Do you mind if I watch TV?"

He didn't mind. She played with the remote control for a while and finally settled on an ancient episode of *Lassie*. An embittered rancher was planning to kill his favorite cow, but Lassie somehow got him to change his mind. Drifting in and out of sleep, Casey

411

couldn't quite follow how she had done this.

They slept for a few more hours, and woke around eight. Ariel always woke up in a loving frame of mind. That's how you discover a person's true nature: by the way she wakes up in the morning.

"Hello, Magic," she said. "Beat you at golf."

They both had things to do. Casey needed to spend a few hours editing articles for the magazine, and Ariel had to take her father to a doctor's appointment.

They made pancakes together.

"Explain your political views to me again?" she said. "My father was asking me."

"Why doesn't he just ask me?"

"I don't know. He fears the rage of the black man."

Casey scowled at her.

"Just jesting," she said.

"What did you tell him?"

"I told him I think you're sort of a socialist."

"That's the right answer. I'm sort of a socialist."

"He seemed to want to know what that could mean, in this day and age."

"A socialist is someone who sits around pondering the question of whether it can possibly mean anything anymore to call yourself a socialist."

"I'll tell him that."

He was surprised the old man was curious. "Why did he want to know?"

"I guess he just wanted to know. I think he respects you."

After breakfast, washing the dishes with rubber gloves, she started doing a bump and grind, slowly peeling off one glove. She looked at him with astonishment: "I'm channeling Gypsy Rose Lee!" she said.

He sat at her table, laughing as he watched her performance, feeling lucky to be there, lucky to have found her again.

54

While Ariel was dressing, Casey read the paper. "Did you know there's going to be a comet in the sky tomorrow night?"

"Is that Russell's Comet? My father told me about it. He saw it when he was a kid."

"We should definitely see it then — we should see it with him. We can borrow a car and drive somewhere."

"Can't we just go to Central Park?"

"It won't be visible in the city. Too many lights."

When they were getting ready to leave, the phone rang.

"Damn," Ariel said after she hung up.

"What?"

"They asked me to sub at the Saint Luke's weight-loss clinic. I've been trying to get my foot in the door there for a long time."

He thought about it. "I can take your father to the doctor."

"Really?"

"Why not?"

There were many reasons why not. He had a million things to do, and he would have preferred not to spend the morning baby-sitting Ariel's father. But he knew it was the right thing to do, and he didn't have a moment's hesitation about doing it.

He picked Schiller up at 94th Street. Schiller was waiting in the lobby, sitting on a backless couch with his walker in front of him, looking grumpy because Casey was ten minutes late. But when Casey helped him up Schiller patted him on the hand and said, "This is good of you." At least that was what Casey thought he said. He had trouble understanding the old man.

They walked out to the sidewalk to catch a cab; Schiller was excruciatingly slow.

They had to wait in the doctor's office for about half an hour. Casey had brought something to read — Eric Foner's book on Tom Paine. Schiller leaned forward and bent up the cover of the book to see what Casey was reading. Then he grunted, either approvingly or disapprovingly, or neither.

He reached into his coat pocket: he had also brought something to read. Chekhov.

The nurse called him in and he disappeared for half an hour. When he emerged, he looked as if he'd been through an ordeal.

Casey raised his eyebrows.

"Don't grow old," Schiller said. "That's my advice."

He didn't say anything else until they left

the building. Then he said, "Let's walk. Exercise."

The last thing Casey wanted to do was waste another hour watching Schiller take three and a half steps. "Are you sure you feel up to it?" he said.

Schiller nodded gravely. They walked up Ninth Avenue, very slowly. Casey found it hard to walk this slowly. He was wondering, half-seriously, whether it would be bad manners to read as they walked.

"Oh my," Schiller said.

"Is anything wrong?"

Schiller's face was contorted; he gripped the pads of his walker.

"My stomach."

Casey didn't understand what he meant at first. Then he understood. Ariel's father had soiled himself.

"My body is not my own," Schiller said grimly. He closed his eyes. "It's time to die."

"It's not time to die," Casey said. "It's time to get you to a rest room."

He had never used the term "rest room" in his life, but somehow it seemed the most tactful expression he could find.

There was a bar across the street. He led Schiller to the crosswalk. Schiller was trying to speed up his pace, but with his physical disabilities, with the awkwardness of the walker, and with the special distress of the moment, he found it difficult. He was sweating terribly. When the effort to walk across the street is almost too much for you — when the effort to control your bowels is too much for you — then it probably *is* time to die, Casey thought.

But is it? Is it really? Casey put his hand under Schiller's elbow to support him as they stepped off the curb, but Schiller shrugged him off. "Thank you, but I think I can make it," he said. From Schiller's expression as he proceeded across the street, you might have thought it was the most challenging task he had ever faced. As it probably was. But did that mean it was time to die? Wasn't the important thing, the impressive thing, the very fact that he was trying to meet the challenge? He was making his slow, implacable way across the street.

Casey helped him into the bar and back toward the bathroom.

"You got a problem here?" the bartender said to Schiller. It was clear that he thought Casey might be the problem.

"We're fine," Schiller said, with his stricken voice, as if he had a bone lodged permanently in his throat.

"Rest rooms for customers only," the man said. He was a red-faced man in his fifties with thick, violent eyebrows. Casey dug into his pocket and slapped a few dollars on the bar. "We're customers," he said, helping Schiller into the men's room.

The room was smelly and ill-tended; the toilet seat was sticky-looking, layered with the urine of men who'd been too drunk or too lazy to lift it. "Hold on," Casey said. He grabbed a few paper towels and ran them quickly under the water faucet and wiped down the toilet seat.

The bartender had followed them in. "Is this guy giving you any trouble?" he said to Schiller.

"This guy," Schiller said, "is my son-in-law."

Casey was touched and uncomfortable at the same time. Schiller, as far as Casey knew, knew nothing about the complexities of his relationship with Ariel.

The bartender shrugged and left the room.

"If you could help me get these down," Schiller said. He was struggling with his pants.

Casey undid Schiller's belt and helped him sit on the toilet seat.

"Thank you," Schiller said. "It seems to be all I can say to you today."

"Let that thank you stand for all other thank yous."

Casey closed the door of the stall from the outside. He heard the liquid gassy sound of Schiller's shitting.

Ariel's father was a very private, very proper man. There could probably be nothing more painful for him than to endure this sort of indignity.

Schiller was breathing heavily. Casey thought the old man might need his help, but he didn't want to barge in.

"Can you use any help?" Casey said.

Silence. Then: "Maybe yes. If you can stand it."

Casey pushed the stall door open. Schiller looked mournful. He gestured with his chin. There was a blob of golden shit on his shoe.

"I'm sorry you had to be here," Schiller said.

"Look, it's . . ." Casey was about to give him words of courage and support, but he thought better of it. Surely the old man didn't need them. If he offered any pithy maxims, he would sound condescending. He wet down a few more paper towels and cleaned off Schiller's shoe, and then he cleaned off his leg.

"Ariel once mentioned to me that you knew Ralph Ellison," Casey said.

"A little."

"I could never figure out why he only

419

wrote that one book. He was so talented."

"His house burned down."

"Excuse me?" Casey stood up and got some dry paper towels and returned to the task.

"His house with his book in it."

"I know," Casey said, cleaning him off. "But that was in the sixties. He still had twenty-five years left after that."

"He was a perfectionist," Schiller said — at least that was what Casey thought he said. It sounded more like "percussionist." "And . . . success. It was hard for him. Second-book jinx."

In the months since Schiller's stroke, this was probably the longest speech Casey had heard him give. He could feel how relieved the old man was that they could pretend to be doing nothing more than having a literary discussion right now.

After Schiller was cleaned up, they left the bar and took a cab uptown. When they got back to the apartment Casey helped him off with his shoes and his socks and his pants and his underwear. He turned his head away respectfully so as not to see the old man's spent sad genitals. He ran a bath and helped Schiller into it, and twenty minutes later he lifted him out and helped him into his robe.

Casey was exhausted. Schiller had a good

420

seventy-five pounds on him, maybe more: all this heavy lifting was an ordeal. The entire morning had been an ordeal.

There was a guest room that Casey and Ariel used when they stayed there. He wanted to sleep for about fifteen years. But he stayed in the living room, thinking he'd wait to take a nap until Schiller took his. He sat on the couch, too tired to move, listening to Schiller moving around in the bedroom. He heard drawers opening and closing.

Finally Schiller emerged, dressed in a tie and jacket.

"I think I'll do a little work," he said. And to Casey's amazement, Schiller, leaning on his walker, set off slowly toward his study. In a little while Casey heard the sound of Schiller at work — the weak but somehow relentless march of the typewriter keys.

He was amazed by the man. To see him struggling on like this was an education.

He dragged himself to the little guest room and closed his eyes.

The last few months had been very different from what he'd expected. He was finally ready to begin a project that he'd been thinking about for years, and he'd been hoping for a few distraction-free months in which to concentrate. But now he was getting dragged into the middle of life's confusions. Worrying about having children with Ariel; worrying about Ariel's father — it wasn't a good time to be dealing with these problems. A part of him wished that he could refuse all this, just close the door on it all and do his work. But of course you can't refuse it; you mustn't even try. You have to let it in.

He woke from what might have been the heaviest sleep of his life to see Ariel sitting on the edge of the bed, grinning at him madly. It was probably her smile that had awakened him.

"Stop glowing at me," he said.

She didn't say anything, just kept smiling.

"What?" he said.

"I talked to my dad."

"And?"

"He didn't seem to want to tell me the specifics. But I think he loves you."

"What did he say?"

"He said you held his hand in hell."

"Not hell. I don't think he said hell. It was Ninth Avenue. He must've said Hell's Kitchen."

Ariel was undiverted by this dodge. "He said you're a good man."

"He's getting sentimental in his old age."

"Maybe," she said. "Maybe."

55

The next day Schiller seemed better. Ariel and Casey were planning to borrow a friend's car that night and drive up to Westchester to see Russell's Comet.

"Do you want to come?" she asked her father.

"Once in a lifetime," he said. "Twice would be greedy."

Ariel was eager to see it — both because she wanted to make this link with her family past, and because the comet, even though it was described in the newspaper as "of only modest brightness," was supposed to be beautiful. The article in the paper said it had a "long blue tail."

There was a state park about an hour north of the city where people were gathering to watch.

Needless to say, it made Ariel sad to contemplate the possibility that no child of hers would see it when it returned during the next century.

Could she live with that? She didn't know.

Casey met her at her father's place as it was getting dark. On the drive up he talked about how he would like to have some of her father's qualities. "He's unstoppable, your old man."

"Sometimes it seems that way," Ariel said.

She wished her father had come along with them, but she understood why he hadn't. It wasn't really because he thought it would be too greedy; it was because he wanted to do his work.

He was working longer hours than ever these days — staying up late in his study, pushing himself to the limits of his strength. It worried her, but she knew him too well to try to persuade him to take it easy. This was the way he wanted to spend the time he had left. He had one task, one passion in life, and he wanted to give it everything he had.

There was hardly any traffic on the way up. It was delicious to be sitting next to Casey, moving swiftly through the dark. It felt exciting, and it felt safe.

They reached the park at about nine-thirty; a series of signs guided them up a hill toward the field where people were gathering.

It was a beautiful clear night; the sky was alive with thousands of stars. She hadn't seen so many since she'd moved back to New York.

She was happy to be here. "We're in the heart of the country," she said.

"I wouldn't exactly call it the country. Technically, I think we're still in Yonkers."

"It feels like the country to me. All of a sudden I feel like a farmer."

Casey was one of those people who never felt comfortable outside Manhattan. "I hope we don't get Lyme disease," he said. "There might be ticks."

There were already a lot of people on the broad field — families with backyard telescopes, couples, lone romantics. She and Casey found a spot that was secluded enough and spread their blanket on the ground. He had brought bread, cheese, cider, and two paper cups; they had a little picnic as they waited.

She didn't quite believe this comet was going to show. When she was in college there had been a lot of talk about Kohoutek: supposedly it was going to be the brightest comet in centuries. But Kohoutek turned out to be all hype. By the time it got close to the earth it had fizzled out; you couldn't even see it without a telescope.

Here in the country, or whatever it was, the stars were throbbing with life. Out here, far from the haze of the city, you could see that they aren't merely white: where the stars are in their nakedness, they are red and yellow and blue.

"I used to know all the constellations when I was little," Casey said. "Mostly because I loved the Greek myths. When Greek heroes and heroines died, the gods would put them in the sky."

He pointed out some of the constellations and told her their stories: Castor and Pollux, the inseparable twins; Perseus and the rescue of Andromeda. You could see Perseus, just above the horizon, reaching out, but Andromeda was hidden below the curve of the earth. She rose into the sky every autumn.

"It should be visible in about five minutes," Casey said. She put her cup aside and lay down to face the sky.

They lay on the blanket, hand in hand, looking up, waiting. The comet, which for some reason she had personified as a lady in her mind, seemed like an exceptionally reliable lady, arriving right on time every sixty-four years, tripping across the night sky with a special subtlety and discretion — beautiful, but only to those who knew enough to look for her. Ariel imagined her as a bride, a perpetual bride, perpetually returning to renew her vows. The night was warm and the sky was thick with stars. She was eager to see the comet — to see it delicately stepping across the sky, trailing its long blue train. But as she waited, holding her lover's hand, she found herself thinking that she wouldn't mind if it never even appeared: the night was astonishing already, just as it was.

The employees of Thorndike Press hope you have enjoyed this Large Print book. All our Large Print titles are designed for easy reading, and all our books are made to last. Other Thorndike Press Large Print books are available at your library, through selected bookstores, or directly from us.

For information about titles, please call:

(800) 257-5157

To share your comments, please write:

Publisher
Thorndike Press
P.O. Box 159
Thorndike, Maine 04986